PUSHING WATER

MARGARET MENDEL

PUSHING TIME PRESS

ISBN: 978-0-578-28710-2
ebook ISBN: 978-0-578-28724-9

First printing: 2017 Muse It Up Publishing

For information, please contact the author:
margaret_mendel123@yahoo.com

Dedicated to Steven, my inspiration. My muse.

I would like to thank Rick Taliaferro for his help with the first edit of *PUSHING WATER*. He gave me some great advice. A big thank you goes out to Liza and Desmond for their long time and sensitive support. While I struggled with the first draft, they surprised me with a pen inscribe with the title of this novel. David was always there for me when I had a computer problem and he never stopped believing that I'd get this novel completed, even when I broke my ankle and could not sit at the computer without discomfort.

There were many people who have stood by me all these years while I wrote. Some simply gave me space; while there were friends who knew I needed to get away from the computer, and get away from the writing. They called me on the phone or sent me emails that simply said, "It's time to play." Thanks Jeri, Pam, Susan, Mary, Robin, Elyse and Debby. And Claudia, Susan and Tricia, my three lovely, creative sisters, have been faithful cheerleaders in my writing life.

"In a river current, it is not the water in front that pulls the river along, but the water in the rear that acts as the driving force, pushing the water in front forward."

—*THE LOTUS IN A SEA OF FIRE,*
    A Buddhist Proposal for Peace By Thich Nhat Hanh

One

"OH LORD, IT'S GOING TO be even hotter today than yesterday," Julia said.

Standing in the doorway, Julia looked more rested this morning than she had when we met up at the airstrip yesterday. There were still dark rings and puffiness around her eyes. It was hard to say how this old friend normally looked. We had exchanged letters occasionally though we hadn't seen each other in over five years. Then out of the blue, a cable came in the mail saying she'd be arriving for a short stay in Hanoi.

Her visit could not have been more poorly timed.

I lived in a small house on the outskirts of a large market district. The street outside my walled-in garden nearly vibrated with activity from before sunup until dusk. The two silk merchants across the way, one with a distinctive screeching voice, constantly competed with each other, vying for the attention of the silkworm farmers carrying fresh loads of raw spun silk thread to the market. Potters and basket weavers balanced mountain-sized bundles of goods on their backs or carried merchandise weighing as much as a mother-in-law dangling from shoulder poles. They shouted the names of their villages to let buyers know that they had brought a special product into Hanoi.

Julia and I sat in my garden drinking coffee, listening to this activity as if today was like any other day. But it wasn't like any other day. This morning Julia would accompany me when I paid a condolence call to a murdered co-worker's family.

Two days ago, I discovered the body of Thien Nguyen, a Vietnamese translator who worked with me at the Archives. He was a lovely person and valued colleague. I'd miss him terribly.

Yesterday after picking up Julia at the airstrip, instead of heading straight back to my place we stopped for drinks at a bar where I hung out from time to time. Between swallows of wine, I made feeble attempts to explain what had happened. Telling the full story was unnerving and painful. My mind stumbled over the unreal situation. The right words would not come. How could something that horrible be explained? So, most of the afternoon was spent with my nose buried in a glass of rice wine, while I listened half heartedly to Julia's stories about her adventures as a correspondent in the Civil War in Spain.

Since finding Thien Nguyen's body, my attention flicked in and out. Most of what Julia said didn't register. The image of this young, dead, coworker lying prostrate between two rows of bookshelves, a garrote twisted tightly around his neck, felt imprinted on my brain. The memory of this scene could have just as well been branded on my retinas because it is quite likely that it would be with me forever.

Waking up this morning was a horror. My heart ached thinking about paying the dead translator's family a condolence call. But what troubled me most about this day was seeing Thi My, the dead translator's fiancé. I'd promised to walk with her to pay the family a condolence visit.

Julia took a sip of coffee. "What do you wear to one of these things?"

Clothing was the least of my concerns. "Wear whatever you want." I stood up. "Time to get ready. Thi My will be here soon."

Leaving the coolness of the garden and walking into the house was like walking into a furnace. I had to agree with Julia; maybe today was hotter than yesterday. Stepping into my bedroom, it didn't matter what I took from the closet. Dressing this morning was a mindless act of necessity.

When I came out to the front of the house, Julia was sitting on the daybed fiddling with her shoelaces. Now dressed in a white linen pantsuit, a beat-up looking camera hanging from her neck, Julia look more like her old self, the reporter I knew back in St. Lewis, Missouri.

We went out into the garden. Neither of us said a word. Thi My was expected to arrive any minute now.

Two

WE DID NOT HAVE TO wait long before there was a knock on the garden gate. Thi My had arrived, accompanied by a nun. This did not surprise me. They had been friends since childhood and it was reassuring to know that this grieving young woman would be well cared for during this trying time.

I introduced Julia to Thi My and the nun. No one said much. The mood was terribly somber.

Thi My handed me a packet of poetry Thien Nguyen had borrowed from the Archives. He often translated the old Vietnamese and French verses into English for me. Some times he took poetry home to share with Thi My. The Archives was not a lending library. I'd been a librarian for ten years back in the States and letting Thien Nguyen borrow poetry felt like a natural thing to do. We had both, on several occasions, gathered bits and pieces of information and handed them over to a professor or a friend of Thien Nguyen's who was writing a scholarly paper. So, there seemed no harm in him reading ancient verse to his fiancé. I couldn't remember when he'd taken this last batch of poetry. It no longer mattered. I took the poetry, hurried into the house, placed it on a counter top and returned back to the garden. It was time to leave.

Lifting the latch on the garden gate, we stepped out into the bustling street. The news of Thien Nguyen's murder had undoubtedly traveled like wildfire through Hanoi. As we walked out into the middle of the street, the din of the busy merchants and shoppers nearly fell silent. Everyone stopped to watch. A large crowd parted to let us pass.

All eyes were on Thi My, now known throughout the city as the murdered translator's fiancé. She lowered her head while the nun lead us in the slow traditional walk to pay our respect to the deceased.

Yesterday the nun had told me that Thien Nguyen's family refused to let Thi My wear the ceremonial funeral garb. The young couple's marriage had been arranged while they were still children. Though Thi My and Thien Nguyen had fallen in love, over the years politics divided the families. Now the murdered translator's family blamed her for turning Thien Nguyen against them. They wanted nothing to do with her. There was no choice but to bear that shame and walk the streets denied the right to publicly display her grief draped in the customary mourner's gauzy garment.

But the death of one individual does not change everything. The poor and the wretched still sat huddled in the doorways and on the curbs with hands outstretched. In the last five years of living in French Indochina, I'd learned to look away from these impoverished skeletons.

We hadn't gone far when two boys wearing not much more than rags ran up the street. As they passed the grain merchant, each child snatched up handfuls of raw rice, kept running and darted into an alley.

"What scallywags," Julia commented.

"They're starving," the nun responded. "Maybe they will eat the rice without cooking it."

Julia and I didn't go through this area yesterday after leaving the airstrip, even though it was only a short distance from my house. Instead, I'd decided to break my friend in slowly to the overwhelming poverty in my part of the city. The hungry peasants were technically not allowed in all areas of Hanoi. But the increasing number of farmers, finding it impossible to stay on their land because of the high taxes that the French Colonial Government levied on property, the taxes on their rice crops, salt, and even a tax on their dead, forced them to give up their land and join the countless poor that now crowded into all areas of Hanoi.

The nun kept moving at a slow, even pace as she maneuvered us through the city streets. To hurry along would indicate a wish to see the deceased quickly lowered into the ground. The French referred to this Vietnamese custom as a respectful stroll. We were expected to walk as though regretting our destination. It was quite common in a funeral procession to see a distraught son walking backward for miles to reach his father's gravesite.

Eventually, we arrived in a neighborhood where I had never been before. Unlike my part of the city, where most homes had turned the front portion of the living quarters into a shop, these houses were more affluent looking. Each residence consisted of two or three stories, which meant that several generations lived together. Trees had been generously planted along the streets many years ago. Now the trees stood as tall as the tallest house. The roads were immaculate with the brush strokes of the street sweeper's broom clearly evident along the dusty curbs.

Several French soldiers stood at attention along the streets. Due to recent increase in rebel activity, the presence of the military had been stepped up. Local officials posted notices throughout the city blaming the rebels for the translator's death. A hefty reward was promised for information leading to the arrest of the murderer. The French jumped at this opportunity to lock up anyone they considered to be a troublemaker or a Communist, and had been throwing people into jail by the hundreds.

We had been walking for well over an hour when I heard faint shrill wailing in the distance. A shiver ran down my spine. This was the crying of the professional mourners.

Thi My too heard the mourners. She grabbed hold of the nun's arm.

Julia looked at me. For a brief moment there was a flash of fear in her eyes.

The nun slowed her pace. Bending forward, she staggered slightly. At first, it looked as though she'd lost her footing, yet the nun continued to walk slowly, uneasily. Thi My held tightly onto the nun's arm as they crept forward. Julia did not slow down in time and nearly stepped on the back of the nun's robe.

A large crowd gathered in front of a house up the street. Men stood in small groups talking; women beat their breasts, weeping uncontrollably. Then they spotted Thi My. A hush came over the crowd. They intently watched her approach. Several women glanced nervously at the opened doorway and then back at Thi My.

When we stood at the edge of the crowd, the nun and Thi My wobbled slightly as if they were about to topple over. Neither said a word. They did not attempt to move closer. One by one, people stepped aside, clearing a pathway. The nun and Thi My then slowly walked to the open door of the house. Julia and I followed.

We stood at the entrance. The mournful wailing and crying grew into frenzy. Then the crying died down, only to build again several minutes later to a fevered pitch. Rising and falling, the weeping had a rhythm all its own. There was a faint momentary trill just before the hysterical crying began. Then the wailing grew louder. Someone called out Thien Nguyen's name. Someone screamed. Then the crying softened to a near whisper.

After a while, Julia and I no longer stood with our heads bowed. Thi My had grabbed the attention of the mourners. We were outsiders. We were not expected to show the same kind of deference as the grieving young woman or the nun.

I glanced into the house. Candles flickered everywhere. When my eyes adjusted to the dim light, four women became visible. They stood shoulder to shoulder with their backs to us. They were the paid mourners. It became obvious that one of these women initiated the crying because just before the wailing began again, a nearly imperceptible whimper came from one of them.

Then from the darkest corner of the room, a man walked toward us… Loc Dang Hung, Thien Nguyen's brother. He had a startling resemblance to his murdered sibling. We'd met on several occasions over the years. Today the poor fellow looked drawn and haggard. He wore the traditional mourning garb, a turban constructed of a white gauzy fabric carelessly wrapped around his head. A long sheet of the same flimsy material was thrown over his clothing. The fabric fluttered ghost-like as he walked toward us.

Stepping over the threshold of the doorway he whispered something to the nun. Nodding, the nun said something to Thi My. The grieving woman stood as though paralyzed. The nun gently took her by the arm, led her to the edge of the doorway and turned Thi My so that her back was to the entrance of the house. Thi My lowered her head and neither uttered a word nor shed a tear, though her rippling silk garment betrayed her trembling body.

"We can go in now," the nun said to Julia and me.

"What about Thi My?" Julia asked.

The nun did not respond but stepped over the threshold and slowly walked toward the coffin.

"Please, get down on your knees," the nun instructed me. "Light three sticks of incense, bow three times, say what you want to the departed, and then step back."

Looking at the closed coffin, a vision of the murder scene flashed across my mind as it had so many times since discovering his body. Kneeling as the nun instructed, my mind raced to find something meaningful to say. Any utterance in these circumstances I knew would sound feeble and hardly comforting. Finally a few pitiful words came to me. "I am so sorry you had to leave us while you were still so young. May you find peace in your next life."

Julia was instructed to kneel next. She bowed her head and spoke for what seemed an awfully long time. Her wordiness did not come as a surprise. After all, being a newspaper reporter for so many years, words never failed her.

The nun, unlike Julia and me, lay prostrate on the floor in front of the coffin and remained there for a long while. The paid mourners softly wept while the nun spoke her piece.

When we turned to leave, Loc Dang Hung stepped forward. "We consulted an elder," he said. "My brother will be buried tomorrow morning."

The nun nodded.

"Thi My will be allowed to attend," Loc Dang Hung continued. "Though we can only allow her to remain at the end of the procession."

The nun bowed reverently. Her expression did not change. "She will understand."

We found Thi My outside the house still standing with her back to the door. A woman huddled close to the Thi My, whispering in her ear. As we approached, the woman quickly turned and ran up the street. The nun took Thi My by the hand and we began the slow trek back to my house.

Part way through the walk Thi My turned to me and said, "My brother wants to see you tonight. A rickshaw will be waiting at the circle intersection."

It was inevitable that Dat Tu would contact me sooner or later.

Julia gave me a curious look. There was no need in explaining to this old friend what was going on. I figured in a short while she'd be taking off for another part of the world to get involved with something else that interested her.

Three

SITTING IN THE GARDEN AFTER returning from the condolence visit, the evening descended on us like a heavy dark cloud. Glasses of wine helped somewhat, though nothing would take away the sadness that sat so deeply in my soul. Thi My did not want to come into my garden and the nun had escorted her home.

Julia wasn't hungry and since finding Thien Nguyen's body my appetite was nearly non-existent. The wine was good enough for me. My legs ached from the long walk today and my energy was draining quickly from my body. Meeting up with Dat Tu this evening would take a great deal of effort. It was impossible to know why he wanted to see me, though it had to be important, or he wouldn't have asked me to do something so risky. He'd been dodging the French authorities for months.

Julia assumed she'd come along with me to meet Dat Tu. "Some hostess you turned out to be," she said when I told her she'd be saying back. Julia lit a cigarette, flicked out the flame of the match with an angry gesture.

I needed to move about undetected. Two American women on the streets of Hanoi late at night would certainly draw attention from the French. Closing the garden gate, Julia called out one last appeal. "I'll watch your back."

I slipped my hand into a jacket pocket; my fingers touching the loaded revolver gave me a sense of security. There was a strong probability that nothing would require me to use a gun. Though I figured no sense in taking any chances.

The dark streets, now lit only by an occasional lantern, hid from my sight what the glaring light of the day could not camouflage.

Beggars sleeping in doorways, entire families weak from hunger, crumpled together, even in this sweltering heat. A child whimpered. A trembling hand reached out to me. A man or woman, who could tell which. Though it was certain that if a coin had been placed in the palm of this beggar, a torrent of urchins, desperate fathers, mothers clutching malnourished babies would crawl out from the shadows. The request for more would have been overwhelming. There would never be enough to go around. In the dark, there were no eyes to look away from, no faces scared and withered from the years of deprivation. Quickening my pace, the child's crying grew fainter until it could no longer be heard and the only sound echoing in the night were my footsteps on the dry dirt-packed street.

A few minutes later came the tricky part of my outing, walking past the local detention center, an immense gray stone monstrosity, one of the many structures the French built to replicate the Napoleonic era. Floodlights drenched this landmark building in a blue haze of brightness. Slipping unnoticed by the small contingency of heavily armed French soldiers at the entranceway turned out to be easier than it looked.

Quickly crossing the street, I passed a rusted-out tank from World War I that had been parked on the side of the street years ago with the intention of frightening the locals. Though this old show of military bravado no longer fooled anyone. The last time the engine was started of this relic had been two years ago on the 14th of July at the Bastille Day parade. You didn't have to know much about heavy artillery to know this show of dilapidated power was laughable.

A pack of rats darted across my path. They squealed and dove into a smelly pile of garbage. My pulse beat so fast I feared the veins in my neck would burst.

Luckily it was easy to spot the rickshaw waiting in the shadows of a huge cluster of palm trees at the other end of the alley. Climbing into the carriage the runner said nothing; he quickly pulled away from the curb and ran up the street. The fast moving rickshaw made the humid night air feel cool against my sweating forehead. A short while later, the rickshaw eased against a walkway near the park that encircled the One Pillar Pagoda.

"Sarah, come quickly," Dat Tu called out.

I couldn't figure out what direction to go in.

He called again, "Sarah, here."

His familiar voice comforted me and I quickly ran into a grove of trees. "I knew you wouldn't have asked to meet like this in the middle of the night if it wasn't important."

"It's about Thien Nguyen," he said.

A pang of sadness shot through me at the mention of his name.

Dat Tu was the first translator I'd worked with some years ago in the Archives.

"I need your help," he said. "Before Thein Nguyen was murdered, he sent a message that he found something in the Archives. Something that would reveal to the world that the French were liars." Dat Tu's tone of voice ratcheted up an octave with excitement.

"He said nothing to me," I replied. "He wouldn't have."

"No, suppose not."

I remembered when Dat Tu still worked in the Archives with me, he'd ask for what he called a favor. "A little information," he'd say. "A map of my country. We have no mapmakers." By that he meant the Vietminh had no mapmakers. At the time it didn't seem harmful to gather a few pieces of information and hand them over to him. We did this even though the French would have viewed my action as treason. Sometimes I worried that things had gotten a little out of hand. But Thien Nguyen and Dat Tu buffered these requests with logical reasoning, making them seem innocent.

"Did Thien Nguyen give you any documents lately?" he asked.

"No." Though my response was simple, the situation was more complicated. Thien Nguyen frequently slipped back into the building after the Archives were closed gathering bits of information he didn't want me to know about. He'd been doing this for quite some time. No one else knew. "But..." Pausing, to think before saying any more, I wondered how much Dat Tu needed to know. A jigsaw puzzle rattled around in my head. I wondered how the pieces fit together.

"The Governor General's office sent someone to the Archives the other day," I said. "They were inquiring about a packet of documents they called misinformation that had been accidentally sent from a

Mandarin's office."

"The French are afraid," Dat Tu said. "Hitler denies his intentions of war against France. Soon enough all of Europe will be at war. The American imperialists are too busy protecting their interests to notice what's going on in this part of the world. The Japanese are battering China and the French pretend it will not affect them and that the Japanese, in time, will leave Vietnam. Yes, I'm sure the French are sending many documents." The anger in Dat Tu's voice made his tone shrill.

"What do you think Thien Nguyen found?"

"Perhaps a direct order," he said. "We've intercepted a few pieces of important information. Reading between the lines it is easy to see that the French have already climbed into bed with the Japanese. At the same time they're trying to look neutral."

"None of this makes sense. I don't understand why Thien Nguyen was murdered. And why in the Archives?"

"Everything eventually ends up in the Archives," Dat Tu said. "You know that. And this is where you come in, Sarah. If Thien Nguyen didn't give you something, then he hid it. We need to find it."

There was no emotion in his voice. He was no longer interested in the murder of his friend. Thien Nguyen was a fallen comrade and Dat Tu's only concern now was to find the missing document. His attitude annoyed me.

"What do you think I'll do? Wave a magic wand and conjure up this mystery document?" This was said in jest, though I understood the weightiness of Dat Tu's mission. I suspected Thien Nguyen had found something important and that he had probably trusted the wrong person, paying the ultimate price with his life. Whatever information he'd found, someone else was also desperate to have it.

"Sarah, I know you will do your best. I don't have to tell you how serious the situation has become." Dat Tu paused for a moment. He sighed. Then in whispered tone he said, "My wife has been detained."

"Oh, no." A sickening sensation struck me in the pit of my stomach. Dat Tu and Van Mai had not been married a year and they had a newborn.

"I sent word for her to meet me before I left Hanoi. She never got my message. The French Police brought her in for questioning. That was three days ago and no one has heard from her since."

"Where's the baby?"

"Van Mai's mother."

"Does Thi My or the nun know?"

"Yes."

"You don't have to tell me if you don't want to, but where were you headed?"

"North."

The answer didn't surprise me. The French authorities had recently banned the Communist party and were ruthlessly hunting down the Vietminh. Hundreds had been arrested. Dat Tu and his wife, both very involved with the rebels, had until now avoided capture by the authorities.

"Surely, you didn't expect your wife and the baby to go with you?"
"No, we both knew that would be impossible. We understood what I had to do and decided that she'd be more valuable as a courier here in Hanoi."

His words sounded matter of fact, the same way they had when he spoke of Thien Nguyen. Though in the dark, words without facial expression had a particularly cold affect on my mind. I shuddered thinking about the horrific rumors of what happened to anyone in a French prison. A sudden breeze blew through the grove as we stood facing each other.

"I'll do the best I can."

"You've gotten good at this," Dat Tu said. "No one suspects you."

Yes, with my help a lot of information had been supplied to the rebels. A lot of people were fooled about my involvement. But for how long, that was the big question.

"Tell my sister I am sorry about what happened to Thien Nguyen, but our country is filled with widows."

"Will you be at the funeral tomorrow?" Though I realized that to do so would risk capture.

"No. I will stay in Hanoi until after the burial. Tell Thi My that I'll try to see her before leaving."

A cat screeched in the distance.

"You must go now," Dat Tu said. "Tell no one that you've seen me except Thi My and the nun. Do you understand? No one." He turned and ran into the darkness.

Walking back to the rickshaw, I had a fright that it might be a long walk back to my house. Thankfully, that wasn't the case. Climbing into the carriage of the rickshaw, the runner wasted no time in maneuvering the vehicle onto the road. The lantern hanging near the foot of my seat lit the way with unnerving shadows that moved back and forth across the street like hands reaching out to touch me.

The rickshaw puller stopped up the street from my house. Handing him a few coins it was only a short walk. The silk merchant who lived across from me sat squatted in his doorway smoking a pipe and drinking tea with the owner of the noodle shop up the street. They watched me pass. In the dark it was difficult to tell if the men were suspicious or curious, but they were definitely interested.

There was a huge surprise waiting for me when the gate swung open. Sitting in the garden with Julia was the man some people had nicknamed, The Bear. He didn't get that name because he was soft and cuddly. Quite the contrary, the name came about because he towered over everyone. He had a long wooly beard, and when he laughed he made a great roaring sound.

Rushing to him, he grabbed me up in his arms and swung me around and around.

"How's my mermaid?" he bellowed, and nuzzled his beard in my neck. Releasing me, I slid to the ground feeling a bit lightheaded.

He kissed me on the mouth long, hard and passionate. Our breath warmed his beard as if it had been plugged into a heater. There were other women in his life, but he made me feel as though he'd saved every bit of affection just for me.

Julia cleared her throat.

"I suppose you two have already met," I said.

"Oh, yeah, we've met."

Julia flashed Albee an icy glance. She lit a cigarette. Something had gone on between these two. It was easy to see that they were probably not going to be the best of friends.

Julia took a long drag on her cigarette.

Albee had been away for months. We had a lot to catch up with, but the most pressing news was Thien Nguyen's murder.

He stood silently for a moment or two after I told him. He sighed heavily. "I heard there'd been a murder in Hanoi. I never suspected it would be so close to home."

"The funeral is tomorrow."

"How is Thi My?"

"How do you think she'd be?" Julia said. "In shock," I said, ignoring the sarcastic tone in Julia's comment.

Albee usually started out his visits by telling me tales of his romps through the villages where white men had never been seen before. These adventures over the years ran together. They explained nothing about what he did in his absence. Sometimes they felt like frivolous tales that seemed to be his way of killing time while we were together. Tonight he looked worried. Tonight there would be no stories.

The evening air felt stagnant and thick. I was exhausted. Even the potted bamboo plant in the corner of my garden, a plant that usually rustled nonstop even in the slightest breeze, stood motionless in this sultry night air.

"We'll have to get up early in the morning for the funeral," I said. "I don't know about you two, but I'm dog-tired."

"Ah, a real bed," Albee said. There was a slight change in his tone of voice. "I'm getting too old to sleep on the floor every night. Lead the way, my love." He took hold of my hand with one of his coarse paws and we walked into the house.

I glanced back at Julia. "See you in the morning."

Four

JULIA WATCHED SARAH AND ALBEE disappear into the shadows of the house. It had been a long day. Her body still vibrated from the miserably long flight from Paris and there was a ringing in her ears. Though for some reason Julia did not feel sleepy.

After Sarah left earlier that evening to meet up with Thi My's brother, Julia tried to finish an article about the Nazis she'd started while living in France. But Albee messed up those plans. He came sneaking into the house, scaring the living hell out of her and then explained that he was only trying to surprise Sarah. Julia nearly cracked him over the head with a vase from her nightstand. There wasn't much writing going on after that.

Julia wasn't crazy about Albee. It didn't matter how friendly Sarah was with this guy, no man should sneak into a woman's house late at night. But it wasn't a surprise to know that Sarah had a lover. Back in the States, Sarah was never without a man.

The night was dreadfully quiet. The only sound now was the periodic footfalls of passing rickshaw pullers. A cigarette burned in an ashtray. Julia took one last puff, snubbed it out on the heel of her shoe and then went into the bedroom to finish writing the article.

Earlier that evening, Julia had constructed a makeshift table by stacking on top of each other the two beat-up cardboard suitcases she'd dragged all over Spain. This made a perfect fit for her Remington portable typewriter. This wasn't the first time she'd done something like this. Sitting on the bed Julia plunked away at the keys.

The three years she'd reported on the war in Spain and the last six months working with the French underground in Paris, taught her to be a better writer and photographer. While she was in Spain most of her articles were sent to several newspapers in the States and one in Canada.

Words had always come easily to Julia. The war, though, had given her a gift born from fear. Tonight there was no hesitation about what to write. Her fingers flew over the keys. Fingers, Julia mused, that had learned to think for themselves. But it was more than that. The snipers, the bombs, the running for cover, and the repeated impact of seeing bodies riddled with bullets or blown to pieces forced her to write quickly and snap the camera shutter, not thinking of her own flesh.

She finished writing the article. Pulling the last sheet of paper out of the carriage, there was no way of her knowing when the article could be sent off to the People's Voice in Canada. Toward the end of the war, while still in Spain, she'd managed to send a few articles with the help of a fellow traveler who, with special papers, moved about freely from country to country. The last she'd heard, he'd struck out for Portugal. No one had seen him since. Scooting into Paris just as the Fascists took over Spain, and with all the chaos, it wasn't easy for any correspondent to get any articles sent over the wire to the States.

When first arriving in Spain, it was hard for Julia to conceive how involved in politics she'd eventually become. And though bubbling over with enthusiasm when setting foot in Spain, Julia left that country a different woman. Cynical and jaded she now wondered if everything she'd hoped would happen in Spain was only an illusion.

Conveying the impact of war in the written word was frustrating. Tragedies easily lost their power if the wrong words were put on the page. A photograph could look trite and posed if the timing was off by a second. Julia folded the article; slipped it into an envelope knowing that by the time it reached the editor's desk in Canada, everything she'd written would probably be old news.

She closed the light, shut her eyes, and laid on the bed. Images in the back of her brain came alive. In the light of day, they could be held at bay. At night they broke free, exploding into fragments of memories, shattering across a private, inner vision. Children screaming, mothers falling to the ground lifeless or maimed, soldiers with arms blown off, men running until they tripped over the bodies of comrades, everyone falling onto one another until they became a massive heap of the dead and dying. Political sympathies and enthusiasm turned into a bloodied initiation that first year in Spain, and from that point, Julia never again referred to herself as a reporter. She'd become a freedom fighter.

Remembering Johnny was the most painful of all memories. They joked about getting married when the war was over. They both knew that probably would never happen. Julia loved him like no other man she'd met, and wished the memory of their last day together would go away. But the explosion and the bloody mess of that day would remain with her forever. Johnny thought of himself as more than a newspaperman. He was drawn to trouble. Julia even suspected that he was addicted to danger. "Why else would I come to Spain," he told her early in their relationship. "I could write war stories from my apartment in Brooklyn. I'm here to give the Fascists hell."

She missed him terribly and began to play a game that in the end she knew would only be hurtful. The memory of his gentle touch drifted around her in the dark. Remembering his hungry mouth pressed against her lips only helped slightly to relieve the pain of the loneliness she felt without him. In the quiet of the night, with eyes closed, Julia could easily wait, anticipating, pretending that Johnny would reach out to touch her breast. There were many nights when their lovemaking drove her wild. Tasting salty tears, Julia reached between her legs.

Five

THE NEXT MORNING WHEN JULIA, Albee, and I arrived at the funeral, Thi My and the nun stood solemnly a respectful distance from Thien Nguyen's home, where the funeral procession was to begin.

"Hello," Albee said. Though his usual greeting for Thi My was a kiss on her forehead, this morning he did not touch her.

She glanced up at him, and then looked back down at the ground.

The bewildered look in Thi My's eyes made a shiver run down my back. This would not be an easy day.

Julia stood quietly by my side. Today I told her to leave the camera at home. She did not protest.

A large group of mourners gathered outside Thien Nguyen's house. Some were friends of the family, though some were quite likely curiosity seekers. The horrible thought came into my mind that the murderer might be among them. Another thought nagged me; had Thien Nguyen trusted the wrong person? Had he unknowingly brought his killer, perhaps even a friend or an acquaintance, into the Archives. Or had he been followed into the Archives and then taken by surprise? It was confusing and terribly disturbing to think about. After last night's meeting with Dat Tu, it was clear to me that he and I both believed that Thien Nguyen was murdered because of what he'd discovered in the Archives. I'd decided to do what Dat Tu had asked, not so much to help him, but to avenge a murdered friend.

Suddenly there was a great commotion at the front door of the house. Someone cried. Several women screamed. Like a body of water, the crowd moved forward. Then there was silence. A monk wielding a huge sword over his head appeared at the doorway. "Open the celestial door," he shouted in Vietnamese. "Close the terrestrial barrier. At the sound of my voice let cruel animals disappear. Let evil spirits fly from our path. Let Thien Nguyen join his ancestors."

The hearse, a large, ornate structure set on a huge stretcher, was hoisted onto the shoulders of six men. Thien Nguyen's body had been taken from the house and placed inside this burial structure. At that point all hell broke loose. Once again someone screamed. Some mourners called out orders as they pointed in one direction and then in another. Everyone talked at the same time in a feeble attempt to confuse any evil spirit that might decide to follow the deceased to the gravesite.

Thi My remained silent and continued to gaze down at the ground.

The monk took his place at the head of the procession. Draped in his chasuble, he came into full view just as he reached a far intersection and slowly turned the corner.

Several people followed behind the monk carrying a signboard with Thien Nguyen's full name, place of birth, age, any notable degrees, and his employment. The spirit house, a replica of Thien's ancestral home containing a full set of miniature furniture, followed the signboard.

Between the spirit house and the hearse, several young people carried a silk banner called the golden bridge. Expressions of praise and admiration for the deceased's virtues were written on the silk ribbon. Thien Nguyen's spirit was to travel across this silken bridge while his body was transported to the burial site. This represented him stepping into the spiritual world.

The funeral procession moved with painful slowness. It would be quite a while before we could join the procession. Julia fidgeted. She walked up the street a short distance and then returned. Albee leaned against a wall. He took out a pack of cigarettes, offering one to Julia. "We still have awhile to wait," he said.

"How long do these things last?" she asked.

"Until the dead ancestors are satisfied that the right amount of respect has been paid."

"The dead ancestors?"

"It's always about the ancestors in this part of the world," he said. With the snap of his wrist he struck a match across the wall; in the sunlight the flame was barely visible. Julia leaned into Albee's cupped hands. She took a long drag then exhaled a huge grey plume of smoke.

At that moment, my landlady, Aon She Beng, came up from behind me. Bumping into my left arm, she pushed passed me. "Why you not visit me?" she growled at Albee. "Am I no longer important?"

"Oh, Aon She Beng, you'll always be important to me," he said. "You're my favorite person in all of Hanoi. But you know I need my rest. You want me fresh and sassy, don't you." He took hold of her shriveled hands that more resembled claws than actual hands, and kissed her palms.

"For big man, your mouth too soft," she replied. "You sweet talk too much. Be in big trouble some day."

"I'm always in trouble," he said, and winked.

A slight twinkle came into her eyes. "Not in trouble with me," she said.

"But you're too much woman for me to handle."

Only Albee could get away with talking to Aon She Beng in this manner. She barked orders and berated all the men who came to visit her, but in her eyes, Albee could do no wrong.

"Tomorrow I make you special tea," she said. "We have nice talk."

"That would be lovely," Albee said.

Aon She Beng abruptly turned. She looked at me; her eyes sharp with anger. "The Communists and bandits have ruined this country."

"It's a changing world," I said.

"Not here," she replied. "They try make us weak by killing innocent people and make families pay so much money to bury the dead. This family poor; they borrow my money to pay for funeral." She shook her cane at the procession. "The communists are a plague. The French will crush them. Then I will sleep and not worry they steal my money and murder me in my bed."

I'd become accustomed to my landlady's rants. Though lately she seemed a little more on edge than usual. She'd lived alone as long as I'd been in Vietnam and I'd never heard her mention family. From what I'd heard she'd outlived at least two husbands. I had no doubt she had a few skeletons hiding in her closet, like the rest of us.

After Aon She Beng said her piece, she turned and thumped down the street maneuvering her way into the middle of a group of elderly women.

A small orchestra of flutes, stringed instruments, and a gong played a slow scratchy dirge.

I'd gotten used to the odd music in this country. Julia probably wouldn't find it such a pleasant sound. The drummers' beat out a slow rhythm, setting the pace for the procession. Thi My buried her face in a silk hankie and cried. Her shoulders shook violently though she did not make a sound.

All funerals in this country traveled along a road that has the most twists and turns in order to reach the burial grounds. I suspected we'd be at it all day and possibly this thing could go on into the evening.

Thi My's presence became more visible as the crowd around the house thinned out with a large portion of the mourners following the monk. Yet, no one looked in her direction. When I thought about it, Aon She Beng had not looked at her, either.

Dang Hung stepped out of the doorway of his house. He stood directly behind the hearse. Thien Nguyen's two sisters, weeping and holding onto each other followed close behind their brother.

Soon a frail, elderly woman supported by two companions came out onto the street and positioned herself in line behind the hearse. The paid mourners wailed with great gusto at that point. I'd never met her, but I suspected this older woman was Thien Nguyen's mother. Staggering, the poor woman nearly fell. The two companions held onto her and together they slowly walked up the street.

A group of elders from the neighborhood, friends of the family, and the curiosity seekers bunched up behind the family, joining the procession.

"Looks like I got here just in time," a man whispered in my ear. Jean George, the Director of the French Archive Project, and his wife, Henrietta, stood directly behind me. I had been so engrossed in watching Thien Nguyen's mother that I hadn't noticed anything else.

In the five years that I'd worked in the Archives, Jean George could hardly be called a boss. He was more of an overseer who made sure that those above him never discovered how incompetent he really was. He'd been appointed by a local French official to keep an eye on the Archives, though he never showed his face in one of the work areas unless he had a gripe or someone above him had been getting on his ass. Then he'd came running to make sure that his problem was everybody's problem.

Henrietta leaned forward, kissed me on each cheek. "How very nice to see you, Sarah."

Henrietta had been in this country far longer than someone with her unfailingly French manners should have stayed. This woman had the faith of a true colonialist and it was clear her intent had always been to turn this country into a little France. She'd sent me numerous invitations to attend her planned gatherings. The book clubs, the discussions on French culture, poetry, and sewing groups had all been grand failures. Luckily I'd never been to any of them. She worked tirelessly with the French bureaucracy to help bring more single French women to Vietnam in her effort to assist in civilizing this country through the feminine touch. My appointment to the Archives, most likely had been seen as part of this feminizing project. Too many men with the pioneering spirit, the rough necks who planted and managed the rubber plantations, the mining engineers, and the Frenchmen sent to Indochina to build the roads had turned this colony into a frontier country with gambling, whoring and much drinking. Now with the blessing of the French Colonial government and the help of people like Henrietta, they were actively recruiting single and widowed women to hopefully become the brides of the rowdy band of foreign men who managed this land and the businesses.

Henrietta leaned forward. In a conspiratorial manner, she whispered, "It was such a terrible thing, the murder of that young translator. Poor dear. And he planned to marry in a month. What a tragedy. Jean George has been sick over his death." There was a pause. She staggered slightly as though for a moment she'd lost her balance. I detected a faint odor of wine on her breath. "We've hired a bodyguard," Henrietta said, and discretely pointed him out to me. "He goes with us everywhere."

No longer in control of her soft tone, Henrietta now talked louder than necessary. "At first I found it really quite intrusive to have this man around all the time, but he is so charming. I've gotten used to him and feel much safer now that he's around." Henrietta stood too close. There was an awkward intimacy that made me uncomfortable.

"Protecting you from what?" I asked, and attempted to ease away from her.

"Why the rebels, of course. They are everywhere. I do worry about Jean George's safety."

Jean George glanced in Thi My's direction and then looked at me. "Guards have been posted all along the way to the burial site in case there is any trouble."

I suppose he thought saying this might comfort Thi My. "Trouble?" Albee snorted, and flicked his cigarette to the ground.

"Murder on French property is a threat to all," Jean George continued.

Albee walked toward us. "Don't flatter yourself," he said. "The French shouldn't be here in the first place."

"Not now," I chided Albee, and glanced at Thi My. The nun quickly positioned herself between Thi My and Jean George as though her body could shield the poor woman from hearing these words.

Jean George straightened his jacket as if Albee had roughed him up. He looked at me. "For a librarian, you keep pretty tough company."

"He was quite fond of the young man," I said. "Grief does strange things to your sensibility."

"He sounds like a rebel sympathizer to me." Jean George looked at Albee and then at me. "The guards are posted in case they try something."

"Who are the *they*?" I asked again.

"The rebels, of course. Who else would do something like this?"

"Why would you think that?" It was very clear to me that the French took every opportunity to blame any trouble in this country on the rebels.

"It's really quite obvious, isn't it? Everything we do to civilize this country, they undermine," Jean George said. "I've told everyone to stay away from the Archives today while the Bureau investigates the murder. And, by the way, I've hired a new translator."

"You certainly didn't waste any time," I said.

Jean George took hold of his wife's arm. Without saying another word he quickly escorted her away to join the crowd of people who had begun to walk behind the family. Jean George and Henrietta would not walk the entire way to the gravesite. It would be like him to have a car waiting for them a couple blocks away.

As the funeral possession began to move, the nun said, "We will have to remain a distance from the others."

Thi My looked so frail, it appeared that even the slightest breeze could have blown her over. We stood in a small group surrounding the poor young woman as though she were in need of protection while waiting for the nun to tell us that Thi My could take her place in the funeral procession.

Six

Is it a dream?
There is the sound of mourner's drums.
Many bowls of rice have been set before me.
Incense burns. Candles flicker.
People are dressed in mourner's garb.
Who has died?
I cannot remember.
Numbness befalls me.
There is nothing but darkness.
Then light fills me again.
It is neither warm nor cold.
A mother cries. Her mouth stuffed with the mourner's rags, yet, her cries rip through my heart.
Who has caused this mother such pain?
Falling, falling deeply into sleep again,
Thi My softly weeps. I reach out to her and the world goes dark.
Stumbling back into the light I am riding on the golden bridge.
The spirit world beckons me.
Thi My whispers my name.

Seven

I'D BEEN AWAY FROM THE Archives two days longer than Jean George allowed. A ton of work was waiting for me. With Thien Nguyen's funeral over there was no reason to put off going back to work. So, with Albee and Julia still sleeping, I quietly dressed, grabbed the packet of poetry that Thi My returned to me, and tiptoed out of the house.

My office consisted of not much more than a small desk in the hallway. Jean George called this the administrative center.

Sliding into the seat behind my desk, Jean George must have heard me come in because he burst out of his office. "Mademoiselle Sarah," his voice boomed in an arrogant, self-righteous tone. "Will you be with us for the rest of the day?"

He pointed to Thien Nguyen's desk where a young wide-eyed, neatly dressed stranger now sat. "This is your new translator." Then without saying another word, Jean George retreated back into his office, slamming the door behind him.

I had deliberately diverted my eyes from the desks on the other side of the hall. The translators sat there when they could manage to get time away from the stacks. Now from the rickety chair where Thien Nguyen once filled out his time card and translated documents, the new translator nervously watched me. Thin and delicate, there was a childlike quality about this young man.

"I guess we'll be working together," I said.

He rushed to my desk. "My name is Le Sing Dong." He looked to be about the same age as Thien Nguyen. They might have even known each other.

"Anyone tell you what you'll be doing?" I asked.

"No. I've been waiting for instructions."

That didn't surprise me. There had been at least a half-dozen translators in the five years since I'd taken this job in the French Archive Project. But this morning I really didn't have the temperament to show the ropes to someone new.

"How many dialects do you know?" I asked.

"Many."

This told me nothing. His response could have meant that he only knew two, and one could have been the dialect from his ancestors' province. Jobs like this one were scarce and many well meaning, yet near illiterate people applied for any work they could find.

"We might as well get started." It would be clear soon enough if this guy would work out.

Most people thought translators only dealt with the language conversion of documents. But in these Archives, it was much more than that. Translators had to carry large bundles of written material back and forth between the storage room and the reading area. Space had become an increasing problem. The documented files, ancient texts and government communiqués took up an unbelievable amount of space.

As we approached the door to the Archives, my hands momentarily froze. The vision of Thien Nguyen's body flashed in front of me. Touching the door frightened me. Coming back to work was not going to be easy. My arms felt weak. Taking a deep breath, I slowly reached up and with great effort managed to get the door to move.

When the door swung open, Le Sing Dong gasped. His response startled me. The top of my head went cold with panic.

"I've never seen so much literature," he whispered.

The first visit to this building could be overwhelming. I'd gotten accustomed to the row after row of shelves filled with stacks of paper, loose papers, papers bundled in old silk ribbon or jute string, books bound in brittle and cracked leather cases, leaflets, copies of newspapers, and publications of all kinds. The French had mandated that eventually every bit of literature in Vietnam be routed though this building, a major undertaking of the Colonial government. It was part of a policy they called their "civilizing mission" in Indochina.

Though I'd worked as a librarian back in the States, nothing I'd ever done prepared me for this job. The climate here is hard on everything and is a major enemy of paper. The rainy season lasts for months and is a perfect breeding ground for molds and strange fungi. The heat and humidity during the rest of the year makes everything dripping wet. The temperature can go so high some days that it feels like the blood is cooking in your veins. These old documents and block prints in my keeping didn't have a chance in hell of surviving. Yet, in the time that I'd worked on this project I had catalogued some documents that were hundreds of years old. Every morning, even before putting my hand on the latch to open the door to this huge room, the air tasted of the disintegrating and rotting manuscripts.

There were other things in the archives, too, not just letters, books and documents. Rodents and insects had long ago set up housekeeping among the sheaves of paper. The staff takes turns doing the janitorial duties. They sweep the floors. No one complains. The most bothersome issue about this building for me is the infestations of rodents, spiders and other crawling things that scurried around in the bookshelves. Periodically throughout the day someone bangs a stick against the floor. Sometimes the whack of the stick is followed by a short-lived squeal. This never fails to unnerve me and a shiver crawls up my back. I hate spiders the most. They get pretty big in this part of the world. I let the staff know what area I will be working in the next day. That way someone will clear the shelves of insects and rodents before I got there.

The new translator stood silently at my side as though in a trance.

"Why don't you take a look around?" I said. "Then we can talk."

Le Sing Dong stepped away. He walked along one of the shelves lightly touching the documents.

At the far end of the room two women sat hunched over a long table. They had worked in the Archives many years. They never needed to be told what to do. They arrived at sun up and without prompting, repaired the bindings of old manuscripts, leaving their workstation only when the light of day disappeared.

"New translator," I told the women.

They watched Le Sing Dong briefly. When he vanished behind a bookcase, they returned to pulling long strands of jute through the broken backs of books.

Some of the books and manuscripts had been squeezed so tightly together in the years before I arrived that it was impossible to separate them from the soft wooden shelves. And Jean George had his own agenda. He'd recently given orders to find first one publication and then another that he wanted removed immediately from the Archives. They were to be made ready for shipping to France. Everyone had to stop whatever they were doing and get involved with these special assignments. He never gave a reason. "Do as I say," were his famous last words. There was never a "thank you."

We were in the middle of one of Jean George's special projects when Julia's telegram arrived announcing she'd be arriving from Paris in a couple of weeks. By then, Thien Nguyen and the other staff knew exactly what to do. But, then Thien Nguyen was murdered the day before Julia arrived. Now, not only did Jean George demand the same output for his assignments, there was a new translator who had to be trained.

Part of my job also included the supervision of building maintenance. Several windows had been broken during the last monsoon. Nailing boards across the gaping holes had been the best that we could do. The roof leaked in a couple of places, and though the repairs had been made, during a heavy downpour, sections of the bookshelves always got soaked. One entire collection of documents had gotten so wet in the last monsoon that we could no longer separate the pages.

Jean George put a rush on getting some of these books sent south to Hue and Saigon where he said better facilities were being constructed. In the middle of getting this job done, we received a shipment of manuscripts from several northern provinces. Managing all these pieces of paper some days bordered on insanity.

I stood contemplating how things could not get much worse when Father Dominique came up from behind me. This priest had a way of gliding across the floor without making a sound. His robe dragged along the dusty floor leaving a trail that looked as though something had slithered into the Archives.

"Ah, Sarah, my child. You are with us again."

"Good morning, Father Dominique."

"Did you meet your new translator?" he asked.

"Yes. And did you get a chance to talk to him?"

"Indeed, I'm the one who recommended him for the job. A very bright young man."

"So then you can tell me if he's as smart as Dat Tu or Thien Nguyen."

"There's no comparison. Le Sing Dong is a very capable young man. I've never met anyone like him before. He will give you no trouble. He learns very quickly. You'll see."

As the priest finished saying this, the new translator came from around the corner of a bookshelf.

"Ah, Le Sing Dong, good morning," Father Dominique called out, and extended his hand.

"Hello, Father," Le Sing Dong said and took hold of the outstretched hand. Le Sing Dong's other hand was wrapped with a handkerchief. A bit of blood spotted through the cloth.

"Well, are there enough books for you?" Father Dominique asked. He turned to me. "This young man has always complained that there was never enough to read. I do believe the Archives will be a heaven on earth for him. He reads books like some people breathe air." The priest turned to Le Sing Dong. "I must not hear any more complaints from you about not having enough books in the world for you to read."

Le Sing Dong looked embarrassed and glanced down at the floor. He pulled the hanky tighter around his bloody finger.

"Are you alright?" I asked. He didn't look distressed though he did look uncomfortable.

"I'm fine. It's just a scratch from something sharp in one of the shelves. Really it's nothing."

"Do you mind if Le Sing Dong and I have a word in private?" Father Dominique asked. The bloody finger did not seem to be of concern to the Father.

"Go right ahead."

Father Dominique encircled Lee Sing Dong in a long sweeping arm. The young man nearly disappeared in the folds of the priest's robe. They walked slowly to the other side of the building, all the while Father Dominique whispering into the new translator's ear.

Le Sing Dong returned several minutes later without the priest.

"So, are you ready to get started?" I asked.

But before he responded, we heard the sound of a stick cracking down hard several times on the floor. There were rapid moving footsteps, another whack, a short-lived squeal, and then all was quiet again.

Listening to the scurry of rodents and staff between the rows of bookshelves made me dread all the more walking through the stacks while explaining to Le Sing Dong the basic workings of the Archives. Not that it was ever easy trying to convey all that a translator needed to know, but on this first day back it seemed impossible.

Le Sing Dong stood patiently waiting for me to say something. He took off the cloth from the bleeding wound. A long, thin cut ran the length of his index finger.

"How did you do that?"

"Something sharp in the bookshelf."

"Where?"

"I'll show you." Le Sing Dong turned and went back along the row from where he had come.

"Wait! No."

I knew exactly where it had happened. It was in the row where Thien Nguyen had been murdered. The morning Thien Nguyen's body was discovered, I had arrived in the Archives early in the morning, and discovered that the tungsten light bulbs hanging between one of the shelves had burned out.

These bulbs were expensive and not easily replaced. Jean George would give me the usual hard time about being frivolous and wasteful. This was going through my mind when I decided to see what the problem was.

It was difficult to see in the dim light but someone lay slumped against one side of the shelves. It didn't register at first who it might be. Was it a man sleeping? He did not stir as I approached. His face was turned away from me. I bent down to take a closer look. I shook him slightly. He still did not awake. Then he slumped sideways. His head banged hard onto the floor. The breath caught in my throat. It was Thien Nguyen. His eyes were opened. He looked startled and he glared at me with bewilderment. A wire, twisted tightly around his neck, his face had an unnatural puffiness.

Little pieces of glass lay scattered all about his body. The light bulbs above his head had been smashed as though his attacker wanted to bury him in the shadows of the shelves.

If at all possible, this was an area I definitely wanted to avoid today. The staff had supposedly cleared the broken glass after Thien Nguyen's body had been removed. If there were still pieces of glass large enough to cut Le Sing Dong's finger; hard telling what else might still be in that area. It could even be possible that there was still evidence hanging around on those shelves.

The image of Thien Nguyen was still too fresh in my mind. Le Sing Dong would have to get his training later. "I really don't have the patience for this today," I said. "Would you mind browsing the shelves on your own? Get familiar with the building. Tomorrow will be soon enough to get you started."

Le Sing Dong said nothing. He turned and walked toward the aisle nearest to where we stood.

It was clear to me now that the best place on my first day back was behind a desk. Making lists had always soothed my nerves in the past. Maybe that would help get my mind off Thein Nguyen's murder. A pad of paper and a pen sat in front of me. And then remembered the packet of poems that Thi My had returned to me, I casually flipped open the bundle of pages. A pang of sadness sat in my heart when I thought about how much Thien Nguyen loved these old verses.

It was not an easy language to learn with so many dialects. The multiple meanings behind many of the words eluded me. To read this poetry, steeped in symbolism and mythology, needed someone like Thien Nguyen or Dat Tu, not necessarily a scholar. It needed someone familiar with the culture to explain the intricacies and the meanings lodged in the verse. Leafing through the bundle, a page of Chu Han literature slipped out. Lately quite a few of these poems and stories had come into the Archives. It was considered serious literature, influenced by Confucianism. Thien Nguyen loved it dearly.

So far he hadn't translated any of the verse into either French or

English, though he had intended to do so. Could this have been what Dat Tu thought Nguyen had found?

Flipping through a few more pages I found a totally unexpected document on official French Government stationery. With the Governor General of Indochina official seal, it was clearly an important communication. It had been addressed to an official in a northern province. Recently the Archives had received quite a few very old royal proclamations and ordinances from this northern province, some of the material dating back as far as the 14th Century. Much of it was in very bad shape.

The title of this communication was, "Agriculture Conversion in Indochina." That certainly got my attention. It wasn't hard to figure out that this had been the document Thien Nguyen intended to give to Dat Tu. I read on:

All available land is to be transformed in use from agriculture to rubber and hemp for wartime production. Any virgin land now being worked by peasants is to be confiscated and will become the property of a European, and preferably a Frenchman, or to a certain rich Vietnamese proprietor who is supportive of the French Colonial Administration.

There was no mistaking the intent of this mandate. It was beyond me to think that the French had been so stupid as to actually write all this down. There was no doubt in my mind that letters like this one had been sent out to other provinces.

I continued to read.

All land debts are to be recalled. Land is to be attained by any means and in such acts any transaction will be looked upon favorably by the legal system.

This was the document the Governor General's office had been seeking when that administrator came to the Archives the other day. "Misinformation, my ass." I slipped the letter back into the pages of poetry and closed the folder.

The intent of the communication stunned me. There was no doubt that this had everything to do with Thien Nguyen's murder. Though for the life of me it was a mystery why it had to happen this way.

I had been sitting at my desk—don't know for how long—dumbfounded about what I'd read, when Jean George stepped out of his office. He hadn't expected to see me and appeared startled. He was about to say something; instead he nodded and left the building.

Time passed dreadfully slow. Thankfully the workday eventually ended.

I slipped the packet of papers back into my pocketbook. No way was this information going to sit around on a shelf in the Archives.

Eight

AFTER WORK EACH EVENING, ONE of the local rickshaw pullers waited outside the Archive building to take me home. All rickshaw pullers wore the same type of conical straw hat slung down over their face. We never looked at each other. They all appeared pretty much the same with their thin bodies and ragged clothing, and we never spoke as they pulled me along the streets.

Leaning back in the musty seat, I watched as the city closed for the night. Even though most of the noodle shops and fresh produce stalls were emptied by the time my work day was over, a passenger traveling in the open air could still experience the fragrance of the day's activities. The lingering aroma of exotic herbs made my mouth water while the rickshaw bounced along the rutted streets.

As one labor pool closed their shops for the day, another work force opened theirs. Evening shadows hung on the buildings like sheets of dark fabric as the rickshaw puller took me through streets where prostitutes—some not much older than little girls—gathered in the doorways of brothels. The demure workers stood quietly watching us quickly move up the street, while the seasoned madam waved and called to the puller.

We passed an opium house, one of Albee's frequent haunts. He'd tried to get me to join him a couple of times, but this never interested me. Booze was my entertainment. I knew what to expect when I drank. Waking up with a hangover in the morning seemed a small price to pay for the simple pleasure of drinking.

When the rickshaw stopped in front of my house, the puller tilted his hat slightly, revealing his face. "I need to speak to Albee," he said.

"Dat Tu…what are you doing here?"

He lowered his hat again. "Please."

"What do you want me to do?"

"Open your gate. Let me take this thing inside. Quickly, please."

"Yes, of course, come in."

Dat Tu pulled the rickshaw into the garden, and we hurriedly closed the gate behind us.

Julia sat on a chair near the small fishpond drinking from a tall glass. Cigarette smoke floated above her head like a feathery bank of fog.

"Glad you're home," Julia said. "Now who on earth have you brought with you?"

I detected a slight slur in her voice.

Dat Tu took off his hat.

I rushed into the house. "Albee, we've got company."

"Who?"

"Dat Tu."

Albee stepped out into the garden. "Ah, you're just in time to eat."

"I didn't come for food."

Albee put one of his large arms around the young man's shoulder. "Eat first, then we can talk." Without much difficulty, he coaxed Dat Tu into the house.

Albee and I usually played a domestic game when he first arrived in Hanoi. The novelty wore off by the second day and then we'd both go back to business as usual. Though lately on his visits, we rarely saw each other after the second or third day, and then he'd take off again for the deserts of China or wherever he was headed.

A pot of something simmered on my small wood-burning stove. Curry smelled like the main spice in whatever Albee had prepared for us. But, I didn't ask, "Curried what?" Albee had lived in this part of the world long enough to understand that eating depended on whatever became available. He lived by the motto, "Don't snub what the Gods provide." Since I'd moved to French Indochina I'd certainly eaten my share of food that I'd labeled "unidentified."

Julia put a record on the gramophone, sat down and eagerly ate her dinner. "Very good," she said. It hadn't taken her long to master the chopsticks, and I watched as my old friend gobbled up the exotic broth with a portion of rice.

Dat Tu ate a small bowl of the food. He'd become quite thin since he'd quit working at the Archives. He hadn't been very heavy to start with, but now his face looked gaunt.

Albee hunched over his bowl and shoveled the food into his mouth. He always ate with urgency. After finishing his portion of the meal, he pushed away from the table. "Okay," he said, "now we can talk."

Taking out a small leather pouch of tobacco, a pack of rolling papers, Albee slowly constructed one of his fat after-dinner cigarettes. He struck a match across the floor and lit the handmade job. Soon a gray-blue haze filled the room. He never said where he got this stuff, but the tobacco stank like burning rubber.

Julia swallowed the last of what was left in her tall glass and put another record on the gramophone. Julia had brought with her a small stack of Kansas City jive records she'd found in Paris. This music used to bring me a lot of pleasure back in the States when Julia and I hung out in the after-hours joints. Now the songs irritated me and sounded totally out of place in this country.

I lit a cigarette, took a drag, and poured a glassful of rice wine. "Jean George hired someone to take Thien Nguyen's place." I said.

"Good," Dat Tu said.

"By any chance would you be interested in coming back to work in the Archives?"

"No way in hell," Dat Tu replied. "I have more important work to do."

I noticed Dat Tu had recently picked up some interesting American slang.

"You going to fix the world, are you?" Albee asked, giving Dat Tu a look that I couldn't quite read.

"Not the world, just my country."

"You're going to get yourself killed," I said.

"If that's what it takes."

Julia remained silent but watched Dat Tu intently.

Albee cleared his throat. "So, why'd you come here tonight?"

The music on the gramophone ended. The silence felt abrupt and threatening as though the neighbors could now hear every word we spoke.

"What's it like in China?" Dat Tu asked. Despite all of his rebel activity, at that moment he sounded like a child asking a parent about life among the stars.

"It's not good. Why? You interested in going there?" Albee asked.

"Maybe."

Albee took a drag on his cigarette and slowly let out a long stream of smoke. He looked down at the table and appeared to absentmindedly play with a couple grains of rice that had fallen from his chopsticks during the meal. "Are you questioning whether you should go or have you already made up your mind?" When Dat Tu did not respond, Albee continued, "Let's just say that the Japanese are bent on taking over this part of the world. Asia for Asians is not an innocent phrase. They want to control all of Asia or they wouldn't have started a war with China. It's dangerous over there right now. It's especially dangerous to get caught in the middle."

This got Julia's attention. Knocking the ash from the butt of her cigarette, she asked, "So what is going on over there?"

Albee glanced at her, almost startled, as though he'd forgotten Julia was in the room. He looked at her for a long moment before responding. "I'm an archeologist who digs up old things, very old things. The truth is, I pay less and less attention to what's happening in the world today. Whatever's going on now, you can trust that someone will dig up the ruins in a few centuries and try to make sense out of what we'd done to each other."

"That's pretty cynical," I said. We both knew that he was full of shit.

He cared very much about what happened in the world.

"Is it any worse than ignoring what's happening around you and doing nothing about it?" Albee asked.

"It's the same thing," Dat Tu quickly interjected. "Cynicism is only an excuse for doing nothing. What the Japanese are doing in China does not matter to me. Vietnam is my only concern. I want the French out."

"That attitude will play right into the Emperor of Japan's hands." Albee leaned closer to Dat Tu. "I'll bet your father gets pretty upset when he hears you talk this way."

Albee knew that Dat Tu and his father fought bitterly about the right for France to control their country. I looked at Albee. He had a familiar smug look on his face. For the life of me it was difficult to understand why he said such a thing, except to stir up trouble, which he certainly liked to do.

"My father's a traitor," Dat Tu snarled.

"Let's just say that you and your father have different ideas about what's good for your country." At this point I felt obliged to smooth out the conflict, though I agreed with Dat Tu. But over the years I'd seen how politics tore this family apart.

"No, let's say that my father knows how to fill his pockets. And the only thing important to work for now is a united and independent country. Nothing else matters."

"Those are fine words," Albee said. "But the French are not the most dangerous enemy right now. The Fascists are the ones to look out for, the true enemy. Once they are defeated, then we can go after the French."

Julia slammed her glass down on the table.

Albee looked at her. "Yes?" he asked slowly and quizzically.

"The true enemy?" Julia said with a sneer. "Who decides who that is? A committee in Moscow?"

"That's right. You take into account the changing objective situation." Albee looked at Dat Tu though I knew that this comment had been directed at Julia. "Right now the Japanese are the biggest threat to this country and the world." Albee shifted his gaze, looking straight at Julia. "You might not like it but you have to think long range sometimes."

Julia took a drag on her cigarette. She held the smoke in her lungs and glared at Albee. "In Spain," she said through clinched teeth, "Moscow's Spanish Communist Party's long range thinking silenced the anarchists, the socialists and even the independent communists. When I first got there it looked as though the communists were the good guys and that everyone would join together and wipe out the fascists. Then it didn't take long to figure out that the only thing your group wanted was to dominate and take control." Julia's voice trembled.

"You can say that because you have no sense of history," Albee said. He knocked the ash from his cigarette onto the floor. "I know you spent six months in Spain—"

"No, Albee, I spent three years there."

"Okay, but you were reporting stories and not dealing with the politics. Right?"

Dat Tu abruptly stood and said, "Spain, Poland, Czechoslovakia, they're all the same. What do I care! I'm not going around the world looking for trouble. It came to my house, to my family, and to my country. France is my enemy and not Fascism. The Japanese can have China. What harm can they do me? The only thing my comrades and I want is to get our country back."

"Boy are you wrong there," Albee said. "I've seen first-hand what the Japanese can do. You think they'll stop with China. They'll come after your country next. They'll move into Burma and Thailand. They'll do whatever is necessary to take control."

"You really don't care about Vietnam or Spain," Julia said. "The picture is so big that the people in these little countries are simply interchangeable characters on your world stage."

Albee smiled. "In a way, you're right. We're all characters in this stage as you put it. We all have a role in building a better society."

Julia glowered at Albee. "And with that notion you plan to sacrifice the lives of anyone who gets in the way, or who thought they were on the same side as you, but doesn't quite buy the entire program laid out by your superiors in Russia?"

"You plan on sacrificing my country's independence?" Dat Tu asked.

"No, just the opposite. We want to make this fight effective. All the sacrifices should be worthwhile, not some romantic gesture. If you're going to fight, fight smart. Know who the enemy is. Dat Tu, it's very possible that the Japanese will take control of Vietnam from the French. Would you accept that?"

"No. But I do not want to fight someone else's battle, either."

I listened to this conversation knowing full well what the French had planned for Vietnam. Thien Nguyen had known this, too. What had he planned to do with the information he'd found in the Archives? He must have told more people than Dat Tu. For the first time it became clear to me how importance this document was. Had Thien Nguyen decided to hand it over to Dat Tu? If the rebels got hold of this information they would use it to convince their countrymen that the French were only interested in exploiting this country. But then I wondered what if Albee got his hands on this document? Would it ever see the light of day? This kind of information would have jeopardized his master plan. It would have redirected the Vietnamese rage away from the Japanese and kept the focus on the French. Albee did not want to see that happen.

"Vietnam does not exist in isolation," Albee said. "It's part of a worldwide system of capitalism and imperialism. Whether you like it or not, its fate is determined by what happens in the world. The major struggle right now is between fascism and their capitalist supporters and the progressive forces which happen to be led by the communist party."

Julia ground her cigarette butt into the ashtray. "A lot of good people died in Spain fighting for the right side." Her eyes filled with tears. "They were betrayed by the communist party." Abruptly standing, Julia left the room and went out into the garden.

Albee watched her disappear into the evening shadows. "Not everyone understands," he said. "In the end, we'll know the answers to many questions. But for now, you have to trust that whatever decision you make, is the right one. You can throw you energy into a bottomless pit or you can join forces with us and do this thing up right."

"I want my country back."

"With some serious work, you'll eventually achieve that goal. But it's going to take a lot of effort." Albee stood and yawned widely. "I need fresh air. Dat Tu, why don't we take a walk?"

I poured myself another glass of wine while the two men maneuvered the carriage out into the street. A serious disquiet hung in the garden after they'd left. Now I wasn't sure to whom I'd show the document. Though it was quite clear to me that whoever possessed this letter, would have some powerful information.

"What the hell is going on?" Julia said.

"Not sure."

"And here I was feeling sorry for my poor librarian friend thinking she was working in this God-forsaken country with no friends and nothing to comfort her." Julia took another drag and gave me a quizzical grin.

I put a Gaulloise into my cigarette holder and struck a match. The smell of sulfur stung my nostrils. "I can't shake the image of Thien Nguyen."

"I know what you mean." Julia looked up at the stars and then she looked back down at me. "I saw plenty of blood spilled in Spain."

Her face changed. There was harshness in her eyes. Her jaws clinched and there was an angry tone in her voice.

"I doubt if they'll ever really know how many people were killed in Spain. The streets got so slippery with blood in some small towns, the military convoys slid off the roads." Julia's voice cracked. She turned away from my gaze.

Julia vigorously fanned herself. Then abruptly changing the subject, she said, "This heat is unbearable. How long have you lived here?"

"I lost count." I took a hearty swallow from my glass of wine.

The expression on her face changed. Now it was kind of a chiding look as if she had a secret. It was a familiar look, a look I remembered from years ago. It seemed that no matter how much time passed between our visits, some things did not change. "How'd you get to Spain?" I asked. "Did a newspaper send you?"

"Hardly. Though when I decided to go to Spain with the International Brigade, I asked my editor if he'd like me to send him stories and details about what was going on over there. He said, sure, but that the paper couldn't pay. A lot of businesses hadn't recovered from the Depression. Kansas City didn't change much after you left. Most folks couldn't rub two nickels together, let alone afford a penny for a newspaper." Julia lit another cigarette.

As I looked at her, even after she'd had several days rest, she reminded me of a woman trying to cover up something with all that face powder. I didn't think traveling told the real story. She didn't look well.

"I kept the letters you sent me from Madrid," I said.

"How sweet." Julia smiled and flicked a long ash from her cigarette onto the garden floor.

"I'm not very good at corresponding."

Julia smiled sweetly.

People like me—I mean normal folks—shouldn't have to apologize for not being able to keep up with people like Julia who could knock out a letter in a matter of minutes.

"In one letter you asked me to join you in Spain. Remember?"

"I got pretty involved there for a while. You have to admit fighting fascism is a pretty good cause. We needed all the help we could get. In the end, the fascists won. I wonder if all those deaths were worth the struggle. Now Germany's gobbled up Poland. Next, mark my word; the Nazis are going to take over France and Great Britain. Look at the world. Where do you think we'll be in ten years?" The dim glow of the kerosene lamp cast an eerie shadow across Julia's face. Her drawn, tired look frightened me.

Many things about this evening unsettled me. And the dinner conversation certainly threw the door wide open to how complicated the times were.

"Excuse me for a few minutes," I said, and standing abruptly, picking up my glass of wine, I went into the house. It couldn't be put off any longer. The document had to be safely hidden, at least for the time being. This old house had a few nooks that would work as hiding places, but this document had to be carefully placed so that the vermin who scurried around in the woodwork wouldn't make nesting material out of it.

Nothing too creative came to mind. Opening the door to my armoire I took out a heavy quilt that was rarely used. It might work, I thought. Carefully clipping at a few stitches on a corner seam with a pair of fingernail scissors I made a small opening in the quilt. Rolling the document into a tight scroll, I carefully shoved the paper into the opening. The quilt could be stitched closed later. Placing the blanket back into the armoire with the document securely inside eased my sense of anxiety a bit, though I wish I'd never seen that piece of paper.

Grabbing another bottle of wine I went back out to the garden.

Just as Julia filled her glass with a large portion of rice wine, a hot breeze blew into the garden. An uneasy tingling crept across my shoulders. Julia fidgeted in her chair. She quickly looked over her shoulder. Just as abruptly as the breeze had whooshed over the garden wall, everything went deathly quiet again.

"Strange," Julia said. "While you were in the house, something rustled in the bushes over there in the corner. It's kind of a creepy night."

I said nothing. Though I had a peculiar sensation that we were not alone. Brushing the thought aside I excused my own feeling of uneasiness to having the document now tucked away in the quilt.

Nine

There is no flesh or bones to catch the breeze.
Great waves of sounds rush at me.
How is it that I move? I cannot feel my limbs.
Sarah's face, calm, her caring words draw me near her.
She can be trusted. I remember those words.
She can be trusted.
But, I have forgotten something.
I live in the beating heart of Thi My.
I gave her poetry.
She gave me strength.
What have I forgotten?
There are secrets?
I see in the night as though in day. Yet, the daylight makes me blind.
What have I forgotten?
I cannot loosen myself from Sarah.
She can be trusted, repeats again and again in my brain.
Sarah, please help me remember.
What I have forgotten.

Ten

AN HOUR LATER, ALBEE CAME back into the garden. "Girls," he called out. "Let's go get drunk."

"I'm for that," I responded.

"Count me in," Julia said without hesitation.

We scooted into a pair of sandals and hurried out into the street to catch up with Albee. It wouldn't have surprised me a bit if Aon She Beng had come running to the peephole in her garden gate the minute Albee's blustering voice called out to us. He knew this, too. He hadn't stopped by her place for that cup of tea as he promised, so when we walked past her house, he gave her closed gate one of his big grins, and called out, "Hello, Aon She Beng. See you later."

A few shoppers still remained in the market place at this late hour, haggling over prices with merchants. Albee, the big and hairy man that was, usually attracted attention wherever he went. Several people stopped what they were doing to gape at him.

As we neared two waiting rickshaws, Albee almost tripped over a small child sitting on the edge of the dusty street. This thin, filthy urchin could have been mistaken for a small heap of garbage. Albee bent down, took a few coins from his pocket, placed them in the child's grubby palm, and whispered something into his ear. The hungry child looked up at this giant. If this poor little beggar could have managed a smile, this would have been enough thanks for Albee's generosity. The boy stood, his stick thin legs poking out from his ragged clothing, and walked slowly down the street, disappearing into an alley.

"Poor little thing," Julia said. "But, why'd you give money to a child. Wouldn't it have been better if you'd given it to an adult?"

"Nothing's going to make a difference in the long run. Though if that child brings the parents a few coins they might think twice about selling him."

"Sell him?" Julia asked.

Her question surprised me. From what she'd said earlier that evening, I knew that she'd seen plenty of misery in Spain, though I wondered what her expectations were of this country.

"Look around you," Albee commanded. He pointed into the shadow where a woman sat in a doorway across the street. "See that woman holding a baby? They have nothing. Do you know how I know that? Because ninety-nine percent of the population in this country have nothing and that woman may have already lost other children to disease and starvation."

Albee's behavior tonight puzzled me. It wasn't so much what he said to Julia, but he had told me many times that handing coins to impoverished people only prolonged the inevitable. He believed that hungry and dissatisfied people fought the hardest for change, and only liberals and do-gooders, in an attempt to appease their consciences, handed out skimpy funds to the unfortunate. It might have been Julia's presence that set Albee off. But there was something different about him this visit. Something was going on. Though if I'd asked, he would have denied anything was wrong. Secrets were as much a part of him as the blood that ran though his veins.

Five years ago when we first met, Albee told me about his work in an archaeological dig in Manchuria. He always had interesting stories about the nomads that lived in the desert. Back then he exuded excitement about his work. Then the Japanese moved troops into that area. Albee changed after that. He had become secretive and definitely more political.

Albee climbed into one rickshaw while Julia and I climbed into another. When we arrived at the Americano Bar, the place was empty except for several men who were bellied up to the bar. They gave us the once-over and then looked away.

"Glad to see you back in town," Bobby called from behind the bar.

Albee gave him a wave with one hand. "How about a beer?"

"Coming right up. And what would you ladies like"

Julia and I ordered wine.

We sat at a table in the farthest corner. Albee took a seat facing the door, a habit he'd gotten into, he said, living on the edge of society for so many years. Always good to know if someone's coming after you was his motto. He had never been attacked from behind, but then a sane person would think twice before tangling with a man his size.

Albee was a world traveler and a man of many habits, and would never think to drink his ale in another bar in Hanoi. If he liked you, he'd be your friend for life and he'd do anything for you. But Albee had a dark side, and I'd learned to never cross him because he found it impossible to forgive a misdeed.

"How long will you be hanging around this time?" Bobby asked as he set our drinks on the table.

"Can't say. Could be a while. Things are getting pretty hot across the border."

"Yeah?"

"China's a particularly unhealthy place to be right now," Albee said. "Has been for quite some time."

"That's what they tell me. What about your work?"

"No more digging. The war's put a stop to that."

"Too bad," Bobby commiserated.

"Does that mean you're out of a job?" I asked.

"No, there's plenty to do." Albee took a swallow of beer and smacked his lips. "Bobby, it tastes like you made a special batch just for me."

"I did. I did indeed," Bobby replied, and then went back behind the bar.

"I like the taste of Bobby's brew, but beer should have a head like back in the States. It was like getting whipped cream with your beer."

"What do you think is going to happen in China?" I asked.

A grin or an angry clenched jaw could sometimes get lost in Albee's tumbled whiskers. It was not easy to tell if he was flashing a smile, but his eyes often betrayed him. His eyes glared hatefully at me.

"Maybe the world's rotting," he said, and gulped the remaining beer. He put the glass on the table with a loud clunk. "For years I've been digging up old cultures that have been buried for centuries. I've held bones in my hands that used to be breathing men, women, and children. I've touched fabric that clothed kings and I've smelled the grains harvested by civilizations that have gone extinct. Scraps. Only scraps left of an entire society. You ask what will happen? If we make it through the next ten years I'd say we're lucky."

Albee raised his empty glass and called out, "Another one, Bobby."

"I thought you were in a good mood," I said.

"Things happen."

"What things?"

Bobby arrived at the table with a small bucket brimming with beer. "I'll just leave this here," he said. Albee had been known to drink from the bucket, but he let Bobby pour the beer into his waiting glass.

"I appreciate this," Albee said.

"I'm sure you're as dry as that desert you just left."

"You have no idea how dry a man can get." Albee did not wait for Bobby to leave the table before he gulped down another mouthful of beer.

"What's going on, Albee?" I asked.

"Never mind me," he said. "I want to hear why your friend came all the way to this part of the world." He downed another quarter glass of beer with several loud swallows and then said, "Tell me, Julia Nevins, what's your story?"

"I'm looking for someone," Julia commented in a demure tone.

I, too, wondered what had really brought her all the way to Vietnam. It hadn't been to just rekindle our friendship.

"Really? You're looking for someone," Albee said mockingly. "And how'd this someone get here?"

"Flew."

"You don't say. Is this someone a bird?"

"No, a woman."

"A woman who can fly. Well, what do you know about that." Albee swallowed the beer remaining in his glass, and then emptied the last of the beer in the bucket into his glass. Bobby had kept an eye on our table and brought Julia and I refills and another bucket of beer. Albee hoisted his nearly empty glass in a drinker's salute to Bobby. He then looked at Julia and said, "Tell me more."

"I'm doing a story on Amelia Earhart."

I hadn't heard this before and wondered if she was serious. Julia drank all the wine in her glass. My glass now, too, sat empty.

"And?" Albee inquired.

"I guess you've been in China too long. You've never heard of Amelia Earhart?" I heard the irritation in Julia's voice. When we'd known each other back in Kansas, Julia didn't take crap from anyone. It didn't sound like she'd changed much. There was no doubt in my mind that Julia could stand up to Albee.

"Can't say that her name's come up in any conversations I've had recently."

Albee's eyes twinkled mischievously. He'd drunk quite a lot of beer by now and everyone in the bar could tell that he was on his way to getting smashing drunk.

"Look, my dear," I said, "I hope you're not going to get so pie-eyed that we'll have to drag you home. You're a big fellow. You just might find yourself sleeping in the street tonight if you can't stand on your own legs."

"I'll let you know when I've had enough," he said.

This was not the Albee that was fun to be with. It would have suited me fine if he fell dead drunk on Bobby's floor tonight. I'd just as soon let the bartender contend with him than have to deal with this big drunken guy.

"So, Julia Nevins," Albee continued, "tell me more about this Amelia woman."

Julia would never back down from anyone, even a big drunk like Albee. From the smirk on Julia's face, it looked like she was even getting a kick out of dealing with him.

"Amelia had planned to fly around the world but her plane went down somewhere in the Indian or Pacific Ocean. They recovered some debris that might have been from her plane. Nothing else. There's some speculation that she and her copilot were picked up by a Japanese fishing boat. Some folks believe the plane was forced to make an emergency landing on a deserted island. I think she's still alive somewhere."

Albee leaned across the table. His scruffy beard brushed against his glass of beer. "What makes you think she's still alive? People do die, you know."

"There were reported sightings of an American woman pilot in a fishing village," Julia said.

"Why come to Vietnam? I doubt very much if she's in Hanoi."

"I had to start some place. I knew Sarah lived here, so I thought, why not."

"Why not what?" Albee said, his voice rising. He picked up his glass and downed the last dregs of his beer.

"Why not visit Sarah," Julia said. "I thought I'd take a look around, see if anyone heard about a woman crashing an airplane."

"Well, you picked a fine time to visit. But then maybe they don't know back in the States that there's a war going on here. You just might get more than you're looking for."

"I didn't come from the States. I came from Spain by way of Paris." Julia looked Albee straight in the eyes. "There's some speculation Amelia might have been conducting reconnaissance work for the U.S. Navy, and the Japanese shot her down."

"You don't say," Albee replied. He studied her face. There was an angry glint in his eyes.

Julia glared back at him.

"Who's paying for this trip?" he asked.

Julia sighed. I suppose she knew that she'd have to explain her financial situation eventually. She shifted in her chair, playing with her empty wine glass, moving it in and out of the water ring on the table. "I'm paying for it," she said.

"Deep pockets?" Albee asked.

"Yeah, I've got deep pockets. Is that a crime?"

"Not a crime, though it does make you suspect. But let's hope that you can learn to live without a fat bank account because the world's on it's way to making some big changes. And those who have, are not going to get to keep."

"So says you," Julia snapped.

I'd seen Julia on other occasions, when people less dogmatic than Albee criticized her for not sharing her wealth in these difficult times. Greedy bitches mostly, Julia called them. I've seen her fend them off with a flick of her tongue. It wasn't her fault she had so much money. It was the misfortune of having an astute father who invested wisely on her behalf, and then soon after that he accidentally drove his sports car off a cliff. I'd met her a couple months after the accident. The money was bittersweet. It never stopped rolling in. Even after the depressions her pocketbook was full of dollar bills. That first night we sat on a bar stool next to each other, after her inheritance had come through, you'd have thought Julia had every intention of drinking herself to death.

"Fancy with words, but you're still a capitalist," Albee said.

"I've probably done more good with my funds than you could ever do with all your political pompous fervor."

"Ah, Julia Nevins' got teeth." One of his big grins that I rarely saw these days, slipped through his tumbled whiskers.

"Oh, cut it out." I'd heard enough. From this point on booze was going to drag the conversation into the toilet. I knew in Albee's inebriated state, he'd make less and less sense.

By now he had drunk three buckets of beer in the same time Julia and I had each downed a couple glasses of wine. Julia and I were doing fine. Albee, on the other hand began to behave as he always did when he drank too much, he wanted to sleep. He laid his head down on the table. If we let him, Albee would spend the night sleeping on this chair, waking up in the morning totally oblivious of what had gone on the night before.

"Come on, Albee, stand up."

"No, not now. I want to dream."

"You can't dream yet," I said. "Wait till you get to my place."

"I want to dream here, next to this nice bucket. I want to dream about how pretty it is."

"You take one arm," I told Julia. "I'll grab the other."

Together we managed to lift Albee off his chair and into a standing position. Then with some difficulty, we managed to each hoist one of his arms over our shoulders.

"You ladies need help with him?" Bobby asked.

Albee had been escorted out of this bar quite often, though tonight he seemed more eager than usual to get drunk.

"No, we can manage," I said. "Though could you get someone to come around and pick us up?"

Bobby hustled out the door and presently we had a couple of rickshaws standing ready to take us home. Bobby helped to maneuver Albee into a seat. If Albee didn't cooperate when we arrived home, I intended to push him onto the ground and drag him into the house. He'd fallen out of rickshaws plenty while in a drunken state. He never seemed to be the worst for it.

I felt a bit tipsy myself. Drinking for me in the last several years had become a solitary activity. Booze made me introspective and sad. Tonight though I felt content. Perhaps it had something to do with seeing Julia again and having Albee around, too. Though it didn't sound like they'd end up being good friends.

As we arrived at my front gate, Albee whistled one of his out-of-tune melodies.

"Shhhh!" I said. His noisemaking could have awakened the dead. On this street where the sounds of the busy market place had long since quieted, his whistle echoed through the night like an exotic screaming bird.

Before we were able to get Albee out of the rickshaw, Aon She Beng opened her gate. A dark figure slipped out of her doorway and hurried up the street away from us.

"You make too much noise," Aon She Beng called out to Albee.

"Ah, hello, Aon She Beng," Albee said. He threw an arm around her. I worried that he might lift her up into the air the way he had greeted me the other evening and hurt the frail old lady. Instead, he kissed the top of her head and said, "How are you, my little chicken?"

"You drunk. Go sleep. We talk tomorrow," Aon She Beng said and then turned and walked toward her gate. "I feel safe with man here," she said. "Drunk man better than no man." She looked nervously out into the street. "Bandits coming into the city. They took from the peasants. Now they come to city, they take what we have." Aon She Beng closed her gate and slammed the bolt tight.

With a great deal of effort, Julia and I managed to get Albee into the house. He flopped onto my bed. Taking up most of the space, he began to snore. Pushing him to one side, I crawled under the covers. A few minutes later, he threw one of his heavy arms across my body.

Eleven

AON SHE BENG HAD JUST finished her evening cup of tea when she heard Albee call out, "Let's get drunk." Such a strong man, she thought. Even his voice made her feel safe. Though he drank too much and that worried her. But if there was trouble, he'd help her, no matter what his condition.

Aon She Ben quickly hobbled to her garden gate and watched through a peep whole as Albee walk past her house. He smiled brilliantly at her and waved as he went up the street.

She hurried back into the house to prepare for her evening visitor. Thien Nguyen's brother, Loc Dang Hung had sent a servant with a message asking for a small bit of her time. His family had been in financial trouble since before their father's death. Aon She Beng knew the purpose for the visit was to borrow more money.

The celebration for her seventieth year would be coming up in a couple of weeks. The preparations had already begun for her party. Good fortune would befall her if an ill-fated person were helped during the days before she entered her next decade. Even though Loc Dang Hung would be granted a favor there was no need to throw her money away. He would pay interest on the money she'd lend him.

Aon She Beng called for her servant to come into the room.

"Clean this mess," Aon She Beng barked. "I am expecting a visitor tonight."

The servant bowed politely, gathered up the tray with the lone teacup and hurried out of the room.

There was a knock on the gate at the appointed hour. The servant rushed out into the garden and escorted the visitor into the house.

"Thank you for allowing me to visit this evening," Loc Dang Hung said. "I hope you are in good health."

"I am an old woman. I agreed to see you out of respect for the dead," Aon She Beng said, then shouted to her servant, "Bring us tea." She motioned for Loc Dang Hung to sit in the seat opposite her. Watching him closely, all the while Aon She Beng wondered how much money he would ask for.

"I am sorry for your mother," Aon She Beng said. "Did they find the killer?"

"No," Loc Dang Hung said. "Such a waste of life."

Loc Dang Hung lowered his gaze to the floor.

"I am a busy woman. Why did you ask to speak with me?"

"My brother's death has put a great burden on my family's finances."

"Yes, I know this all ready. Your father's debt is still not paid." Aon She Beng watched her servant pour tea into the small china cups. "You are too slow, woman. You take too long to do everything." Aon She Beng lifted the teacup to her lips. But hearing a faint scratching sound in a corner of the room, the old woman shouted, "Come in here you stupid servant woman! Now! Something ran behind that vase."

The old servant woman came running to the front of the house.

Aon She Beng pointed to a corner of the room where a large porcelain vase stood on a black lacquered table. "Look behind that vase."

The servant woman looked where Aon She Beng pointed. "There is nothing," she said.

"Something is there."

"I see nothing," the woman insisted.

"You look," Aon She Beng said to Loc Dang Hung.

He got up from his chair and looked on all sides of the small stand. He peered inside the porcelain vase. "The woman is right. There is nothing."

Aon She Beng shouted, "Find that creature. l will not have filthy things in my house."

The servant hurried about in the next room making a great deal of noise opening and closing cabinet doors, shoving furniture about. It pleased Aon She Beng to think that everything would be turned over and poked and prodded until that horrid creature was either found or chased out into the street. She looked at Loc Dang Huang, her anger and discomfort growing. "I cannot drink my tea. Tonight you have brought too much trouble. No more talk. I will give you money. Then you will leave. I know what to give you. I know everything. You will not cheat me. You pay me what you owe."

Loc Dang Hung sighed. "I understand."

"When I open my purse. You will pay interest. You make me risk my money."

Aon She Beng stood up and went into a back room where her servant was on hands and knees looking into the closet. "You stupid woman," Aon She Beng shouted. "Find that disgusting creature. Kill it." Unlocking a cabinet door, Aon She Beng took out a roll of money, counted out a sum of bills, and then returned to the front of the house. Handing Lok Dang Hung the money, she said, "Now leave. I am a tired old woman."

"Thank you for this kindness," Loc Dang Hung said. "This will put my mother at ease."

"You are wrong. Your mother had a foolish husband. He squandered the family money. He put the family in debt. Now your mother has the shame of murdered son. She will never be happy again."

Loc Dang Hung did not respond. He opened the gate and just as he ran up the street someone whistled.

Aon She Beng recognized Albee's whistle and knew that he had returned home drunk again.

"Aon She Beng," Albee called out. His hulking body was stooped over and supported by Sarah and that American woman. A rat scurried along her garden wall. "We will kill you tomorrow," Aon She Ben muttered and took a few steps toward her noisy neighbors.

Twelve

THE MORNING SUN LEAKED THROUGH the curtains in my bedroom window. The heat and the monsoons earlier in the year had shrunk one of the wallboards and now a thin sliver of sunshine slipped through a narrow gap in a far wall, casting a finger of light onto my dressing table.

Julia came out of her room, put one of her 33 records on the gramophone, and I could hear her pecking on her portable typewriter.

Albee lay so quietly next to me. I thought he was still sleeping. I'd seen him sleep for a day and a half sometimes after arriving in Hanoi. He especially slept deeply after drinking too much beer the night before. But rolling over to face him, his eyes were wide open.

"When I don't see you for such a long time," he said, "I forget how beautiful you are." He grinned mischievously, pulled me close, and slid his hand under my nightgown.

He made me remember how delicious it felt to lay next to a man's body. In his absence, there were opportunities to get involved with other men, mostly French officers. I turned them all down, but not out of loyalty to this big man. I'd decided years ago to limit my entanglements with the opposite sex. Albee had been perfect…neither one of us wanted a commitment.

I eased one leg over his huge thigh. My sexual desires remained dormant between our visits, though when this man crawled into my bed I felt like a cat in heat.

He put his lips on one of my breasts. His beard brushed against my skin like coarse prickly wool and though we usually made love in silence, this morning Albee moaned softly as he sucked on my nipple. He reached up and kissed me hard on the mouth. "Give me what I want," he whispered.

"What?"

He eased himself into me. "That."

My rickety bed creaked and groaned as our bodies thrust against each other. The sweat dripped from under my arms. Albee's heavy breathing in my ear drowned out the early morning noise of the merchants outside on the street.

"Now that's what I call a good morning," he said, and fell back onto his pillow.

We lay together breathing heavily, slowly stroking each other. He had such amazingly soft spots on his inner thighs, his arm pits, secret silken patches that the desert of China had not reached, while his hands, rough, dried, and cracked like a river bed, scratched my skin when he dragged his weather-warn paws across my belly.

"I don't know about you," he said, "but I'm hungry."

"Then it's time to get up."

When we stepped out of the bedroom, Julia did not look up but continued to read from a typed written page.

"Good morning," I said.

She did not respond.

"Want some breakfast?" I asked.

She looked up. "Tea or coffee would be fine." Then her gaze turned to Albee. It was easy to read the anger in her eyes.

"Oops," he said. "Did I say something last night?"

"No, you were only slightly offensive."

"That's good. Sometimes I'm a lot more than slightly offensive." "Can't say that I like you when you've had too much to drink," Julia said with a nasty edge in her voice.

I built a fire in my small wood stove and filled the kettle with water.

"So what'd I do?" he asked. There was no sincerity in his voice.

"It's not what you did. But do you remember anything that you said last night?"

"Sort of," he said.

This old lover of mine tried to get out of every tight spot with an innocence that I'd learned over the years did not exist. He had a way of absolving himself of any guilt. Usually he remembered what he'd done or said the night before, even when he'd gotten smashingly drunk. Though after all the years of traveling through the world and slipping in and out of people's lives, he believed that he left no trace of his existence. Consequently, he thought there was nothing to apologize for.

"Forget it," Julia said. "No harm done. You've just been out of the world too long." Julia looked at her paper. "Digging up dried bones," she said, "boozing it up and banging women are probably about all you know how to do."

"Hold on there, woman of the world. What makes you so high and mighty?" Albee stepped closer to her.

The water in the kettle hissed as Albee and Julia glared at each other.

"Tea's ready," I said. No way was I stepping into this one. Julia could be quite sensitive and though there had been no mention last night about how Albee's comments had offended her, there were some obvious ill feelings. I wasn't good at this kind of thing and tried like hell to avoid confrontations. Julia, though, walked straight into them. That's where this old friend found it most comfortable. Back in the States, Julia always seemed to find herself in the middle of one storm or another.

"There's bread and jam in the cupboard," I said. "Help yourselves. I'm going out into the garden."

"I'll join you," Julia said, and poured a cup of tea.

"Bread and jam," Albee said. "Just like back home."

Julia sat in the chair next to me. Albee settled himself in the doorway chomping on a slice of French bread thickly slathered with fruit jam. On the street, merchants called out for the passersby to purchase their wares, shoppers chatted, children laughed and played as they walked to school. I put a match to a cigarette and wondered how long Julia could hold her tongue. She'd most likely be the first one to break the silence and I was right.

"So, tell me, Albee," Julia said. "Do you take any woman seriously?"

"I take everyone seriously."

"Then what's so hard to believe I'd be interested in writing an article about a missing female pilot?"

Albee swallowed some tea. "It's not hard to believe at all. But did you look at a map before you started out? That Pacific Ocean is pretty damn big. Did you think you'd climb into a sampan and sail out to the middle of wherever this pilot was supposed to have gone down?"

"I thought, for your information," Julia said, "that I'd use Sarah's location as a jumping off place."

"The only place you're going to jump into around here is the middle of a very dangerous watering hole of the Japanese. The British and Americans are in a frantic race to evacuate the non-Chinese from Shanghai. The Imperial Navy has threatened to blow them out of the water and you're thinking about taking an excursion along the coast line to find a downed airplane?"

Julia put her teacup on the small table next to her chair and said, "They're not at war with us."

"The hell they're not," Albee snapped. "They just haven't gotten around to declaring it yet."

"Japan promised Roosevelt they wouldn't attack us or any of our territories. A country doesn't say that publicly, then turn around and start a war."

"And you believe that bullshit?" Albee snarled. "You said yourself they thought this aviator might have been involved in reconnaissance. You're not following your own logic. How long have you been a reporter?"

"Irrelevant," Julia almost screamed. "How long have you been getting your brain fried in the desert?"

"I've seen what Japan has done in China," Albee said. "It's bloodier than anything you could conjure up. They make it a point to wipe out entire villages. They take no prisoners. Women, children, the old, it makes no difference to them." Albee glared at Julia. "It might already be too late. They're on a roll. They've joined forces with the Fascists. There'll be no stopping them now."

"Water and oil. The Japanese joining forces with the Fascists will never happen."

Albee took a big bite of his bread.

"Well, looks like you two are going to be great friends," I said. "And I can't tell you how glad I am that you're both staying with me."

"I arrived first," Julia responded.

There was playfulness in her voice, though I knew Julia hadn't finished with Albee. And the odds were pretty good that he would not let the subject drop, either. In the last year he'd become convinced that Japan had set their sights on not just taking over China, but that they wanted a great deal more. According to him they wanted the world.

Albee stood, stretched, and said, "Well, I have some business to take care of. See you when I see you." He threw me a half-hearted kiss and walked over to the garden gate. He unlocked the latch and when he stepped out into the street, a dusty cloud stirred up by a passing rickshaw floated into my courtyard. He looked at me. He appeared to want to say something else, but instead, turned and closed the gate behind him.

Thirteen

JULIA SIGHED AND SIPPED HER tea. It felt like there was much more space in the garden now that Albee left.

"Remember how we used to take rides into the Missouri countryside?" Julia asked.

"Yeah," Sarah replied. "Boy that was a long time ago."

From what Julia could tell, Sarah lived quietly and comfortably in this little house with its small garden. Albee appeared to be her only extravagance in her life. Julia knew Sarah would not mention the argument she had with Albee. Sarah, never a big talker, kept a lot of stuff bottled up inside. Julia placed her teacup on a nearby table and asked, "Well, what's on the agenda for today?"

"Work," Sarah replied.

"Mind if I tag along?"

"Suit yourself."

"By the way, is there a post office around here?"

"Postal service here is lousy. I suppose you could send something through the Archive office."

"Perfect. I have to get these things off my hands."

"What things?"

"Articles for newspapers back in the States and one for Canada."

"It'll be old news by the time it reaches them. Our stuff goes by freighter."

"As long as it's out of my hands, I really don't care how it gets there or when it arrives."

The heat didn't feel quite so oppressive to Julia this morning. If she had learned anything from traveling, it had been to acclimate quickly to an environment. In Spain, she'd spent a lot of time moving about in the dry, thin air of the mountains. She not only learned to tolerate the high altitude but also the dust that was so thick some days it looked and felt like a dry fog. And while in Paris, her long walks along the Seine in the blistering summer heat became as natural to her as taking a stroll down one of the main streets in Kansas City in the spring.

From the day Sarah told her about the murdered translator, she wanted to take a look at where the crime had been committed. As a reporter back in the States, she had covered her share of homicide cases. Death had become a familiar sight in the years while living in Spain. She had seen her share of corpses, whether a murder victim in an abandoned building on the wrong side of the tracks in the U.S.A., or after a gun battle or bombing in one of the war-torn villages in Spain. Death was final, but as a reporter there was always a story connected with it. She looked at her hands. Her long fingers had typed many images of death and a fascination for this dark side of life had grown in her where there had once only been a vague curiosity.

Julia and Sarah walked along the busy street to where a couple rickshaws usually waited. This morning there were only single-occupancy rickshaws available. They each climbed into a vehicle. As quickly as Sarah climbed into her seat, the runner took off with a galloping head start. Julia's runner was in no hurry to get anywhere. Luckily Sarah had instructed the runner to head for the French Archives building or Julia would have been at a loss where to tell this guy to go.

Sarah's rickshaw turned a corner and then disappeared down a narrow street. Julia wanted to tell her runner to go faster, to catch up with her friend, though she realized he probably did not understand English. There was nothing for her to do but hope for the best.

He finally caught up with Sarah's rickshaw where several vehicles, rickshaws, and military trucks waited for their turn to merge into the circular intersection. Julia felt relieved spotting Sarah caught in the traffic jam.

"How much farther?" Julia asked.

Sarah's puller took off again. "We're almost there," Sarah called back to Julia.

A few minutes later, Julia's rickshaw eased alongside a stark building, square and washed smooth with dull stucco. Sarah stood at the front entrance, waiting while Julia climbed out of the buggy.

Julia followed Sarah into the building and immediately tasted a musty quality in the air. They walked down a short hallway with several doors on either side, and as they passed a desk, Sarah picked up a few papers from a small shelf. "Most of the work is done through here," Sarah said and opened a door.

Julia entered a world like none she'd ever experienced before. She'd seen plenty of dead-letter file rooms in offices, and the newspaper business had its share of stored records. This cavernous room was beyond belief with shelf after shelf, row upon row of books and towering stacks of papers lining every available floor space.

Sarah grinned. "Well, what do you think?"

"Wow. What are you supposed to do with all this stuff?"

"We translate some. Keep local documents regarding recent political concerns, land deeds, birth and death records, but most of that's now being sent either to Saigon or directly to Paris."

Several men walked along the shelves in one corner of the huge building. They looked at Sarah and then disappeared through a side door. A thick film of dust covered the windows letting in so little light that the entire area looked like it was bathed in a dreamy stream of sunset glow.

Sarah greeted two women sitting at a large desk. They were stitching together the pages of very old manuscripts. One of the women pointed to several boxes on the floor. Sarah bent down and curiously looked through the contents. "Well, I've got my work cut out for me today," Sarah said. "You'll have to entertain yourself."

"No problem."

"Do you want someone to show you around?"

"I can do it solo. But, tell me, where'd you find the translator's body?"

"Fourth row, middle."

Two young men entered from a side door carrying large bundles of papers tied together with twine. Sarah sighed. "Let the games begin."

Julia left Sarah at the end of the fourth row. It looked like a place where a murder might have taken place. Each row except this one had several light bulbs glowing overhead. Yet, in this row a long shadow ran the full length of the walkway between the shelves. Julia stepped slowly into the shadow. Unlike the other shelves, this area had a careless appearance, with booklets and papers pushed in sloppy mismatched stacks as though someone might have been hurriedly hunting for something.

She ran her fingers along the edge of the wooden shelf unsure of what to look for. Glancing down at black scuffmarks from rubber-soled shoes Julia knew what this meant. She'd seen it before. If the young man had been alive, he surely would have struggled and his kicking and flailing would have indicated this by showing an interruption in the drag marks. There was no sign of a struggle.

Julia looked up. A broken light bulb hung above her head, a few jagged edges of glass and filaments dangled from the end of a cord that extended down from the ceiling. The broken light was obviously more than a coincidence. There were no pieces of glass on the floor or any remnants of the light bulb on the books. Julia slowly ran her hand along the back of a stack of books. Something jabbed her. Carefully feeling around for more sharp objects, she paid close attention to what else might be back there. There were shards of glass behind the books, though there was no broken glass on the books.

"Careful you don't cut yourself," someone said.

She quickly turned.

"I lifted a book out of these shelves the other day and cut my finger," the young man said.

Julia removed her hand from the bookshelf.

"I am Le Sing Dong, a translator. Do you work here, also?"

"No. Just visiting."

"You are from America?"

"Yes." Julia looked down at the young man's hand and wondered if this young man thought his cut might have something to do with Thien Nguyen's murder.

"I would like to go to America some day. I've heard they have many libraries."

Julia picked up one of the manuscripts. "Did you know the murdered man?"

Le Sing Dong glanced over his shoulder as though he heard footsteps and said, "Yes. We went to school together. Thien Nguyen was very respected."

"Were you friends?"

"We often studied together." Le Sing Dong seemed to lose interest in the conversation and quickly turned to leave. "I must get back to my work."

Julia strolled amongst the shelves and stood wondering what she'd do with herself for the rest of the day, when there was a commotion coming from one section of the building. The entire workforce had gathered around a table. Julia approached the group. Sarah was reading from one of the documents.

"What is it?" Julia asked.

Several people stepped aside. Tears ran down Sarah's cheeks.

"Dat Tu's wife is dead," Sarah said.

"How?"

"The report says suicide," Sarah hissed. She turned away from Julia and continued to read the long list of names.

After reading the last name, the group returned to their workstations. Le Sing Dong looked at Julia with cautious eyes, turned, and walked away.

Julia placed a hand on Sarah's shoulder. Physical attempts at solace were never her strong point; they felt contrived and feeble. But her words were sincere. "I am sorry," she said.

Sarah looked at Julia. "She didn't commit suicide. They killed her." Sarah angrily brushed at her wet face with the back of her hand. "The world's going mad. The French are following the Nazis' example, covering their actions with reports like this one, listing all the deaths as accidents and suicides."

"What are you going to do now?" Julia asked.

Sarah glanced at the women pulling jute thread through the broken backs of the manuscripts. "They wonder about that, too," she said.

"Do you think Dat Tu knows?"

"He knew before it happened and so did Albee. We all hoped she would be released, a little beaten up, but alive. This news breaks my heart." Sarah paused. "Listen. Do you hear how quiet it is? That's the sound of tragedy. Everyone here has felt the kick of a boot."

Julia removed her hand from Sarah's shoulder. Anger did not accept or need comfort.

Fourteen

Time?
There is none.
The world swirls around me.
It turns upside down.
I hear the wind howl. A woman screams.
Words make no sense.
Sarah, you have the key.
You've brought me to this building.
I remember now.
Everything ended here. This is where…
Sarah, tell me what it is that I have forgotten.
I've become like smoke.
I cannot hear my footfalls on the floor.
This world frightens me; it used to bring me joy.
Something terrible has happened.
I used to sleep and dream in poetry. Now there is terror in the darkness.
The woman's screams have stopped.
I find no comfort in this silence.
Someone, please, release me from this awful dream.

Fifteen

THE REMAINDER OF THE DAY was a blur. I watched Julia walk back and forth through the rows of shelves. She spoke with some of the staff that understood a little English. The grief I'd first felt when reading Van Mai's name on the list of the dead quickly turned from numbness to anger. I learned years ago, the mind could only take so much tragedy before it shuts down. Thien Nguyen's murder ripped a gash in my soul where I'd so carefully stitched closed an old wound. The losses and hurts had begun to mount up. I feared that the worst was yet to come.

When we arrived back home in the evening, we heard a great deal of commotions in Aon She Beng's garden. The preparations for her birthday celebration had been set in motion. A fanfare of cooks and helpers came and went, banging pots and pans, a noisy bunch who called loudly to each other.

Albee had not been home all day. I had no idea when he'd be back. Neither Julia nor I had much of an appetite. We nibbled at some bread and jam, and then went out into the garden with a bottle of rice wine.

"So, what did you think of the Archives?" I asked.

"It's not something that I'd like to spend my days doing. I never knew that a librarian could end up in such an exotic place."

Just then, Aon She Beng shrieked. Someone threw a heavy object at the common garden wall that I shared with her.

"What the hell's going on over there?" Julia asked.

"Sounds like Aon She Beng's got them chasing a rat."

For the rest of the evening neither one of us said much. We kept our glasses filled with wine and listened to the racket going on next door.

Then, thankfully there was a lull in the commotion.

"I love your staff," Julia said as though she had kept track of where our conversation had left off before Aon She Beng started to make all that noise. "Every time I moved from one row of shelves to another, someone came rushing with a dust cloth or broom to clean the area."

"I'm afraid they've cleaned away any evidence that might have helped find Thien Nguyen's killer."

"Well, they're not that good at cleaning. I found glass on the shelves from the broken light bulbs. I'll bet we could find other clues if we poked around a little more."

"But, for what purpose?"

I should have told Julia that the only thing I wanted at that moment was to forget the vision of Thien Nguyen's body.

"Interesting question," Julia said. "I guess purposes make themselves known. The closer you look at something the more you see. For instance, did you notice the scuff marks on the floor?"

"Yeah, I saw them," I said, and then wondered what Julia would think of the document the nun had given me that was now tucked away in the quilt in my closet. "You're right…why the scuffmarks?"

This question baffled both of us. Though we clearly understood what the scuffmarks meant. Sitting in the garden, a glass of wine in hand, a concrete wall encircling us in a false sense of security, the terror of the murder now only a question of scuffmarks.

A calm came over the garden while the air grew irritatingly more humid. Julia sat so quietly that if I'd closed my eyes, I could have almost believed I was alone. By the time we finished a second bottle of rice wine, it sounded as though Aon She Beng had given up trying to capture the rat and gone to bed.

Julia shifted in her chair. "You ever think about Buster? He sure pined away after you took off."

"Can't say that I've miss anyone from back there."

"Not even me?"

"You're hard to miss."

"Thanks. I think." There was a slight slur in Julia's voice. We both had drunk more than we should have. And we'd both probably have a bitch of a hangover in the morning, too.

"You seeing anyone else besides Albee?"

"There are a couple guys who come around." I said this knowing that was something she'd like to hear.

"Sounds promising. You got any you could share with me?"

I wondered if Julia really thought that we could start up our old life again. Buster had been as much hers as he had been mine. That really meant he had been neither of ours.

The quiet, the dark and the booze thankfully dulled my senses and I desperately wanted to sleep. We both decided it was time to go to bed. Julia could not find her way to the back bedroom and collapsed in the front room of the house on the daybed. Groaning a couple of times, it didn't take long before her heavy drunken breathing punctuated the humid night air. Stumbling into my room, I didn't even remember falling onto the bed.

Sixteen

Sleep, Sarah. Sleep.
I know what has happened to me.
I am dead.
My body grows like wild rice in an abandoned paddy.
Reaching for the sun there is no warmth.
My throat is parched, yet water satisfies nothing.
These human yearnings are still strong in me.
Sarah, help me.
There are others like me. They are everywhere.
A woman, a familiar face, now walks with me. Crying for her baby,
blood runs from her eyes like ruby tears.
An old man hides in your cupboards.
He no longer asks for answers, but cowers from everything.
He says do not trust the rat for he only tells lies.
Sleep, Sarah, sleep.

Seventeen

THE BRIGHT MORNING LIGHT FELT like knives jabbing into my eye sockets. My head throbbed with pain. There was a faint recollection of a dream that someone stood over my bed during the night, softly speaking to me while I slept.

Julia lay across the daybed now clad only in her bra and panties. The coarseness that had grown on her face from all her years of hard drinking and living a raucous nightlife receded in her slumber. I wondered, as I watched her sleep with a child-like innocent face, whether my old friend had little girl dreams?

Not only did my head hurt like hell, but there was also a dreadful taste in my mouth. From past experiences I knew that even brushing my teeth wouldn't remove the scruffy tang of last night's booze from my tongue. Though maybe I'd get lucky today and a strong cup of coffee would do the trick.

I built a fire in my stove knowing the noise would probably wake up Julia, but there was no choice. I filled a pot with water, measured in a hefty portion of ground coffee, and put it on the stove to boil.

Julia moved slightly. First her head turned from one side to the other, then a leg slipped off the edge of the daybed. "Oh, God, what time is it?" Her voice was croaky from smoking too many cigarettes the night before. "Am I going to die?"

"You'll be fine," I assured her. Reaching into the cupboard for two cups, I had the strangest sensation that something stared back at me. This morning the hangover was playing tricks on my mind. I quickly grabbed the cups and strained the dark brew through a cloth bag.

I handed Julia a full cup.

"You expect your man any time soon?" Julia asked.

"I have no idea when he'll show up. You better slip something on just in case."

Julia threw on a robe and we took our coffees out to the garden. The workers in Aon She Beng's garden made a racket opening and then banging shut my landlady's gate. Aon She Beng shouted orders. There was no longer any mention of a rat.

We had just finished our coffee when Albee opened the gate and sauntered into the garden. He had a familiar look in his eyes. He'd been to Madam Rebecca's, his favorite opium house. Though he'd probably slept for several hours, his eyes were still filled with the dreams brought on by the drug.

"So, lost dogs can find their way home," Julia said.

Ignoring Julia's comment I asked, "Want some coffee?"

He smiled. "I need nothing."

At that moment Aon She Beng shouted at one of her workers.

"Quiet Aon!" Albee bellowed. "You're disturbing my peace!"

The morning noises outside on the street and my landlady's garden immediately fell silent, as if Albee had fired a gun. The vendors on the street stopped calling to each other. Then within a few seconds, the clang and clamber of the market's activities started up again. Aon She Beng from that point on toned down her shouting a bit.

Julia and Albee disrupted my simple life. The last thing I wanted now after Thien Nguyen's murder was living with these sensitive hung-over houseguests.

"Albee, if you need your peace and quiet, go inside and take a nap. No one wants to deal with your bullshit."

"I don't need a nap. I'll be fine," he responded. "There's work to be done."

"Like what?"

He looked at me, his eyes still glassy from the opium, and said, "I got people to see, places to go."

I'd read somewhere that talking about a tragedy lessened its power. It was difficult to comprehend this because my mind continually bounced back and forth between Thien Nguyen and Van Mai's murders. It wasn't just getting drunk last night that messed with my thoughts this morning, but since the murders, finding the right words eluded me. Every phrase became strangely wrapped around my sense of loss. There was a near desperate attempt not to touch the hurt. Then realizing that Albee did not know about Van Mai's death, sadness washed over me and my body went limp.

"The list came out," I said.

There was no need for me to say any more. He knew what list. The expression on my face probably said more than any words I could have found and I suspected that he already knew.

"She's on the list?" he asked. Though this did not sound like a question.

"Yes. Suicide. According to the records Van Mai committed suicide."

"Bastards," he snorted.

We sat silently for a long while. The racket continued next door though the noise now sounded muffled to me, trivialized by the death of another dear friend. The fact that the cranky old woman next door was making preparations to celebrate entering another decade only saddened the loss of Thien Nguyen and Van Mai.

"I think I'll get that coffee now," Albee said.

He stood and slowly went into the house. As he passed there was a faint odor of a campfire. This man lived on the edge of many worlds. In the last year, though his visits had increased, he'd become more secretive. Several minutes later he emerged from the house with a cup of coffee in hand. He squatted in the doorway as limber as a man in his twenties. And though he never told me how old he was, I estimated him to be at least twice that age.

We drank our coffee listening to Aon She Beng's shrill complaining.

Albee chugged down the last of the brew in his cup. "So, ladies," he said, "want to go for a ride? I've borrowed a car."

The crowds of people in the city were wearing on my nerves and the prospect of getting away from all this noise appealed to me. Though wherever we went my sadness would be dragged along with me.

"Good," Albee said when neither of us responded. "I'll just splash some water on my face and then we can be off."

Julia pulled the robe close around her body. "I can't go like this."

"Well, you better shake your tail, sweetheart. Time's a-wasting."

"He'll wait, don't worry. He's lucky to have such charming company," I said. "We going north or south?"

"You'll see."

"Is anyone else coming along?"

Ignoring my question, he said, "I'll bring the car around. Don't take too long." Then almost as an afterthought, he said, "We might be spending the night. Better bring a few extra things. Sarah, do you have any perfume?"

"Yeah, why?"

"Bring it."

"Ah, isn't that romantic," Julia said, and went into the house to get dressed.

It didn't take much for me to get ready these days. Lately, the only thing I usually did was drag a comb through my short-cropped hair, slip on a pair of slacks and a clean shirt. Nothing fancy.

It took Albee longer to get the car than he'd said. Julia and I both smoked another cigarette before we heard the sound of a car horn outside on the street. When Albee last visited Hanoi he also had errands to run in the country. He could always get someone to loan him a car, usually a Peugeot.

Julia handed her bag to Albee then climbed in the back; a long-legged woman, Julia stretched her body across the seat. I'd sat in the back of this car before, and though the springs in the seats were a bit worn down, on the straight asphalt roads the ride was pretty comfortable. Most of my traveling had been in rickshaws. Riding in a car was by far easier on the rump. The Michelin Tire Company had invested heavily in the local rubber plantations and they exported a great many tires back to this part of the world. Even rickshaws now had rubber wheels. Once I'd ridden in a very old and tired rickshaw with metal rims. Can't say that I'd ever want to do that again.

Albee took my small traveling case and stuffed it between two large duffle bags. I'd seen these duffle bags before. I had a strong suspicion Albee was up to something.

"Where's the perfume?" he asked.

"It's in there."

He dug around inside my case, found the small bottle, and nestled it on top of the luggage.

This was a curious thing to do, though nothing Albee did surprised me. He closed up the trunk, climbed into the driver's seat and turned the key in the ignition.

"So, where we headed?" Julia asked.

"Out of town," Albee replied, and slowly eased the car through the narrow streets of my neighborhood, an area that the French called the native district. Families like Aon She Beng's, artisans, merchants and moneylenders settled in this section of Hanoi centuries ago. Potters, weavers, and silk merchants made up most of the businesses in the area. Over the years, the buildings had become so jammed together that it was sometimes daunting to determine which door went with what shop. The French hadn't messed too much with the architecture on these streets, though the Colonial government had constructed many buildings in other areas of the city. If it weren't for all the Chinese and Vietnamese people milling around some of the more modernized and fancier streets in Hanoi, you could have believed you were strolling the avenues in Paris.

Soon Albee maneuvered the Peugeot out of the narrow streets. This was not an easy task considering that the automobile was sometimes nearly the same width as the street. Within several minutes, we were traveling north on a newly constructed, wide, asphalt roadway.

Cars were a novelty in this part of the world. Only the wealthy could afford such a luxury. Automobiles symbolized the division between the French colonists and the peasants. Many roads were so narrow; motorcar drivers could sometimes be stuck for hours behind a farmer headed to market pulling a cart full of goods. But the poor endured the drudgery of a long, slow trek while the motorist impatiently raced from one location to another.

When first arriving in Vietnam, the good quality of the roads in some areas that led out into the countryside surprised me. Many of them were far better than the roads I'd traveled on back home in Missouri. It wasn't difficult to figure out that these good roads were intended for the transportation of raw material from the mines and the rubber plantations. These grand roads only led to the railway stations and the seaports, and were designed to assist with the export business. The streets inside the poor districts of Hanoi and the roads that led to the villages were still cobblestone or muddy, rutted dirt roads that had to be repaired after every monsoon season.

I accompanied Albee many times on his trips into the countryside. From the road we'd taken, I knew we would probably end up in the village that we often visited. The French had recently increased the checkpoints along the main roads. There would probably be at least one or two roadblocks before we arrived at our destination. Three-quarters of the way from where we'd turn off the asphalt road, a military vehicle and two French soldiers blocked our way.

"What's this?" Julia asked. "Trouble?"

"Shut up," Albee said.

"What the…" she replied.

Albee got out of the car.

"Bon jour, *Monsieur*. Papers, *s'il vous plait*," the young soldier said.

"Yes, of course." Albee removed a small packet of folded papers from his shirt pocket and leaned casually against the car.

"The Madams' papers, now, s'il vous plait?"

Julia and I handed the young soldier our passports. I took out my working documents and gave those over, as well.

The soldier flipped through the pages. He handed everything back to Albee. The soldier walked to the back of the Peugeot. "Open this, please," he said. Though he used the word please, it did not sound polite. It was an order.

Albee unlocked the trunk.

Then I heard a delicate tinkle of glass break on the road.

"Oh, I'm so sorry," Albee said.

"Idiot!" the soldier shouted. "You ruined my boots. The devil with you, get out of here."

The heavy aroma of my favorite perfume filled the air. A drop or two would release the sweet scent, but a full bottle—if what I thought had happened had taken place—would make this road smell of imported French decadence until the next monsoon.

Albee climbed back into the front seat. He hung his head like a scolded child. "I am sorry, sir," he said, nearly whimpering.

"You fool," the soldier said.

The cloying fragrance of my perfume filled the car.

Albee put the car in gear. "He's going to be very popular in the barracks tonight," he said and gave me a mischievous grin.

"What did you do?" Julia asked.

"A little distraction. That's all."

"I don't think I like that perfume any more," I said.

We still had quite a long way to go. Julia sat quietly in the back. Once and awhile she dozed off. But Albee got her attention when he turned onto a dirt-packed road. The car heaved back and forth through huge ruts that would only get worse the closer we got to our destination.

"You sure we should be on this road with a car?" Julia asked. Her head smack against the side window as the vehicle drove into a particularly deep washout in the road.

"We've always made it before," Albee replied.

"How about the passengers? They live to tell the tale?"

"Ask Sarah."

"Yeah, a little bruised. But you'll survive."

Albee eased the car to the far edge of the road to let a man leading an ox pass. The man raised his head ever so slightly, looked out from under his cone-shaped straw hat and made eye contact with Albee. Albee nodded. The ox, a giant next to our Peugeot, passed us with wild eyes and long strands of drool dripping from both sides of its mouth. The beast never looked in our direction but continued walking as though our automobile was as natural as an indigenous tree.

"How much farther?" Julia asked. It was easy to detect her impatience for the long ride.

"A little ways, yet," Albee replied.

The road soon became even more rutted. The car pitched violently from side to side. We were not traveling very fast to begin with, when Albee slowed down even more when the bottom of the car scrapped across a rock that stuck up in the middle of the road.

"Hope that didn't break the oil pan," he said. "You ladies wouldn't mind spending the night out here if I had to go back to Hanoi for car parts?" Albee gave me a wink. "Just kidding. We're fine."

Albee maneuvered the car over another difficult stretch of road. Julia's head hit the back window again.

Several minutes later, a familiar cluster of trees came into view. The rice paddies on either side of the road were flooded to the top of the dikes making the surrounding land saturated with water and soggy as hell. Albee pulled the car over as far as he could to the edge of the road and stopped the engine. "This is where we get out," he said. "We walk the rest of the way."

This was a familiar routine to me. Walking across these marshlands would feel more like taking a stroll in a field of shallow quicksand.

The first time Albee brought me here, sloshing across this water-soaked land felt mysterious. I hadn't been in Hanoi that long and though I had a crash course in the language, there had been no references to the people who lived this far out of the city. The French acted as though nothing significant happened in this country before they arrived. In my own naiveté I imagined that these villagers lived in a similar manner as farmers back in Missouri. But crossing under the stone arch that led into this village, I knew I walked into an existence like nothing that I could have ever envisioned.

Albee opened the trunk of the Peugeot, handed Julia and me our overnight cases and then took out the two heavy canvas suitcases.

"What do you do here?" Julia asked.

"Business," he replied.

We followed Albee down the embankment. Julia nearly slipped once but managed to remain upright.

A high brick wall enclosed most of the village. Dense growth of trees and bamboo hedges separated the inhabitants from the rice paddies giving the little enclave an appearance of being sheltered from the world. As we crossed under the brick archway, a scruffy magpie in a bamboo birdcage flitted back and forth nervously calling out a warning.

The decaying walls of this ancient village left a dusty taste in my mouth. The hard-packed dirt streets twisted and turned, deliberately designed hundreds of years ago so as not to disturb the legendary sleeping dragon believed to reside beneath the village. The maze-like streets frequently took twists and turns that resulted in abrupt dead ends.

A group of men advanced toward us led by the village elder. We'd met on several occasions. He was a slight, bent-over man with eyes so dark they caught the daylight as though they were cut onyx. Several young men, boys really, stood to one side, rifles slung over their shoulders.

"Welcome," the elder said.

I could have never guessed the age of this old man, or any adult in this village, for that matter. They were not an ageless band of people but their weathered and deeply wrinkled skin and their stooped bodies from working in the rice paddies, made them look ancient. They were tough like timber and everyone in this compound looked as if they had worked a hundred years in the bleaching sun.

"Why the big show of security?" Albee asked.

"Our visitors from the mountains trust no one. They know that you are a friend, but they remain cautious."

"They're right," Albee replied. "They should trust no one."

"Please, come." The elder led the way to the dinh, a community house where all business was conducted and where guests were taken.

Albee nodded a polite greeting to the young men holding the guns as he walked past them. I diverted my eyes to the ground and followed close behind Albee. There was a sense of uneasiness in the village. Even the children did not laugh and play as they had usually done on my other visits.

Julia could not contain her excitement. Her eyes darted everywhere.

The community house, dark except for a few flickering candles, smelled strongly of tobacco and incense. Though women were not usually invited into the dinh, they had always made me feel welcomed, probably because I accompanied Albee.

A small group of men smoking cigarettes, sitting on their haunches, clustered around a low wooden table filled with teacups.

All heads turned in our direction when we stepped over the threshold. When I saw Tran Cuong Gia sitting at the far end of the room I knew why we had traveled here.

Albee set the duffle bags on the ground in front of Tran Cuong Gia.

Tran Guong Gia stood up. He opened first one canvas suitcase and then the other. He looked up at Albee and smiled broadly. "Thank you."

"I knew you'd be pleased," Albee said.

Tran Cuong Gia motioned for one of the young men standing in the doorway to take the duffle bags. "When will there be another delivery?"

Even before that incident at the checkpoint with the perfume, I suspected that we were most likely carrying guns. Julia didn't need to know. No sense in worrying her. She'd figure things out soon enough.

Tram Cuong Gia pointed to Julia. "Who is this other woman?" he asked. "A new wife?"

"Her name is Julia," Albee responded. "An American on holiday."

"The Americans have made promises," Tran Cuong Gia said. "I hope they keep their word." He stood in the doorway. The bright afternoon sun illuminated his handsome profile. He was a metisse, what the locals called a person of native and French mixed racial heritage. He was tall with light honey-colored skin and slightly almond shaped eyes. Lean and muscular, there was an animal quickness about his movements and he had become a trusted leader amongst the rebels.

Albee and Tran Cuong Gia stepped out of the dinh and walked up the street.

"Who was that?" Julia asked.

"A friend from the mountains."

"Did Albee bring him what I think he brought him?"

I did not reply.

Really, what else could it have been, but guns? Julia had only asked the question, as any reporter would have done. Julia already knew the answer. She was simply seeking confirmation. She'd done this before, playing at being stupid to get more information. This situation had been a bit tricky and neither Albee nor I wanted to start a discussion about what he'd brought to this village. It would have been a different story if we'd been caught carrying the weapons. But thankfully we weren't.

I watched Tran Cuong Gia's strong, erect body quickly move up the street. He walked with absolute determination. And though Albee was a huge man, somehow Tran Cuong Gia's smaller, but sharp, tight body was an even match.

The other men in the dinh got up and walked out, also. The brilliant light of the afternoon sun poured in through the doorway.

"What now?" Julia asked.

"We entertain ourselves until it's time to leave."

Julia leaned one shoulder against the doorsill, her face split in half, one side in the bright sun light, the other half buried in the dark shadow of the dinh.

"So, how long have you been running guns?" she asked.

"I don't run guns."

"Well, what else would you call it?"

I looked out into the village street wondering where the children were today.

Julia moved into the full sun. "Your friend Albee is certainly involved up to his neck."

"Yeah, he's in this for real."

"And you? You in this for real, too?"

"Can't say. Time will tell."

"Fair enough. Though next time let me know if my life is in danger. So, please share with me if your boyfriend is hauling guns. I can handle myself."

For the remainder of the afternoon, we strolled through the village. Several women squatting in a doorway, watched as we passed. Farther up the street, a woman paused for a moment to watch us before flipping wet clothing over a jut line stretched between two poles. We turned down a street, following it for a while until we found that it circled back to where we began. So, we walked back to the dinh and waited for Albee.

"You haven't said much about your experience in Spain," I said. "We've got plenty of time now. Want to tell me about it?"

"There's nothing to tell," Julia said. She abruptly took out a pack of cigarettes and offered me one.

We leaned against the building smoking our cigarettes. A soft twilight blush washed over us as the sun slowly descended behind a long mountain range. We heard the laughter of a few children playing somewhere in the village, but we hadn't seen any on our walk.

The late afternoon dragged on forever. My legs were tired and just as I was beginning to think that I could wait no longer, Albee stepped out of one of the buildings and walked toward us.

"We've been asked to eat at Phu Van Ho's home this evening," he said.

"That means we'll be spending the night," I explained to Julia.

"Where'll we sleep? Not in that car." Julia looked a bit apprehensive.

"One of the families will offer us a mat in their home," Sarah said.

"You've stayed here before?"

"Several times."

Albee took hold of my arm and softly said, "I need to speak with you."

"What's up?"

"Not here," he said and we strolled up the street leaving Julia behind. "Tran Cuong Gia is taking off after sundown," Albee said. "I'm going with him."

"Did you know about this before we left Hanoi?" Albee had pulled this kind of thing on me before. A one-day visit sometimes turned into a three or four-day excursion. Though this would be the first time that he left the village.

"In a couple of days there's going to be a meeting. Some important decisions will be made. I have to be there. And, no, I didn't know about this before we left. You know it's always a possibility that something will come up."

As usual he did not apologize.

"So, we're stuck here until you return?"

"No, we're going on foot. You have the car. You know how to drive. Take it back to Hanoi.

"I suppose we have no choice, now do we?"

"You always have a choice."

It was very clear that he'd used Julia and me as decoys. The French police saw men traveling alone as potential trouble, even if they were in automobiles. And if it hadn't been for his female companions coming along, he probably couldn't have pulled off that cute trick with the perfume at the roadblock.

"I guess we served our purpose."

He turned and walked away.

I returned to the dinh. A slight odor of lemon grass and fish sauce perfumed the air. Neither Julia nor I had eaten anything since that morning. My hangover was history. My stomach was grumbling like crazy.

"Something sure smells good. I hope that means we'll be eating soon," Julia said.

Albee stepped out from one of the doorways up the street and motioned for us to join him. Julia put out her cigarette and we hurried to meet him.

"I'll be leaving as soon as the sun goes down," he said.

"What do you mean, you'll be leaving?" Julia asked.

"He's got some business."

"What about us? Are we going, too?"

"No. We go back to Hanoi tomorrow morning."

Julia looked at me curiously. No doubt she had a hundred questions.

When we stepped through the doorway of Phu Van Ho's home I could tell by the delicious aroma that this would be a great meal.

Covered clay pots and heaping bowls of rice filled the table. Tran Cuong Gia sat at the far end of the room.

When everyone had been seated on the ground, the lids were removed from the clay pots. Steam billowed up from the containers like escaping apparitions.

Tran Cuong Gia lifted a small portion of rice to his mouth and chewed slowly.

No one said a word through the meal, including Phu Van Ho.

When we'd finished eating, Tran Cuong Gia said, "It's time."

Albee stood and the two men walked to the door.

"We'll go with you to the end of the village," Phu Van Ho said.

Tran Cuong Gia stepped out into the evening. I stood close to Albee while Julia hung back a bit. A small parade of people had gathered on the street and now slowly moved along behind us.

We reached the edge of the village where an opening in the wall met an adjacent rice paddy. Several of the young men with guns hung over their shoulders, stepped over a ledge. Albee and Tran Cuong Gia followed. Then like shadows slipping away from their owners, the silhouettes of the men vanished into the darkness.

Eighteen

AFTER ALBEE AND TRAN CUONG Gia were no longer in sight, everyone turned and walked back to the main section of the village. We hadn't gone far when an ancient-looking woman took hold of my arm and Julia's hand, and pulled us into a doorway. The old woman pointed to the two mats on the floor. This is where we would spend the night.

I smiled and nodded in agreement. The old woman grinned broadly exposing her betel-stained teeth.

Julia looked a bit bewildered.

"This is as good as it gets out here," I said.

I sat on one of the mats. Julia lay down on the mat next to me.

The old woman rolled out a straw mat on the other side of the small room and then blew out the candle leaving us in near total darkness. There was the sound of joints cracking softly as the old woman lowered herself down onto the floor. The room fell silent except for the shrill nasal breathing of our hostess.

"It's clearly lights out," Julia whispered.

"Up with the sun and down with the sun. It's a simple life in these villages."

"So what's Albee up to?" Julia whispered.

"No idea."

"Is this the last we'll see of him?"

"He'll be back. Can't say when, but I'm sure he's going to hang around Hanoi a bit longer."

Night in a village could hardly be compared to that of a noisy city. Here, no one walked the streets after a certain hour or chatted so that everyone heard what they were saying. On my other visits to this village, I'd learned that the splash of a fish in a nearby pond could seem as close as the breathing of the person sleeping on the mat next to me. The sounds in the villages changed with the seasons. The monsoon would not arrive for several more months and any noises in the village now were those of the dry season. In a monsoon the downpour smothered the croaking frogs and the splashing fish in the rice paddy. But the chirp of crickets, the buzz of insects, the troubled cry of a child, even the sleeping breath of an entire village could be heard in the dry season. And yet, even with these minute sounds, a solemn quiet laid across the land, lulling the unaware into believing that nothing would ever alter the peaceful quiet of this country.

Listening to the insistent croaking of frogs it was difficult to believe that I'd ever fall asleep. But then before that thought was finished the world went black.

At one point, I was awakened suddenly with a sense of danger. My mind was alert while my body was paralyzed. The rough wooden floor beneath me radiated warmth from the day's heat. The room was so dark I felt as if I'd gone blind. Julia still slept on the floor beside me. I heard her heavy breathing.

From somewhere in this small room, a man said, "Do not move."

An animal growled. A crouching shadowy figure moved toward me. At first I thought it was the legendary dragon living beneath the village that had come to life. Glistening green eyes peered down at me. Its face, so close to mine that its whiskers brushed against my cheek. The animal's breath, a foul stench of rotting flesh filled the room. Julia awoke. She screamed. I made no sound, though my pounding pulse betrayed my fear. The man stepped forward. "You smell of the French," he said. The man's eyes were now visible in a slight glint of moonlight that had now crept into the room. They were angry, mean eyes. He took hold of the animal's collar and pulled it away from my face. "I should let him eat you," the man said.

The croaking of a frog, insistent and determined to be heard, woke me up. My clothing was soaked in sweat. A rancid smell lingered in my nostrils. I lay on the mat for the longest time until sleep eventually overcame me again. Throughout the remainder of the night, animals and strangers, laughing children, and buzzing insects wove themselves into pockets of dreams, nothing making sense, sticking to my mind like a warning.

At dawn, I awoke to the smell of fish broth simmering in a pot over an open fire in a corner of the room.

The old woman, her nose inches from the open fire stirred the broth with a long wooden paddle. Julia rolled over, sat up and stretched her lower back. Her neck made loud cracking sounds. "Getting old," she said. "What time is it, anyway?"

"Does it matter?"

"No, guess not."

After we got up from the floor, the old woman brought us each a bowl of steaming broth. Long strands of green herbs floated in the soup and small chunks of white bean curds sat on the bottom of the bowls clouding the lower half of the broth as though there were two distinct flavors in the one dish. The old woman motioned for us to drink and when we responded to her wishes, she smiled and looked pleased with herself.

"Time to hit the road," I said after we finished the soup and rolled up the bed mats.

"Thank you for everything," I told the old woman. She smiled broadly and we stepped out into the street.

As Julia and I headed for the edge of the village, we passed a long line of well-wishing villagers. Phu Van Ho's wife, a woman of great dignity, handed me a basket containing one large pummelo, a fruit that looked similar to a grapefruit but weighing a great deal more and tasted sweeter. She also put into the basket large banana leaf packages that most likely contained sticky rice and mung bean paste. Taking the basket, I said, "You are very kind. May the seasons repay you a hundred times."

As we reached the car, a portion of the village, adults and children, followed us across the marshland. Julia and I climbed into the car. Turning the key in the ignition, the engine easily started up. Children scrambled up the embankment to watch our Peugeot drive along the upper portion of the dyke.

Nineteen

JULIA WATCHED SARAH TURN THE car around. She looked out the window at the rear tire. Her side of the car had a good grip on the ground, but it sounded like Sarah's side was having difficulty grabbing some traction on this muddy road. Every time Sarah stepped on the gas, one of the back tires spun like crazy. The car began to slid sideways down the embankment.

"We're headed for that rice paddy," Julia said and held tightly onto her seat.

Several men ran to the car and pushed on the back of the vehicle.

Sarah stepped on the gas once again. All four wheels grabbed hold of the earth. Turning the steering wheel quickly to the left the car headed back in the direction that they had come.

"See, trust," Sarah said and then sticking her head out the window she waved farewell to the villagers.

"I'll never doubt you again," Julia said playfully.

Though if Sarah could have read a deeper meaning into Julia's tone, she would have picked up the relief Julia felt to be traveling away from the village. Until now Julia hadn't let herself admit how claustrophobic this community made her feel. In some ways this place reminded her of the small mountain towns she'd traveled through in Spain. Simple lives disrupted by politics. It looked to be such a hopeless cause with sticks, rocks and a few flimsy suitcases of guns pitted against world powers.

Julia felt old this morning. Her back ached after laying on the hard floor all night. She'd spent many nights in Spain curled up in miserable situations. She'd lost her patience for lousy sleeping arrangements. A persistent mosquito had buzzed around her head for hours during the night. Now there was a collection of itchy spots where the insect had feasted on her during the night.

Julia stretched and sighed heavily. It felt good to put more distance between her and the village. Hopefully they would have an uneventful ride back into Hanoi. Then Julia noticed four men and one woman walking ahead of them, taking up the entire width of the rutted road. Sarah slowed the car to a snails pace.

"Sound your horn," Julia said.

"They'll move. We're in no hurry."

A short distance later, the group stepped off the road and took a narrow path that ran along the irrigation system. One of the men looked back at the car. He lifted his conical hat; angry eyes peered out at them as the car gradually picked up speed.

When the car drove across a deep rut, Julia's head bumped against the doorsill. "Were you aiming for that?" she grumbled.

Sarah ignored Julia and held tightly on to the steering wheel.

Julia opened her mouth to say something else, but the car rocked from side to side, forcing her to grab hold of her seat, bracing herself so as not to hit her head again.

When they reached the main route back to Hanoi, a convoy of Japanese military trucks had taken up the full width of the road blocking their way. Sarah pulled up the handbrake and turned off the engine.

"Headed to China?" Julia asked.

"Where else? Like Albee said, they've threatened to escalate the war. The French haven't officially given them permission to use these roads. But it looks like that doesn't matter."

Several farmers sat on their haunches watching the convoy go by.

Julia had seen this in Spain: truckloads of troops rolling past her on the open roadways, soldiers with grimy hands holding tightly onto guns, eyes blankly looking out at the changing countryside. She'd always wondered how many of these men and boys were ready to die that day.

"The Japanese are using the coastline of Vietnam to move troops into China. They call this a military privilege," Sarah said.

The loud drone of the truck engines nearly drowned out even the simplest of thoughts. Julia looked at Sarah, her eyes, angry and intent, betrayed her calm demeanor. When the last truck of the convoy passed, Sarah said, "Catroux, the Governor General of French Indochina, has lost control. He cannot even get his own government to help with Japan's aggressive attitude. I heard he appealed to FDR for assistance, but the US refused to get involved."

"It's not their war," Julia said. "The same thing happened in Spain."

Sarah started the car engine. "The world's going to hell in a handbag, my dear, and no one wants to get involved."

Several other peasants gathered on the roadside to watch the trucks go by. When the last vehicle passed, the peasants stood in a close circle chatting, and then they each went off in a different direction.

Sarah drove the car out onto the road just as a light rain began to fall. Soon a deluge of water poured from the sky making it nearly impossible to see the road. Sarah slowed the car to a crawl. She'd seen this before, unexpected short bouts of heavy rain in the middle of a dry season. "What else could happen?" Sarah mumbled.

"You could hit a water buffalo," Julia said jokingly.

"Please, keep those thoughts to yourself."

Peasants walking along the road held woven straw mats over their heads to shield them against the downpour. A group of children, huddled in the back of a cart peered out at the Peugeot from under a woven mat, giggling and pointing. A stooped old man, braced on a crooked walking stick hobbled along the side of the road. No one but the children looked at the car.

Julia and Sarah remained quiet until they passed the spot where Albee had been pulled over by the roadblock. There was no sign of French soldiers today and Julia suspected they had been given orders to let the Japanese military convoys travel the roads unobstructed.

"So, why do you think the translator was murdered?" Julia asked breaking the long silence.

"I really don't know."

Julia thought Sarah's response had been too quick and too matter-of-fact. Of course, she had thoughts about what had happened. "Well, it doesn't look like the authorities are in any hurry to investigate his death," Julia continued.

"Small potatoes in this country," Sarah said. "There's too much going on."

"Well, I guess that leaves it up to us. Don't tell me you haven't thought about it."

"Truthfully, I've thought of little else since his death. But I don't know where to begin."

"I'm offering my help," Julia said. "That's part of what I do as a reporter. Dig around, look for information, and talk to people."

"So, then, you're not sailing off in search of Amelia Earhart?"

"Not likely," Julia replied. "I just said that to give Albee something to chew on."

The rain subsided. The air inside the car was humid. Julia opened her window. A few drops of rain landed on her lap. Soon the sky went from angry black to a dirty light gray. Steam radiated up from the pavement as if the earth had been on fire and now lay smoldering in front of them.

Sarah sighed heavily. "Sometimes the weather here feels like a shroud."

They traveled for another hour on the well-constructed French road. After reaching Hanoi and driving on the cobbled street for a short while, Sarah eased the Peugeot onto the street along the back wall of her house. But before they gathered up their possessions from the trunk of the car, Aon She Beng screamed.

"She's still at it," Sarah said.

"You mean—"

Another desperate scream echoed along the street.

Sarah jumped out of the car and hurried up the street fearful that something dreadful might really be happening to her landlady this time. But when Sarah rounded the corner and saw the crowd of shoppers and local vendors gathered outside Aon She Beng's courtyard laughing, it was easy to see that the old woman was not in any danger.

"What's going on?" Julia asked.

"Beats me," Sarah replied. "But she's certainly fired up about something."

"You going to see what's the matter?"

"We'll know soon enough."

Sarah opened the gate to her courtyard. Nearly noon, the sun now beat straight down into the small garden. The shrieks and howls that came from the other side of the common wall soon subsided. Later that afternoon, Julia heard whimpering.

"I'm going to have a lie-down," Julia said. "That is if your landlady doesn't start up again. That woman is getting on my nerves." Trickles of sweat ran down the small of Julia's back and the heat in her bedroom was even more miserable than standing outside in the sun.

Her typewriter sat on the suitcase where she'd left it. Plunking down on several keys, Julia wondered what she'd write about next. There were no assignments, no deadline to meet, and there hadn't been contact with an editor in months. What frustrated her more than the heat and humidity was the realization that though she played with the idea of looking for Amelia Earhart, it was more than that. Here intention in traveling this far had been to simply keep moving.

Twenty

AON SHE BENG'S HARANGUING WAS getting on my nerves. But there were more important things to do than worrying about this old gal's problems. While Julia settled in for an afternoon nap, I quickly wrote a note. Opening the garden gate, I gave the paper to a local man who would gladly deliver a message for a few coins. "This is for the nun," I said. There were few secrets on these streets. He asked no questions. He knew which nun I meant and where to find her at this time of the day because the ritual of chanting brought all Buddhists to a temple in the afternoon.

After closing the gate, Aon She Beng began talking loudly again in her garden. It was difficult to tell what the woman was saying, between thee loud outbursts, and then her whimpering that had a pitiful pleading tone.

Gathering up a few sticks of kindling from the corner of my small kitchen, I started a fire and soon had a kettle of water bubbling on the stove.

I hadn't been sitting long in the doorway of my house sipping a cup of tea and listening to the brittle bamboo leaves clacking away, when the nun and Thi My arrived. I'd sent the note to the nun not expecting Thi My to come along with her. Tradition frowned on too much public exposure during the mourning period. But then these were not ordinary times.

The nun stood in my courtyard, a portion of her Buddhist garb draped over her shaven head to protect her from the unforgiving sun. Thi My looked more peaked and fragile than when I'd last seen her.

"Let me fix you a cup of tea," I said and hurried into the house.

Julia came out of her room. "Sleeping in this heat is like going into a coma. How long was I out?"

"Not long. The nun and Thi My are here. Want some tea?"

"Too hot for that," Julia said and went out into the courtyard.

The one thing I'd learned from the years of living in Vietnam is that when the summer season hits, there's no relief anywhere from the heat. My guests could choose to sit in the blistering afternoon sun that poured down into my courtyard or they could come into the stifling humid atmosphere of my house. Either way, we'd be miserable. No one followed me into the house and it appeared that even the glaring sunshine was preferred to the coffin-like stillness inside my house.

When I came back out into the garden with the cups of tea I sensed an uneasiness in the air. I handed a cup of tea to the nun and one to Thi My. Something had happened in my absence. Their demeanor had changed. Thi My no longer looked haggard. Her eyes were brighter, even her pallor had gone from ashen to a more natural tone. The nun took the cup of tea. Glancing up at me there was a spark of hope, or perhaps it was excitement in her eyes.

There was no easy way to bring up the topic of Van Mai's death, which was why I'd sent for the nun. We'd all become so entwined in each other's lives that I felt the reported suicide of the nun's sister as profoundly as if the woman had been a close relative of mine. The trip into the country with Albee had most likely been a diversion, an excuse to keep from dealing with another death. It had now been several days since I'd seen the prison report. In all that time I hadn't the courage to contact the nun before this. It was cowardly of me knowing that if anyone had notified her of the death, it had most likely been a colonial officer who had told her the terrible news.

"I was so sorry to hear the news about you sister, Van Mai," I said.

The nun's usual soft, gentle breath caught in her chest. Words are cruel and useless at times like these. My intent in sending for the nun was to give my condolences. Yet, the mention of Van Mai invoked the memory of what we all knew was another painful loss. The nun said nothing. Thi My said nothing. We sat half-shrouded in the growing shadow of the garden wall as the sun slowly moved across the cloudless sky. When we finished our tea, Thi My suddenly looked over her shoulder startled, as though someone had come up behind her. She quickly glanced at the nun.

"What is it?" I asked.

The nun said nothing.

Thi My closed her eyes, her face relaxed. Tears softly fell across her cheeks. "He's here," Thi My whispered. "He's here in your garden."

"Who?" Julia asked.

The nun glanced nervously about the courtyard. "You are probably just tired, my dear," the nun said.

"No, he's here," Thi My said. Standing up, her eyes darting everywhere; the pond, the noisy cluster of bamboo stalks in a corner of the garden, the gate and then Thi My fixed her gaze on the common wall that separated Aon She Beng's garden from mine.

A hot breeze lazily pushed its way across the garden, brushing against my face. The dry bamboo leaves chatter became shriller. At that moment, I could have almost believed there were such a thing as a ghost.

Aon She Beng let out a blood-curdling shriek and shouted, "Get out! Leave me alone."

"What is with that woman?" Julia asked.

"Lately it sounds like she's finally gone off the deep end," I replied.

"I'll go see," the nun said. Putting her teacup on the ground, she went next door.

Thi My did not move, her breathing heavy, her eyes hopeful.

A short while later, though Aon She Beng no longer shouted, her voice remained at an irrational shrill pitch, pleading. We could not make out what the nun said, but her tone was calm, like a single chord held through a discordant song.

Thi My sighed deeply, lifted her head and wiped at the tears with her delicate hands. Her eyes moved across the courtyard again, seeming to search for something.

The nun returned shortly. It was difficult to determine from her expression what had transpired in Aon She Beng's courtyard. Though something had happened. Nuns and monks are not sworn to secrecy as a priest is, but Buddhist teachings, from what I've learned in dealing with them over the years, encouraged discretion. The nun chose silence. Looking only at Thi My, she offered her hand to the poor girl, and the two women went out into the street.

Twenty-One

Chaos.
The world has turned upside down.
The sweet soymilk of my childhood smells of urine.
Sunrise brings bats to my door.
Sarah, the frightened monkey living in your kitchen cabinet has watched for years as wars floated above his head.
Hidden, he's seen the corruption.
It rumbles like thunder in a blackened sky.
I watched my lover.
Thi My heard my words.
I lay in the folds of her garment, her tears falling on me like a soft rain, and in your garden we were wedded in a sorrowful ceremony.
There is no returning to my grave.
My choice is made.

Twenty-Two

A WOMAN'S SCREAM ECHOED INSIDE a cave. I lost my way in the dark. I wondered if the scream would help me find the light again. A fearful thought struck me. What if the scream came from deeper inside the cave? A pulse pounded inside my head. Something slimy brushed against my leg. In the distance there was a flicker of light. The woman called once again for help. Startled awake, I realized the screaming woman was Aon She Beng.

It was the middle of the night and Aon She Beng was at it again. "Stop it, Aon She Beng," I shouted though it would have been impossible for her to hear me from my bedroom.

"Sounds like someone's trying to kill your landlady," Julia called to me.

Hurriedly wrapping myself in a robe I rushed out of the house still groggy from my dream. Julia followed dressed only in silk pajamas. We ran out of the courtyard and into the street. Several lights glowed in the windows across the way.

"No, not you," Aon She Beng called, and let out another ear-piercing scream.

I banged on her garden gate. "Aon She Beng, it's me, Sarah! Let me in."

Aon She Beng did not respond. I banged again. "Aon She Beng, open this gate!"

Someone fiddled with the lock. Aon She Beng not only bolted her gate, lately she placed a board across the door each night. Finally, the gate opened. Her usually carefully managed hair hung across her shoulders like long shreds of grey rags. Her eyes glistened wild with fear in the flickering candlelight.

Julia and I looked around the garden for intruders. The bright moonlight cast deep shadows across the courtyard like fallen bodies.

"What on earth is the matter?" I asked.

Her heavy breathing obstructed her speech. "He's come for my money," she managed to say.

"Who?" Julia asked, annoyed.

Knowing Julia, the reporter part of her was probably disappointed that we hadn't stumbled onto something more sinister.

Aon She Beng glared at Julia and said, "That's my business."

"Oh, no, you don't get off that easy," I said. "You scream your head off, waking half of Hanoi, and you won't tell us what's going on. You want to play that game, fine, we'll just leave and go back to sleep."

"No! No leave."

"So, who's scared the pants off you?" Julia asked.

Aon She Beng's eyes darted around in the dark as though looking for someone or something. Tilting her head as if straining to hear a sound, Aon She Beng staggered slightly forward.

"What's going on?" I asked. "You're trying my patience. I'd much rather be sleeping than standing in your garden playing guessing games with you."

"I thought it was a dream," Aon She Beng finally said. "My husband wait until everyone sleep, then complain I bad wife."

"Your husband is dead. You were dreaming." This was unbelievable that we were standing here in the middle of the night dealing with this old lady's bad dreams. "Go back to sleep," I said. "In the morning you'll see how foolish this is."

"I don't dream," Aon She Beng screamed. "No dreams, not dream for many years." The flame on the candle trembled in her shaking hands.

"Calm yourself. You'll have a heart attack."

"He look for my money."

"I'm going to tell you again, Aon She Beng, your husbands, all of them, are dead."

She turned to face me. Her eyes glistened with anger. "Yes, I know," she said. A chill crept up my spine.

"That's ridiculous," Julia said. "You're imagining things."

"You know nothing, you stupid woman," Aon She Beng shouted.

"Calm down," I said. "We'll go into the house and have a look around."

"You won't find anything. He tricky devil. He wait. When I think he gone, he jumps out."

"You're serious, aren't you?"

"I know what I see."

"Okay, show us where you think he was." We had to put an end to all this nonsense and get back to bed.

"In kitchen, pulling up floorboards."

"I'll check it out. You want to come with me, or stay out here?"

"Let's all go," Julia said. "We want to see this ghost in action."

I had no doubt that Julia's tone irritated Aon She Beng, though the old woman said nothing and followed us.

I took the candle from Aon She Ben. It flickered and nearly went out as we stepped into the house. Holding one hand in front of the flame, we slowly crept into the kitchen, a small area where the cooking was done in the back of the house. I bumped into a few pieces of furniture, but nothing presented a problem. When we entered the cooking area, Aon She Beng lit another candle and pointed to the floor in the corner near a cabinet. Large splinters of wood had been pulled up from the floor. It looked like a dog or a large cat had been digging at the boards and left deep gouges in the wood.

"How did this happen?" I asked.

"Dead husband."

"Why would he want to pull up your floorboards?"

"He wants my money."

"Why would anyone think you had money under the house?" I asked this though the truth was that everyone in the neighborhood knew the answer to that question. Of course, this old miser hid money under her house, and probably under her bed and just about anywhere that she'd think no one would look. Yet, it did appear that something had been scratching at her floor.

"It was probably one of your neighbors cats that got into your kitchen and did all this damage. It wasn't a ghost."

"No cat!" Aon She Beng shouted. "A spirit, a ghost hiding in my house. When you go, he come back. He sneaky spirit. Soon bring all my dead ancestors to live in my house. You stop him." Her hysterical tone of voice intensified. Even in the dim candlelight, I saw her cheeks flushed red, her eyes intent and angrily glaring at me. "Stop him," Aon She Beng shouted, stomping her foot as though it were a command.

"What do you want me to do?"

"Get spirit out of my house."

"This is ridiculous. Either you go back to your bed or come to my place and spend the rest of the night on my couch. I'm tired. This is enough foolishness for one night."

"I not sleep in your house." Aon She Beng grabbed the candle from my hand. A bit of hot wax dripped onto my thumb, but that would have been the least of what could have been a most miserable experience if my landlady had taken up my offer.

"As you wish. But, please, no more screaming."

"Albee return soon?" Aon She Beng asked in her usual demanding tone.

"I suspect he will."

"He chase demon away."

"If you say so." I said.

I'd had enough of Aon She Beng's nonsense and headed for the front of the house. As Julia and I stepped out of the front door, something scurried into a corner; something far too small to be human I suspected this was the culprit that had been giving Aon She Beng so much trouble the last couple of days. Julia quickly looked over her shoulder. She'd heard it, too.

"A rat?" Julia whispered. "Probably."

"Should we stay and help?"

"Help do what? If her servants haven't caught the stupid thing, what are we going to do?"

Julia shrugged in agreement. "I sure hope she doesn't start yowling again."

I opened the courtyard gate. Several more lights now glowed in our neighbor's windows. One man sat on his haunches in the doorway of his house. The red glow of a cigarette faintly illuminated his face as he puffed away.

Before we stepped back into my house there was another loud crash, but no one called out.

"I'm stuffing cotton in my ears," Julia said and stumbled off to her room.

Twenty-Three

AON SHE BENG WAS QUIET for the next couple of days. Something crashed against the wall a couple of times. At one point someone shouted, "Die! Die!" But other than that, the preparations for my landlady's birthday, or what they called in this country the longevity celebration, continued without too much trouble.

It was late, nearly midnight. Julia sat with me in the garden. We'd finished a bottle of wine when we heard Albee's familiar whistle just before he waltzed into the garden. There was a familiar look about him, and I knew he'd stopped off for a taste of opium before he got to my place. He walked differently when he'd been smoking the stuff. There was an agile smoothness to his gait. His big body seemed to hover a bit off the ground.

"Hello, ladies," he said. He waved to Julia with one of his big paws and when he hugged me it felt as though we lingered longer than usual in an embrace. Without saying another word, he went into the house.

"Aon She Beng's going to be happy to see him," Julia said. "But she's been so quiet, it doesn't sound like she's going to need him to chase away her dead husband's spirit."

"Don't be so sure. Aon She Beng gets pretty needy when he's around. Once that old gal faked a fall just to have him sit with her for an afternoon."

"Doesn't sound like something he'd put up with."

"He knew what had happened. Nothing else was going on that day, so he sat with her drinking tea and listening to her stories. Those two have an interesting relationship."

Julia yawned widely and then swallowed the last of her booze. "So it seems," she said. "I'm going to hit the hay. See you in the morning."

I was tired, too. Though sharing a bed with Albee tonight would be impossible. He usually took up more than his share of the bed and it was too hot to lie close to any man tonight.

"A penny for your thoughts," Albee said. He stood in the doorway, his bulk nearly filling the entryway.

"I thought you were sleeping."

"Changed my mind."

"So, what have you been up to?"

He sighed heavily. Stepping out into the garden, he sat in the chair next to me.

"Dat Tu came back with me," he said.

"Has he heard about his wife?"

Albee rubbed his hands together, something he did when words were not easy to come by. "Times are not good," he finally said.

"What's going on, Albee?" Asking him a direct question sometimes brought an answer and sometimes only a well-rehearsed blank look.

"Can't tell you anything my dear, you know that. But, soon there's going to be some drastic changes. After tomorrow, it's best I find somewhere else to hang my hat."

"Aon She Beng is going to be very disappointed."

"And you?" he asked.

"Sure, I'll miss you, too. You kind of grow on a person."

"Like a fungus?" he joked.

"Yeah, like a fungus."

The night was so quiet we could have believed we were the only people awake in this part of the city. And then we heard the soft padding of a rickshaw puller running up the street. Albee sat straight in his chair. He looked at the garden gate.

"You expecting company?" I asked.

The rickshaw continued up the street. The night was silent again.

"Never can tell," he said.

Albee and I never pretended that we'd ever be more than part-time lovers. Tonight though, there was something out of the ordinary in his voice. What I knew about this man had more to do with suspicions than actual information. He came and went. I rarely asked questions. I knew enough not to expect him to tell me any more than he thought necessary, and often wondered if he ever gave me a straight answer.

It was doubtful that we'd make love tonight. Opium usually dampened his libido and though he affectionately held my hand as we walked into the bedroom. He seemed preoccupied. But then when he lay next to me, he became as gentle as a small creature, his kisses like whispers in the dark.

He did not smell of perfume as he frequently did when he returned from one of his opium jaunts, but there was an aroma of damp earth in his clothing. He pulled me close. His hot breath smothered me. There was always a sense of urgency in this man as though he needed to be someplace else. This was how he let go of people. He drew them near to him, held them tightly, until they were almost suffocated, and then he'd let go and walk out of their lives. He'd done this to me before. Soon he'd become a stranger, a shadow. I wondered if this might be the last time we would lay together.

I returned his kisses and with my fingers, traced the muscles of his large arms, noting his imperfections, the patch of moles on the top of his shoulder, a long scar on his right bicep, and the bristly hair that grew across his chest.

The morning would come soon enough. I knew that in the next day or two, Albee would simply walk out of my life. We knew that this would eventually happen. He brushed his lips against my ear, sighed, and no longer rushed at me. Neither of us said a word, and for the first time he gave his body over to me in a way that he had never done before, though I knew it was only temporary.

Twenty-Four

THE MONSOON SEASON HAD NOT started in earnest yet. It looked as though Aon She Beng would have a dry day for her longevity celebration. By early afternoon I realized that I'd put off attending my landlady's party long enough and asked Julia if she wanted to come along with me.

"You kidding, wouldn't miss this for the world," she said.

Albee had been quiet most of the morning. When I asked if he planned on going, he merely grunted.

All morning, we heard the padding of rickshaw drivers outside on the street as they stopped to let guests disembark. The chatter in the adjoining garden built to such a level that I could no longer make out individual conversations. Unlike Julia, I certainly did not look forward to attending this thing today, though I knew if I didn't go I'd never hear the end of it.

So the three of us headed next door. And as soon as Aon She Beng spotted Albee, her eyes sparkled and a big smile spread across her face. More than a dozen people stood around in the garden waiting to speak with her. They admired her beautiful porcelain vases, her elaborately decorated garden, and her expensive brocade garment. She ignored them all in favor of Albee, and waved frantically for him to come and sit beside her.

"What can I say," he murmured, "When you got it, you got it." He put on his big toothy grin and walked to where Aon She Beng sat on a newly purchased chair that looked more like a throne than a piece of furniture. She appeared quite pleased with herself gazing down on her guests. But all dressed up in her regal gown, her wrinkled and squished-in face reminded me of the carved apple dolls that my grandmother used to make for me when I was a little girl.

Several farmers, with their conical straw hats in hand, brushed passed me as they left the garden. Aon She Beng probably owned their land and they most likely, out of respect, brought her offerings of rice or fruit. The farmers diverted their eyes to the ground and hurried to get out into the street.

Henrietta, Jean George's wife, called to me, "Oh, Sarah I have someone I want you to meet."

"Good Lord," I said under my breath. "Here we go."

"So nice to see that you brought your American friend," Henrietta said. "I am sorry that we didn't get a chance to speak at the funeral of that poor fellow. I'm Henrietta." She reached out a gloved hand to Julia.

Julia's no fool, and I believe she took an instant dislike to my boss's wife, because she grabbed Henrietta's hand with the vigor of a lumberjack and tightly squeezed those French fingers. Henrietta winced ever so demurely and quickly pulled her hand away. Then with ladylike decorum Henrietta cradled the poor wounded paw in the other hand.

"Nice to meet you Henrietta," Julia said. From the grin on her face I could tell she had a good time of it. "Degrees of feminine superiority" Julia used to call it when she out-muscled another woman. Some women were fair game to Julia, and Henrietta fit the mold perfectly.

Henrietta did not look again at Julia and directed her next comment to me. "May I introduce Mme. Blossom Debuce. She is newly arrived from Paris and will be setting up a dress shop. Jean George is helping her with all the pesky details."

I smiled politely and bit my tongue to keep from saying something snide because in the past three weeks I'd seen this woman leaving Jean George's office quite often. They looked pretty chummy if you asked me.

"So, how long have you been here?" I asked.

"Four weeks," Blossom responded. Our eyes locked and I knew she recognized me.

"Why'd you choose a dress shop?" I asked. "With all the tailors and seamstresses already here, it doesn't seem necessary to open another one."

"They know nothing of fashion," Blossom replied. She gave my body, clad in baggy pants and buttoned-down shirt, the quick once-over, seeming to evaluate whether she should cultivate me as a customer. "I've brought the latest designs with me and very soon all the women in French Indochina will be wearing only the best that Paris has to offer."

"How nice for us," I said.

"Yes, isn't it just wonderful," Henrietta replied and then turned to Blossom. "There is that officer I told you about. I do want you to meet him. He is very available. His wife, such a delicate creature, died two years ago. Sometimes he looks so lost and bewildered. You must meet him. Please excuse us Sarah." Henrietta took hold of Blossom's hand and hurried her off to the other side of the garden.

"That available man is an opium addict," I whispered to Julia.

The guests stood in clusters. The French administrators and their wives huddled near the garden gate in what looked to me like a closed circle of children telling secrets. Several local merchants stood shoulder to shoulder in the middle of the garden, looking amused by something, grinning, and their feeble attempts to appear respectful didn't fool me. They'd endured Aon She Beng's antics for days and I wondered if they weren't waiting for her to start up with some of her craziness. A Mandarin dressed in a beautiful silk-embroidered robe stood isolated from the rest of the guests and paid little attention to anyone. He looked as though he might stand patiently forever waiting his turn to pay his respects to Aon She Beng, who probably owned most of the land in the province that he managed.

A French and a Japanese military officer stood near a large vase filled with lotus blossoms. I hadn't noticed them until one of the French officers shifted and turned to face the garden gate. I thought his initial look was one of surprise, which I guess is what had gotten my attention. Then his expression quickly changed to one of interest. I looked to see who had entered the garden.

Thi My, dressed in a white silk garment stood in the entrance, her father on one side of her, the nun on the other.

I glanced at Albee sitting next to Aon She Beng. They both saw the new guests. A hush came over the garden. All eyes were on Thi My as she walked across the garden. She carried a small package wrapped in gold embroidered fabric and offered it in both hands to Aon She Beng.

My landlady hesitated at first. Then with slightly trembling hands, she took the parcel from the young woman. Thi My then turned and walked back to where her father and the nun were waiting. I had met her father on many occasions, though today he did not look in my direction nor did he glance at anyone else in the garden. He simply remained focused on his daughter and when she once again stood at his side, he turned and accompanied by the nun, walked back out into the street.

I heard Julia sigh. Henrietta whispered in Blossom's ear as soon as the garden gate was closed. The two military men appeared not to be fazed by the incident, while the merchants lowered their eyes to the ground.

Everyone was expected to present Aon She Beng with some kind of gift or offering. Until this morning, I had no idea what to give my landlady. Then I decided on a piece of jewelry my mother had left me, a cameo set in a gold brooch. It had been stuck in a box since her death almost 20 years ago. I knew I'd never wear it.

When finally there was a break in the line of people waiting to pay their respects to Aon She Ben, I took hold of Julia's hand. "Come on," I said. "Let's get this thing over with."

Albee vanished at some point after Thi My made her entrance. No one had seen him since. He had looked quite out of place sitting next to Aon She Beng with his hulking size looming over her frail wrinkled body. Though Aon She Beng looked quite pleased with her favorite person sitting by her side.

Julia and I approached Aon She Beng. I held out my gift wrapped in a small square of brocade cloth. "This is very precious to me," I said. "It belonged to my mother."

Aon She Beng took the offering, unwrapped it, and asked, "Is this gold?"

"Yes," I replied. Her question amused me. This old fox knew better than I did whether something was a precious metal.

She nodded her approval and then she looked at Julia. "What she bring me?"

"I will take your portrait with my camera," Julia responded.

"Good," Aon She Beng said. Her small dark eyes sparkled and she smiled broadly.

She leaned forward. "Where Albee?"

"I don't know. I guess you scared him away with all your powerful guests," I replied.

"Now you see I important woman."

Giving Aon She Beng an amiable smile, I nodded in agreement. I couldn't wait to get out of there.

Julia and I stepped aside to let the patient Mandarin have his turn.

"Oh, Lord, I need a drink," I said.

"Let's go. I've seen enough," Julia said. "Though I'd certainly like to know what those two military guys are talking about and why they're even here."

"Aon She Beng's obviously not one of their strategists, but I'll bet she's got something they want. Rumor has it she's got bags of money stashed everywhere and somehow she has been able to acquire more land than anyone else, not only in Hanoi, but in the south, too."

I shared Julia's curiosity about the military's presence. But I found Albee's disappearance more upsetting. Last night was most likely our last goodbye. He'd always found his way back to my door, but these were changing times and I had a sinking feeling that he'd left my life for good.

Julia and I eased our way through the crowd. Jean George, his wife, and Blossom had insinuated their way into the tight circle of French administrators, ignoring anyone who came in through the gate.

Stepping out of the garden, we met Thien Nguyen's brother coming up the street. He walked alone and, still dressed in his mourning turban, he looked as though he had not slept in days.

He nodded politely.

"Good day," I said.

He halfheartedly smiled.

"How is your mother?" I inquired.

"She is not well. Our physician has been treating her, but she refuses to get out of bed. Her body is weak." He said this, and though I would have expected any mother to react this way to the murder of a child, there was something else in his comment, something that I could not quite grasp.

"I hope she recovers soon," I said, but he did not respond, and proceeded to walk through the gate and into Aon She Beng's garden.

Twenty-Five

I WAS UP TO MY neck in work at the Archives. Every conceivable type of document, including poetry, novels, and administrative communications began to arrive from the northern provinces. Jean George said nothing about why this was happening, though we both knew the increased presence of the Japanese had everything to do with this activity. Boxes of documents and tied bundles of papers were strewn everywhere in the main storage building. The monsoon season would be here any time now. We were going to be in real trouble trying to find dry places to put all this stuff once the rains started.

Father Dominique hadn't been around for a while. That was always a good thing. He frequently traveled to the outer provinces checking on what he called charitable work. I knew better. He kept meticulous records of new converts and he'd most likely gone out to gather more statistics to impress the diocese. He would usually be gone for a week or two. When he returned, we'd see him in the reading room bent over a ledger writing the names of new converts in neat columns. I often wondered if he kept track of his parishioners' sins this way, as well.

Le Sing Dong turned out to be a pretty good translator after all, though I still wouldn't trust him any more than I did the priest. He was an eager young man, ready to learn the workings of the Archives, completing in short order any task handed to him. The thing that pleased me most about him was that he didn't ask any personal questions. I worried when he was first hired that he might be a bit too nosy about my private business. Thankfully, he wasn't.

After Albee took off, my personal life calmed down. Dat Tu also disappeared about that some time. The news of Van Mai's "suicide" frightened her family and when the body was turned over to her wid-owed mother, a quick burial was arranged outside the family plot and nothing more was ever said about the dead young woman. Dat Tu's infant son remained with the maternal grandmother. It was doubtful that father and son would ever see each other again.

Julia, bored with sitting in my garden every night, went to the bar by herself. The next thing I knew, she befriended an American re-porter recently arrived in Vietnam. So, Julia was out of my hair most of the time now, too. She came home drunk many nights after I'd already gone to bed, bumped into things, but it never sounded like she had come home dead drunk the way I remember she did when we lived together back in Kansas City. I kind of had my old life back. It felt good. Christmas came and went with only a few extra drinks in the garden and even Aon She Beng was unusually calm. It seemed that those ghosts my landlady had been so worried about had left her alone and now she was preoccupied with her business. The war in Europe had not let up from what news we could get and I read in one communiqué that Canada was sending troops to Britain to help fight the Nazis.

I often thought about Thien Nguyen. The authorities hadn't come up with any information that would solve his murder. Julia apparent-ly had also given up interest in helping to solve the crime. The letter from the Governor General's office remained tucked away inside my quilt in the armoire. I still wasn't sure what to do with it.

Jean George continued to keep the bodyguard and by now the guy was like a piece of furniture posted outside his offices. Blossom vis-ited Jean George several times a week. It was quite clear they were doing more than just going over paper work for her dress shop. But, if Henrietta knew what her husband was up to, she probably preferred that he stayed out of her hair.

Things were so calm and quiet that it was hard to believe there was serious trouble in the world, and that the threat of war was simply a passing blip in time. But that was only wishful thinking. Julia made sure that I knew differently.

"You've stuck you head in the sand," she said to me one evening, as she got ready to meet up with her new friend. She put a Jelly

Roll Morton record on the gramophone. The piano keys beat out a snappy tune.

I looked forward to sitting by myself this evening in my quiet garden once the music stopped and Julia had gone off to drink with her buddies. I'd gotten accustomed to once again drinking myself into a comfortable blur. Anyway, that had been my intention, but Julia was good with words. I objected to her insinuation that I cared nothing about what went on in the world. "I care very much," I said. "I just no longer know what I could do about it. Anything that I've done in the past had been with the assistance of either Albee or Dat Tu and since they've both left the area, I guess I'm waiting for someone or something to come along and give me direction."

"Why not come with me to the Americano Bar and meet my friends," Julia said. "I think you'll find it interesting."

She'd talked plenty about her new friends. I guess I agreed to go with her out of curiosity.

The joint hadn't changed. It even smelled the same. It reminded me of the days when I first met Albee and listened to him recount his adventures in China. Julia now made this place her hangout. The music hadn't gotten any more updated, either, with tunes from the '20's bringing memories of a time gone by.

Bobby waved a greeting. I don't think this man had ever met a drinker he didn't like.

Julia quickly walked to a back table where two men and a woman sat. The woman, her back to the door, leaned forward talking intently to the men. One of the men waved to Julia. The woman turned as we neared the table. She gave us the once-over and as soon as Julia sat down, the woman quickly stood up and left the bar.

"So, what was that about?" Julia asked.

"We'll fill you in later," the younger of the two men said. He looked freshly out of school, and far too young to be traveling in this part of the world. From the look of his smooth baby face, it didn't appear he had been shaving very long, and his slicked back hair reminded me of what a grandmother would insist on when sending a boy to Sunday school.

Bobby came to our table. "How you been, Sarah?" he asked.

I smiled, shrugged.

"The usual?" he asked.

"Yes," Julia and I said at the same time.

"You got it ladies. Two wines, coming up," Bobby said and went behind the bar.

"The arrangements have been," said the young man with the soft young face.

"It's done then?" Julia asked.

"Yep," he said and smiled broadly.

I didn't say anything, waiting for either my drink to be delivered or for more information to come my way. The drink arrived first. When Bobby left our table, I asked, "What's up?"

"We're going north," Julia replied.

This didn't surprise me. Not too much surprised me any more. "When?" I asked.

"I don't know," she said, then took a large swallow of her wine.

"Day after tomorrow," said the young man.

Julia looked at me. "I was going to tell you."

"What's the matter, not enough excitement around here?" I asked.

"The real action is at the border," the young man said. "This country is just a landing field for Japan, and France is letting it happen."

"How long have you been here?" I asked.

"Four weeks," he replied.

"I suggest you wait around and check out the action in a couple months."

"You're talking about the rebels? They haven't got a chance in hell. And if Japan gets its way, France is going to be out of here in a couple years and this country will be the property of the Emperor of Japan."

"What fortune teller gave you this information?" I asked.

"There's a bigger story out there. Nanking, Shanghai, and Manchuria have all been overrun by the Imperial Army and someone has to write about it."

"Good luck," I said and took a hefty swallow of my drink.

"Want to come along with us?" Julia asked.

"You can tell me all about it when you get back." I said. That sounded hopeful, though I shuddered to think Julia might not find her way back out of China.

It was easy to see that Julia was quite excited about the prospect of going on this next adventure. She made short order of her glass of booze and then motioned for Bobby to bring another round of drinks to the table.

"Gentlemen, I suppose it's time for introductions," Julia said. "This is my friend Sarah. She runs the Archives project for the French."

"You must get a lot of hot information," the young man said.

"I get a lot of crap," I replied.

Julia put a hand on the young man's arm and said, "This is Sherman."

I nodded politely, but at that point introductions were not necessary. It was doubtful that we'd ever meet again and I really didn't care if we did. I wasn't impressed.

As Bobby brought the next round of drinks to the table, Julia pointed to the other man sitting across from me. "That handsome guy, we call Tex. He's not from Texas but it fits his southern accent."

He tipped a make-believe hat and gave me a wide toothy grin. Clean-shaven, dapper, he looked like someone who had a lot of practice at appearing worldly. His shirt collars were neat, pointed down perfectly and though he did not wear a tie, he wore a suit coat of expensive fabric. His hands were clean and one arm rested atop the chair next to him in a relaxed arrogant manner.

He extended his hand. "Pleased to meet you." It only took this short phrase for me to agree that he sounded just like he'd stepped out of the southland.

"So where do you come from?" I asked.

"Germany."

"Surely I would have said Georgia or Tennessee."

He smiled. "Maybe a while back. I could be from anywhere when you read my articles, but this tongue of mine only knows one way to wrap around a phrase."

"Tex is a fantastic journalist," Julia said. "I read his stuff while I was in Spain, brilliant, just brilliant."

"So, why didn't you stay in Germany?" I asked. "Must be plenty happening there to keep you guys busy."

"I never intended to stay in Germany," Tex said. "My destination has always been this part of the world. Sherman also has business in these parts. So we hitched a ride on an American air ship headed this way. Here we are now in Hanoi."

"Simple as that?" I replied.

"Well, not so simple. But we managed to get our tails out of Germany thanks to a few contacts I had with a ragtag team of fly boys."

"Don't let him kid you," Julia said. "Tex hops around the world like a kangaroo. He's all ready been to China and back, a couple of times. That's how we got our contact. A year ago he did a piece on Madame Chiang Kai-Shek, something about not wanting her public to think she wore real pearls, but that her necklaces were all fakes."

Tex leaned back in his chair. "I got a lot more than that, but my editors wouldn't print the rest. A year ago, Japan had not only been bombing the hell out of Nanking, Shanghai, and Canton, they were gathering forces in the northeastern provinces. They were helping their German buddies by setting up attack lines along the Soviet Manchuria border. Even the Japanese newspapers were publishing stories about the troop movement. But the paper I worked for thought the information I sent them was too controversial and they wouldn't publish it. That's when I went out on my own. Now I write whatever I want, from wherever I am."

Sherman looked admiringly at Tex. "Now, we're going to get the real story."

"So, China," I said, and I guess it came out as a question, but as a librarian it really was meant as a point of reference.

"Yep," Tex replied.

"I'll pack you a lunch," I said.

"You could come with us," Julia responded.

"No thanks," I said. Then jokingly added, "Say, 'Hi,' if you run into Albee."

A couple days later Julia took off for China without much fanfare. One morning we had breakfast together and then she was gone. After she left my little house felt hollow when I arrived home from the Archives. It wasn't that the place seemed empty, but it was more like something was missing. Everyone that I cared about was no longer in my life.

The weather, the noise outside on the street, and the work at the Archives were all the same. There was no separation. The days ran together; the nights were a jumble of dreams and sleeplessness.

Twenty-Six

ARRIVING HOME FROM THE ARCHIVE, so tired, so bored; rather than fix something to eat, I took a nap instead. The heat in my bedroom never let up no matter what time of the year. I lay in bed; beads of sweat ran down my scalp. It didn't take long before sleep overcame me and I found myself tangled in a dream.

The dream began in my ears with the faint sound of the crackling of wood burning. The world was completely black. Then a red glow of fire exploded in the darkness. The Archive was on fire. Shadows moved back and forth, backlit by the flames, dark silky silhouettes of men and women poking at the fire. Sparks rose up into the black sky, inexplicably forming a bed of stars above my head.

Thien Nguyen stepped out of the flames. Smoke floated around him as though he was about ready to go up in flames. He staggered towards me. A dog howled. Glass shattered and crashed to the street. Thien Nguyen came closer. His mouth moved. I could not hear his words. A large figure rose up behind him. Sharp licks of flames reached high into the black sky. The shadows grabbed hold of Thien Nguyen. I watched helplessly as they dragged him back into the fire. There was a loud snapping of flames and then he disappeared, consumed in the burning Archive.

I woke drenched in sweat with a nagging feeling of guilt. Months ago, Julia and I had feebly attempted some detective work to find the murderer. Nothing ever came of that. It seemed now that we would ever know who killed the poor fellow.

The horrible image of Thien Nguyen dragged into the fire haunted me. The house was silent. The sun had long ago set, leaving the corners in the bedroom etched with dark shadows. The street outside was quiet, except for the occasional sound of a passing rickshaw.

Getting out of bed I prepared a cup of tea, cut a slice of French bread, slathered it with a spoonful of marmalade, and went out into the garden.

Even though the days seemed to run together, there was an increasing uneasiness in Hanoi. Earlier in the week, the French rounded up a large number of suspected rebels, communists and communist sympathizers. One day I heard a terrible noise coming from the street. At first I thought my landlady had gone off her rocker again and was running up and down the market place hollering. It didn't sounded like her, but until now she'd been the only screamer in the neighborhood. I opened the gate and saw a large group of French soldiers manhandling one of the local silk merchant's sons. His mother was on her hands and knees crawling after the soldiers pleading with them to let go of her boy, screaming as though she'd been stabbed with a soldier's bayonet.

Sitting in the garden, the memory of the woman crying and the dream of Thien Nguyen still so fresh in my mind, it felt as though I would never find peace of mind again. I made another cup of tea and sat in the doorway of my little house until the dawn broke.

Finally it was time to get ready for work. When I entered the Archive building, I heard Father Dominique and Jean George arguing. Initially, as their words echoed back and forth, it sounded as though they were singing. So intent in arguing, they took no notice of me. Until now they seemed to agree on everything.

"Your request is impossible," Jean George shouted.

"Collaboration is out of the question," Father Dominique yelled.

"This is not collaboration."

"The Church will not allow you to do such a thing," the priest shouted, his voice reaching an unusually high pitch for such a stout old man.

"The Catholic Church has no jurisdiction over the Archives," Jean George snapped back.

"You are talking about information that's related to all converts in Vietnam and that's Church business. These records are protected and must not be disclosed."

"All records sent to Hue are safe," Jean George shouted, his angry face turning nearly as red as the French wine he drank throughout the day. He looked away from the priest. Our eyes met.

Father Dominique's robe slightly billowed out at the floor and gave the illusion that he might be hovering above the floor in his righteousness, struggling with the devil for the souls of his converts. Jean George, on the other hand, looked totally out of character in his anger with eyes wide and the veins protruding on his neck. He reminded me of a spoiled child throwing a tantrum.

"These records will not leave my keeping," the priest said in a definitive tone.

"We shall see," Jean George said.

"I will burn every last page before handing them over to you or anyone. I have been entrusted with these souls."

Jean George turned his back on the priest, threw open the door to his office, and slammed it shut behind him.

"Britain and France have declared war on Germany," Father Dominique said. "And now the Japanese are marauding across this land like a pack of jackals." The priest whom over the years seemed a pious old man, stood in front of me trembling, his dark eyes glared angrily and he said, "God help us all. We must all pray very hard. This country has been in the hands of God since the French arrived. Missionaries died bringing the sacred word to these primitive people. Now the fascists want everything that we've worked so hard to build. I will not betray the names of the souls that I have collected."

"The Archives has been sending documents to Paris or Hue for years," I said. My intention was not to defend Jean George's latest order, though this is probably how it sounded to Father Dominique.

"Until now, all Church business has been under my charge," the priest replied. "I store files here, but that does not mean the government owns them. I've instructed Le Sing Dong to gather everything that belongs to the Church. We will not wait until the Japanese loot the Archives. My work is a sacred trust and it is even more important now that France is at war."

I had always thought Father Dominique believed himself to be above the politics of the colonial government and that at any point he could hide behind the skirt of the Church. Until now, he appeared untouchable. But it sounded like he'd just got a good slice of humble pie and he obviously didn't like it. He expected me to side with him, help with his cause. He already had Le Sing Dong working on his behalf, and it appeared that the Archives were about to embark on a season of anarchy.

Father Dominique shook his head. "The world may be going mad, Sarah. Are you prepared?"

"I've got a gun."

We'd heard plenty about current events in China. Now there was the war with Germany. We both knew that any information in the hands of the fascists could be dangerous.

"I won't get in your way," I said.

Father Dominique turned and said in a conspiratorial whisper, "Thank you, Sarah."

I hadn't expected to run into this kind of trouble in the Archives this morning. It was disturbing to think that France being at war now with Germany had something to do with Jean George's order to collect the priest's records. The Archives had provided information to the Japanese on a few occasions. They were interested in maps of roads and rivers that crossed into China and Burma. With the insistence of their ambassador, we had been forced to hand them over. Thein Nguyen and I stalled these requests often turning the simple task of finding information into a major mission. We figured every little bit of resistance helped the cause. Jean George had been quite eager to help the Japanese. Too eager, and it would be interesting to see how he'd handle the Japanese from now on.

The only thing that interested me now was looking for clues that might be related to Thien Nguyen's murder. The image of him in the dream of the burning Archive haunted me. Hopefully Julia and I had somehow overlooked something. Though it would be a miracle if any clues still remained. The floor where Thien Nguyen's body lay had been walked on a hundred times by now. The shelves in that area had become covered with another layer of dust. It was doubtful that anything still left in that area could be tied to his murder. Not to mention my paltry detection skills. I could have been looking right at a major piece of the puzzle and not known what it meant.

The day plodded on, and after checking and rechecking the shelves and floor for any missed detail, it was obvious that nothing was left anywhere in the Archives that would tell me about the murder. The scuffmarks remained on the floor but the broken bits of glass had been cleared away, even the small shards that had landed behind the books were gone, and the light bulbs had all been replaced. The disintegration of the paper in the building continued, too, and a liberal dusting of decayed pulp particles lay atop the area again like a sprinkling of powder.

Le Sing Dong busied himself all day collecting Father Dominique's papers that the priest had stored in a specified area of the Archives. It hadn't been difficult to gather them, though it did surprise me to see such a great mound of papers that were considered Church records. I turned away, made no objections, leaving Le Sing Dong to do as the priest instructed.

Jean George didn't show his face again in the Archives the rest of the day, which was curious. He knew the priest would not follow his instructions. It would have been like him to come rushing out of his office, grab Father Dominique's records, and possibly even have the priest arrested for meddling with official documents.

By the middle of the afternoon, Father Dominique, Le Sing Dong, and a couple other custodial workers had carried the last of the Priest's files out through the back door and into a waiting car on the street behind the Archives. It appeared that as long as Jean George kept his door closed, he could pretend that he knew nothing of the priest absconding with the Diocese records.

A light rain fell as I left the Archives in the evening. I had every intentions of going back to my empty home. The quiet would be welcomed. Though seeing Julia again after all these years had brought up far too many old memories. Her visit had opened wounds that had never healed. The years of boozing and hanging out in dance halls with her back in Kansas City seemed like another lifetime. Back then, I'd worked as a librarian, stuck all day in the endless stacks of books while at night booze soothed me into a place where nothing mattered. Traveling to France was my attempt to put to rest the sadness that hung around my neck like an albatross. WWI ruined my life.

Since then I lived in a private hell. No one knew the pain that sat in my gut gnawing at my heart. Not my parents, friends, and especially not the drinking buddies that sat at the bar with me each night. I had been so young and naïve when my fiancé was killed in a muddy trench in France. His death left me limp with grief. My life never felt whole again. After too many years of grieving, I thought traveling to France would rid me of this never-ending feeling of pain and emptiness, but it didn't.

Then while in France, learning about a position as a supervising archivist in French Indochina, I thought this would resolve my problem. Maybe, I thought, living in a place that could be deemed the end of the world might relieve my sadness. Nothing changed. The sadness continued to linger though, in all truthfulness, I scarcely remembered what that poor young soldier looked like.

With Albee and Julia now no longer in my life, traveling, God knows where, I needed to touch base with someone I cared about. Turning my back on the flurry of activity that Father Dominique caused, I climbed into a rickshaw and decided to visit Thi My.

Thi My and her brother, Dat Tu, had grown up in a large two-story house surrounded by a high wall that enclosed a beautiful garden. The brother and sister were both young when their mother died in the flu epidemic of 1920. Their father never remarried, devoting all of his time to business matters. Dat Tu was sent away to be educated in Paris with his father's hope that one day his son would take over the family business or possibly become an administrator in the French colonial government. Thi My had not been formally educated but instead groomed to be a wife. This was not an uncommon story. Their father worked hard, believing the colonial government's promise of milk in the morning and champagne in the evening. But Dat Tu, like many young people, grew weary of what they saw as empty promises and wanted the French out of his country.

Standing in front of Thi My's house, I lifted the huge metal knocker and let it fall against the thick wooden door. It made a hollow sound that echoed away from me, getting softer and softer until it seemed to evaporate. Thi My opened the gate. The poor young woman looked deathly pale and though Thi My had always seemed quite delicate, it appeared she had lost more weight since we'd last seen each other. When our eyes met it was clear to me why I had not come to visit sooner. It had not been the rigid mourning rituals that I'd been afraid to violate. I did not want to see how grief had left her vacant. "Sarah," Thi My said.

I had a strong urge to hold her in my arms, to selfishly cradle away her sadness so that I wouldn't have to see the despair in her eyes.

"I hope I'm not intruding."

"Please, come in."

I had been a guest in this house many times. I'd even spent a few nights during one nasty monsoon season when the rain had flooded the streets.

Stepping into the house, it was obvious that the door had not been opened frequently since the funeral. The air smelled stagnant, heavy with the odor of incense and the sharp smell of simmering Chinese herbal medicine.

"My father is very ill. The Chinese and French doctors have looked at him, each prescribed medicine, but nothing has worked. Each day he is weaker."

"What is the problem?"

"No one knows. He will be pleased to see you."

Thi My led me up the narrow well-worn staircase to the second floor where the family's sleeping rooms were located. During my earlier visits with this family, several elderly relatives, an aunt, a grandmother, and a grandfather also lived in the house. Dat Tu and his father were on speaking terms back then. So much had changed since those days. The grandparents passed away four years ago, joining the long line of ancestors whose spirits are now prayed for each day. A great deal of sadness lived in this house. I wondered if a fortuneteller could have predicted the circumstances that now beleaguered this domain; a daughter-in-law's alleged suicide in prison leaving an infant son in the care of the dead woman's widowed sister; a daughter wasting away grieving for her murdered fiancé; and a son who abandoned his family for a life of revolutionary activity.

Before reaching the top step, we heard the old man's dry hack. Thi My stood outside her father's room, waiting for him to compose himself. He coughed so hard at one point it sounded as though he was choking, but slowly, and with what must have taken great determination, he became quiet again.

Thi My opened the bedroom door, "Father, I've brought a visitor to see you."

Like his daughter, he had also changed a great deal in the short time since we last met at Aon She Beng's birthday celebration. He was thin then, but now he looked emaciated. A very traditional man, had he not been so ill, I'm sure he would have never consented to have visitors in his bedchamber.

"I am sorry I am not more presentable," he said, extending a withered hand in a courteous Western manner.

A wave of guilt washed over me clasping this old man's cold bony hand. I'd come seeking solace, though after stepping into this stifling environment, I no longer had the courage to mention Thien Nguyen.

"Is there anything that I can do for you?" This was my feeble attempt to make my visit worthwhile.

Coughing overtook him again. He rose up in bed, his chest heaved violently against his silk nightshirt. Two women hurried into the room, one carrying a basin of water, the other an armload of white cloth.

He coughed so hard he could not catch his breath. Small speckles of blood flew from his mouth, spotting the bedding.

The two women removed his shirt, and then sponging him with damp cloths while his hacking cough raged on.

Tears welled up in Thi My's eyes.

"There is nothing we can do for him when he gets like this," Thi My said. "The French doctor gave him something to help calm the cough when it gets this bad. He'll sleep for hours." She turned away. "I cannot bear to watch," Thi My whispered. "He has become like a ghost in the house."

We went back down stairs.

"Please, do not leave," Thi My said. "Keep me company for a while."

"Yes, of course."

The lack of fresh air and the dark interior of the house made me feel as though we'd been entombed in a coffin. The shutters were pulled tight against the windows. The only light, a lone candle on a small table in the middle of the room, cast jittery shadows across the walls. The old man's coughing echoed down to us like the whelp of a dying wolf.

"Does Dat Tu know his father is ill?"

"Yes, but there is nothing he can do. He has gone to the city of Kuming in China to join with other rebels."

These words were simply stated. There was no anger or resentment. We both knew that for Thi My's brother to remain in Hanoi would have certainly meant his arrest.

"I've seen Dat Tu's son," Thi My said, "A beautiful child. His aunt has taken him into the mountains. We may never see him again. My father would have nothing to do with his grandson, but I think this tragedy is killing him." Thi My paused and looked up the stairs. "I will make us tea."

I could not tell how long I'd been in this house. The lack of light, the air heavy with the smells of medicine, incense, and misfortune… time had been turned upside down in this ghostly place. The old man continued to cough. Then suddenly it stopped. The two women scurried about on the floor above us.

Thi My returned shortly with our cups of tea and a plate with sliced fruit.

"I have made some decisions," Thi My said. "And I need your help." She poured tea into our cups. "Since my father has fallen ill, he receives visits from other businessmen, some French, some American. We've even had several Japanese generals come to our house. I sit at his bedside and record the transactions. His condition has become so weakened that very soon he will no longer be able to see anyone."

"How can I help?"

Thi My sipped her tea and said, "I have a plan." The angry look in her eyes startled me. There was no long the soft sadness that I'd seen earlier.

"It is easy to do nothing and pretend as my father has done all these years that the French have our best interests at heart. Dat Tu is right. I know that now. This is not your country and there is no reason for you to get involved." Thi My paused. She looked toward the staircase.

The two women stood on the small balcony that overlooked the living room. The woman holding the washbasin said, "Your father is resting."

"You can leave," Thi My said. "I will take care of my father this evening."

The women descended the stairs. They went to the back of the house. Several minutes later, they came through to the front of the house, opened the door, and stepped out into the night.

"It has been very difficult knowing who to trust," Thi My said. "Maybe it's best to live as Dat Tu did, confiding in no one."

"Do you think you can trust me?" I asked.

"If I cannot trust you, there is no one else."

"So, what is it that you have in mind?"

"Sitting with my father all these weeks has taught me about his business. He never explained to me what he did. Maybe Dat Tu knew and that's why he was so bitter toward our father. Now I know, too. I keep looking for shame or regret in his sick eyes. There is none."

The house groaned and creaked. Thi My sat straight in her chair as though someone had entered the room. Sometimes when I visited this family, strange little unsettling noises moved through the house, something unseen, softly walking from room to room.

Thi My looked at me. "I used to think my father trusted that the French would leave our country when they thought we could manage on our own. But they will not leave. I believe my father knows that now, too, yet he continues to hide under the protection of the colonial government. The world is now more complicated than he can handle and he has nowhere to go."

"You sound like your brother."

Thi My nodded.

"So, what do you want from me?"

"I know how to stop some of this madness."

Even Albee, as involved as he had been with the rebels, never spoke this openly to me. Dat Tu, Albee, and even Thien Nguyen disclosed nothing. They'd always said that the less I knew, the less I could betray.

"You look surprised," Thi My said. Her posture, her tone of voice, and the hard quality in her eyes gave me the impression that she knew what she was talking about.

"I guess nothing should surprise me these days."

"No, you're wrong. You should be surprised…and suspicious of everything. Nothing in this country is as it seems."

"What is it that you want me to do?"

"For weeks I've sat at my father's bedside listening to him talk with his visitors. His simple business of transporting food and other goods from the South up to the North has turned into a military operation. The trucks and trains that used to ship rice up from Saigon are now only transporting tanks of ethanol. Most of the rice production is not exported. It is not being sent to the marketplace. Instead, the rice is transported to a processing plant in Saigon where it is converted into ethanol and then shipped back up to Tonkin and sold to the Japanese."

Thi My was right–that news did surprise me. Though what was unexpected was her angry tone. Until now this delicate young woman seemed to be someone caught between a father and brother who constantly bickered about the promises that the French made to their country. Until now, Thi My had been the peacemaker, a person seeming to be without any substantial opinions.

At that moment I had an epiphany. Now so much made sense. "You knew about that communiqué Thien Nguyen took from the Archives. You put it in that bundle of poetry for me to discover."

"Yes," she said. "My eyes were opened after Thien Nguyen showed it to me. Everyone in our country is starving but I couldn't understand why. Rice production has more than tripled in the last couple of years. Listening to my father, it became clear that the increased rice production was not to feed people but was to be converted into fuel to help the Japanese in their war with China."

"What do you want me to do?" I asked.

"These trains that carry the ethanol do not travel on the regular timetables that are posted in the stations. They are transported at night on special schedules. The tankers are disguised to hide what they are carrying. The Americans are angry that so much ethanol is being released to the Japanese and have threatened to stop these transactions. Thien Nguyen had not been able to get hold of a copy of this special train schedule."

"You want them, or do the Americans want them?"

"The Americans are of no interest to me, neither are the Japanese." Thi My paused, a trace of sadness crossed her face. "I have decided to finish Thien Nguyen's plan."

"Your brother suspected that Thien Nguyen trusted the wrong person. I'm concerned about your safety." I said this as a warning. It wasn't meant to be critical of Thien Nguyen. Yet, I feared that these words had come out awkwardly and unfeeling.

"I don't know if he told anyone else," Thi My said.

"We must be very careful."

"Then you will help?"

"Yes, of course."

"All I ask is that you find these special train schedules. Dat Tu has given me the names of people who will take care of the rest. You don't want to know any more."

A lone cricket just outside the door called for a mate and then the sharp hacking cough of Thi My's father sounded throughout the house with an unsettling disquiet.

"I must go to him," Thi My said.

I left the house and stepped out into the night that had now become as black as tar.

Twenty-Seven

DURING THE RIDE BACK TO my place, another rickshaw traveled suspiciously close behind mine. Then at another point the same black automobile passed by several times. It was easy in these uncertain times to feel paranoid. It was a relief to arrive home, even though the dark corners of the rooms in my house gave me the willies. Once inside, I quickly lit several oil lamps.

A funny thing though…usually when I first arrive home I grab the bottle of rice wine. Instead, this evening I put the kettle on and made a cup of tea, cut a slice of French bread and slathered it with jam. Everything that had happened in the last week spooked me, and yet that bottle of booze in the cupboard did not interest me in the least.

Sitting on the daybed my thoughts were only about where to look for that special train schedule. The Archives had become the recipient of much clandestine information. The French continued to amaze me with how stupid they were about waving covert information under the noses of potential spies.

In the morning, it seemed that the situation Thi My presented me with the night before, had been solved in my sleep. I knew exactly where to look for those train schedules.

The Archives was humming with activity when I arrived. The boxes of manuscripts that were to be sent to Saigon were now being deposited back into the main building again. A new load of cartons arrived and they were stacked three and four high next to the repair table.

A porter came through the back door carrying a large cardboard box loaded to the top with documents.

"What's going on?" I asked.

He shrugged, put the box on the floor, and went back out the door again.

Le Sing Dong came into the Archives, struggling to get through the door with his heavy carton. He quickly lowered it to the floor. "Jean George wants to see you," he said.

It certainly was going to be interesting to hear what this was all about. I knocked and went straight in.

"What's going on?" I demanded.

"Change of plans," Jean George said. "The records we sent to Saigon and Hue will now be returned here. The war with Germany has caused our government to rethink how to safeguard important papers. Some documents from Paris might also be shipped here."

"Is the war going that badly?" I asked.

"It's only a precaution. France is strong. Our military is one of the best in the world."

It was difficult to know whether he believed what he'd just said. In the meantime, war or no war, I got the lousy job of finding places for all these incoming documents.

"What are we talking about? A few more boxes than usual, or truck loads?"

"It's unknown how many will arrive. Saigon airlifted some documents last night. That's what's coming in now. I'm sure you'll do your best. I'm buried in paper work."

He gave me a cocksure grin. His desk was littered with handwritten pages. He wasn't fooling anyone. This paper work had nothing to do with archival business. He was writing what he called his memoir. Henrietta had clued me in a while back about her husbands project. There was no reasoning with Jean George, so I went back out into the main building to figure out how we were going to manage all these incoming documents.

Looking at the boxes it was interesting how little it all meant to me. When I first began to work at the Archives, I took pride in my new position. Lately, it didn't matter to me how the place looked or how fast the work got done.

In the afternoon, when it looked as though the deluge of boxes had stopped arriving, I told everyone to take the rest of the day off. This had never happened before and they looked at me as though I'd gone crazy. But they left and I had the Archives all to myself. Though if Jean

George decided to pay a visit, which was doubtful, my explanation would simply be that everyone had done double what was expected of the staff today.

I knew where to look for that train schedule. Bracing myself, I headed to the section of the shelves where I'd found Thien Nguyen's body. There had to be something on those shelves. Julia and I had searched this area several times for clues. We didn't know what to look for. Now, it was pretty certain that he had left us all the information that we needed.

This section now looked like the rest of the Archives, dusty, slightly disheveled with new light bulbs casting a dull glow along the shelves.

It had always puzzled me why Thien Nguyen had been murdered in that particular area of the Archives. Had he been chased there? Or had he been hiding and his killer came upon him? Maybe he had unknowingly brought the killer into the Archives. With all these possibilities swimming around in my head, the job now was to methodically pull from the shelves each manuscript, document, and folder to find that train schedule.

After several hours, the light changed as sun moved behind a huge gingko tree in the back garden, as it usually did this time of the year. Even in this old building, the seasons beat out a rhythm. The sunlight blocked by the tree in the back garden became the first sign that we were in early spring. The monsoon was only a few weeks away.

The light was so poor now in the Archives that my eyes felt as though they were about to pop out of their sockets. My arms ached from reaching into the shelves and lifting out the hundreds of bundles and bits of paper. I'd gone though more than half of the documents in this area. The project seemed futile.

Then, there it was…the French communication that set the special transportation plan in motion. This document at first glance looked no different from the others, an official seal with the Governor General's signature.

But in a few short paragraphs, this document laid out the plan that the rebels had suspected all along. The reason for the rampant starvation was that the rice shortage was a plan of the war. It was as Thi My described.

Three nights a week were set aside for what the document called "selective transportation." The train tankers filled with ethanol were to pull out of the Saigon depot at sundown on Monday, Wednesday, and Friday. Before dawn each morning, the trains were to pull into the nearest station and not move again until the next nightfall, allowing other train traffic to travel with fewer interruptions, but most importantly, to avoid detection.

The French were in such a hurry to appease the Japanese that they hardly complied with one request before they gave into another. And rather than carefully filing this paper work in the government office, they shoved these documents into the Archives, as so much paper work completed. It was almost as if these documents were buried in a mountain of papers, out of the sight of anyone who might go nosing around in the French Colonial offices.

There was no need to take this document out of the Archives. The instructions were simple enough to remember. The last thing I need now, considering the way things were going lately, if the French police stopped me, I certainly didn't want to have this document in my pocketbook.

As I left the Archives, the last of the sunset exploded in the sky with a brilliant ragged arrangement of orange and yellow tones. Jean George was leaving then, too, accompanied by a woman. It wasn't Henrietta. Jean George took the woman's arm, opened the car door, and just before she slid onto the back seat he gave her bottom a soft caress. He then climbed in next to her and the driver quickly scooted out into the evening traffic.

Twenty-Eight

I'D LOST MY APPETITE AND even though I felt a bit light-headed, I decided to push on to tell Thi My what I'd found in the Archives. Riding in a rickshaw, heading for Thi My's home, I wondered how involved I'd get in all this intrigue.

Even as engrossed as Albee had been with his political work, he had asked very little of me. He took comfort temporarily in my bed, in my arms, requesting only small favors from time to time. We never talked too much about what he did, and when he left, I never asked where he was going. It was an arrangement we were comfortable with. Dat Tu had also made simple requests of me and I hadn't questioned those, either. Times were more complicated now. Standing on the sidelines waiting for someone to throw me tidbits of information was no long an option. I wanted to be involved.

A Japanese officer stepped out of Thi My's doorway as my rickshaw approached the house. He bowed courteously to Thi My and got into a waiting car. I did not step out of the rickshaw until the vehicle turned the corner up the street.

"You had a visitor?" I asked.

"Yes, though they come less frequently now that my father has become so ill."

"How is he today?"

"This has not been a good day for him. The French doctor said there is nothing more that he can do. My father drinks the teas that the Chinese herbalist brings but his condition only worsens."

She looked nervously in the direction of the staircase. The boards creaked. It sounded as though footsteps walked toward me, though no one was there. Then the house fell silent, even the old man stopped coughing.

"I found the information you asked for," I said.

"You are very efficient."

"It wasn't difficult." There was no need to tell Thi My where the train schedule had been located. There was also no need for her to know how careless the French had become recently with these kinds of communications, thanks to Jean George. We both knew that Thien Nguyen had found that confidential letter because Jean George was a sloppy and lazy administrator. He never took the time to analyze the dangers in allowing such information to be stored in one place. It was a power play for him. As long as no one found out just how incompetent he was the Archives would continue to house information that should have been left in the care of the Governor General's office. No one questioned Jean George's ability to keep the Archives secure. The growing mountain of paper made him look important. That was all he cared about.

"I will make us tea," Thi My said.

The house smelled strongly of the old man's Chinese herbal medicine. I'd once taken these remedies, at Aon She Bengs' insistence, for a cold. The concoction of herbs worked quite effectively though it was not only nasty smelling, it tasted foul and was nearly impossible to swallow.

"I went to the market today," Thi My said as she returned a few minutes later with the tea. "I met one of Dat Tu's contacts. All he needed was a bit more information, though he already suspects how the trains are being moved. He just needs confirmation."

Thi My poured the tea. Her father's coughing echoed throughout the house.

We heard the scurry of the caretaker's footsteps above us. Then the house fell silent again and we drank our tea.

"There is no exact schedule," I said. "It's a simple plan to travel under the cover of darkness."

"My father probably suggested this. He is very clever."

The sound of the old man's coughing was relentless. The odor of boiled herbs and the dim candlelight depressed me. It had initially been my intention to spend more time with Thi My, to comfort her, yet I had the strongest impulse to leave. It was like sitting on the edge of a dying man's coffin.

Thi My and I sat facing each other silently waiting for the old man's coughing to subside. Then Thi My looked at me as though something startled her.

"What is it?" I asked.

She continued to hold my gaze with such a horrifying look that I thought the poor woman had fallen ill herself. Thi My grabbed at me with trembling hands.

"He's here," she said.

"Who?" The look on her face startled me.

"Thien Nguyen, he's been here every day now for over a week. I thought it was my imagination at first. But, it is him."

"I don't understand," I said. As crazy as it sounded, I too felt the sense of an unusual presence in the room.

"I've seen him," Thi My said.

I hesitated to respond. Her dark eyes nervously looked from one area of the room to another. "No one else knows," she whispered.

"He's here now?"

"Yes."

Many things were difficult to understand in this part of the world. Often asking questions only brought answers that a Westerner like myself could not comprehend. I did not believe in spirits. Yet, recently I had experiences that could not be explained. I dared not ask where she thought Thien Nguyen's spirit stood at that moment or if Thi My actually saw him. But there was no doubt that she felt his presence. We both wanted him to be alive. But I wondered if her sorrow had turned into madness.

My tea had become cold by now and slightly bitter.

The house was quiet again. Even the noisy cricket that lived under a rock at the entrance to the house did not make a sound. The room felt airless. Thi My sat still, her hands now resting on her lap, eyes looking out into the room seemingly mesmerized by a flickering candle, when one of the women upstairs screamed, "Thi My, come quickly!"

We jumped up from our chairs and hurried into the old man's room. He lay in his sweat-soaked bed gasping for breath. His bony chest heaved up pitifully from under his covers. Thi My rushed to his side and took his hand.

"What can we do?" Thi My asked.

"We've done everything," one of the women said. "The French doctor will not come back as long as your father is letting the Chinese herbalist give him the teas."

Thi My looked down at her father. "I trust neither of them," she said. "All they want is his money."

The old man coughed and choked violently several more times. He fell back onto the bed motionless. His eyes were closed. His breathing was so terribly shallow it appeared that he had died.

Thi My let go of her father's hand and sighed heavily. "He will rest now." She turned away from the bed and left the room.

I followed.

She stopped halfway down the staircase and asked, "Do you think I am mad?"

"No," I said. Her question startled me and I felt as though she had read my mind.

"You may find it difficult to understand," Thi My said. "But I believe that Thien Nguyen chose not to join his ancestors and to remain on this land as a spirit."

"Why?"

"In death, as well as in life, I know he is committed to the struggle that will bring this country independence."

"Is he here now?" I diverted my eyes from Thi My to the bottom step.

"I don't know."

There had been a strange energy in the room before the old man went into his coughing fit. Now I felt nothing.

"When I die, I will make the same choice," she said.

"Don't talk that way." A shiver ran down my back.

"I've made up my mind," Thi My said. "Thien Nguyen and I will go up into the mountains together and join the struggle."

"Please, I don't want to hear any more of this."

"All spirits have become restless. You sense something, too. I've seen it in your eyes."

I wanted to tell Thi My that this was nonsense and to ask if she thought an army of ghosts could carry guns and fight against the French. "You are tired," I said. "You've been under a great deal of strain. In time, your heart will mend and you'll meet someone else."

"No. I will not." Thi My turned and continued down the stairs.

It broke my heart to hear such a young woman talk this way.

"I must be getting back to my place," I said. "Please come to visit me sometime soon. It has been a while. We can sit in my garden and listen to the frog sing to us."

"Yes," Thi My said. "I would like that very much. Your garden is peaceful. Have you seen Aon She Beng? How is her health?"

"I believe she's doing fine," I said.

Our conversation had drifted into polite cordialities. Thi My had opened a door of trust by telling me about Thien Nguyen. Quite likely my response had disappointed her. Stepping out into the night, I wondered if she had actually expected me, a Westerner, to take her seriously.

Twenty-Nine

THE ARCHIVE WAS INSANE WITH so many boxes arriving that I could hardly find space to walk.

The last time I'd seen Jean George, had been a couple days ago when he had been smoothing down the skirt of a lady. According to the staff, no one had seen him for a day or two, either. He wasn't missed. This wasn't unusual. He never came into the main building except to complain or reprimand the staff. No one went out of their way to find him.

Le Sing Dong looked bewildered much of the time as he looked for logical places to put the never-ending shipment of documents arriving from Saigon and Hue. Father Dominique, as far as I knew, never showed up again after he'd managed to get the Diocese papers out of the Archives. And it's a good thing that he'd taken all of what he thought was his because those papers would have been buried under the documents that now overwhelmed the building. The funny thing is that after all that fuss about his precious documents, nothing was leaving the Archives.

The Archives had now become a warehouse. All the work that had been done over the years—the cataloguing, the careful consideration in filing and making order out of the chaotic collection of French texts and the priceless ancient manuscripts—now appeared to mean nothing. Saigon and Hue, in their rush to make room for the shipments expected from Paris, had disregarded every procedure to safeguard even their oldest manuscripts while in transit. The corrugated boxes that arrived, containing poetry dating back hundreds of years, had been torn in transport, pages slipping to the floor as though they were bothersome bits of nothing.

I couldn't stand to see this happen. The trained staff had been turned into warehouse laborers, unloading and stacking now instead of repairing and managing the manuscripts and documents as they had been trained to do. With ever-increasing rumors about the war in Europe, the deluge of boxes coming into the Archives added to the sense of panic.

At home, I hoped that I could at least catch my breath and figure out what to do next. Though making plans in these unstable times seemed crazy.

Arriving home after a grueling day of paper management at the Archive, Aon She Beng greeted me as I got out of the rickshaw.

"You come to tea tomorrow afternoon?" she asked, her tone unexpectedly sweet. Though this was posed as a question, there was only one answer she expected.

"Yes," I said, though the last thing I wanted to do was sit around, listening to her harangue the staff. But, perhaps I agreed to this tea party to learn what she might know about what was going on with local authorities and the Japanese. This lady made it her business to get the latest information.

My house felt terribly empty these days. I had little interest in doing anything. Food didn't interest me. Even a glass of rice wine at the end of the day had become unimportant.

Exhausted from the day's activities I deciding to go to bed early. Fixing the blanket on my bed, I lay down and listened to the frog croaking in the bushes near my fishpond. It was impossible to know if this creature understood how fortunate it was. Because it was quite likely that if it lived in another pond, it might have long ago been served as a side dish on the dinner table? Maybe it did know this and that's why it stuck around.

In the still of the night I missed Albee and wondered if we'd ever be together again. I missed the feel of his coarse hands as he moved them across the small of my back. He had a simple way of touching me, making my flesh shiver, as his fingers traveled across my body. He didn't have fancy moves. Frequently he expected nothing in return. Often it seemed as though he missed the intimacy of touching because on many occasions he'd talk to me slowly and softly about his travels while moving his hand back and forth across a part of my body until I felt mesmerized.

The sheet felt cool, almost damp. The air stood perfectly still. The night was now unusually quiet. Touching myself where Albee's hands had once been, a pleasant, quivering chill ran up my back. Instinctively my thighs tightened. Teasing fingers slid between my legs. Spreading my thighs wide, exposing tender flesh, an ache erupted inside my groin. Probing deeper, my salty fingers devoured the moist flesh. The end came quickly, in an explosion of conflicting sensations that made me feel as though I had just been born while at the same time I'd experienced the intensity of my death.

Outside a soft rain began to fall.

Thirty

IN THE MORNING, I WENT out into the garden with a cup of coffee. The air smelled fresh. The rain from the night before had been absorbed by the thirsty soil. The only sign that there had been a little storm was the clusters of raindrops glistening on the bamboo leaves in the morning sunlight. Over the years, I'd watched the shadows move across my garden as the seasons changed. At noon, the sun would beat down with such intensity that there would be no place to sit without thinking that the light from the sky was surely trying to cook my body. This morning, everything felt perfect with the smell of fresh air and a soft warm light of a new day's sun.

I lounged around the house the rest of the day and only got dressed shortly before it was time to have tea with Aon She Beng. Rather than rush next door, I sat in the garden and listened for the servants to open and close my landlady's garden gate, greeting the guests. I was not going over there until I'd heard that at least one other person had arrived.

And then I heard the unmistakable voice of Henrietta. "Wait there for me," she commented. I knew that she had just given an order to her driver.

I hoped that this tea party would be more than a gossip session and that there would be more than Henrietta at the party. Aon She Beng loved to hear about all the mean and nasty personal business of the colony, and she knew that once Henrietta got started she wouldn't shut up.

Henrietta's eyes lit up when she saw me come through the garden gate. "Oh, how delightful to see you," Henrietta said and clapped her hands together in a girlish manner. "This will be just perfect. Who else will be coming?"

"Only you," Aon She Beng said. "Sit, Sarah. We drink tea."

"It's always such fun at these intimate gatherings," Henrietta said and extended her limp gloved hand to me. "It's been too long, Sarah. You promised to come see me more often."

"Yes," I said. Taking hold of her hand, the glove fabric felt damp from sweat. Appearance was everything to Henrietta and I wouldn't have been at all surprised to learn that even in this heat she wore a corset under her afternoon party dress.

"We have tea in garden," Aon She Beng said.

Henrietta pulled off her gloves and carefully laid them on top of her pocketbook. "Oh, how wonderful, you have little cakes, too. I do love sweets. If there is anything that I miss living here, it's a good French bakery. I love marzipan the most. I do miss an almond fla-vored cake. Have you ever tied marzipan?"

"How your husband?" Aon She Beng asked. It didn't sound like my landlady would suffer through much of her guest's small talk.

"He is fine and sends his regards."

"Good."

"He would have come but the Governor General sent him to a meeting in the north."

"You no go with him."

"He thought I'd be bored."

"You need leave Hanoi. You need rest."

"Perhaps, but then I wouldn't have been able to join you for tea." Henrietta looked quite pleased at her clever comment.

"Yes, this true. You not afraid to be alone?"

"No," Henrietta said. She winced ever so slightly and then lifted the teacup to her lips. "Not at all. The bodyguard has been left behind. He looks after my safety."

"You have thoughtful husband," Aon She Beng said and took up the plate of cakes and offered Henrietta the first choice.

Henrietta appraised the cakes and took the smallest one on the farthest side of the plate. "Oh, these do look so good. What a difficult decision this is."

"They expensive," Aon She Beng said.

Henrietta nibbled on her cake. "Delicious."

"How friend dress shop?"

"She has many customers."

"I sorry you not bring her with you today."

"The poor thing was very upset that she could not come, too. But there was important out of town business."

"In the north?" Aon She Beng asked.

Henrietta took another nibble from her cake and without looking up from the table said, "I don't know. I think Hue."

Listening to this conversation I wished desperately that I'd declined Aon She Beng's invitation.

"Hue has much cheap silk." Aon She Beng said. Then without appearing to take another breath my landlady asked, "How is war in France?"

"I don't know."

"I no believe you. Your husband very important man. He hear many things. I old lady. I worried. I no sleep at night."

"He doesn't tell me anything."

"Think. I alone. No one protect me." Aon She Beng leaned forward. I watched as she transformed herself into a sad old lady, though all the while her eyes danced with excitement.

Henrietta took a bite of her cake, chewing so slowly it seemed as though eating that the sweet morsel had become an occupation.

I took a sip of tea and nearly choked when Henrietta said in almost a whisper, "Jean George is so important." She looked at me and then continuing in a conspiratorial tone, she said, "Sarah, you've seen how terribly hard he works. He does hear things though. He shares some bits of news with me. I am sworn to secrecy but maybe it wouldn't hurt to give you some information that might ease your fears, nothing too top secret. He listens on his short wave radio."

"I no make trouble for your husband. He must know many secrets." Aon She Beng lifted her teacup. "I worry in the night." Aon She Beng looked down into her beverage. She sighed heavily and said, "Night is most difficult."

Henrietta put a hand on Aon She Beng's arm. I watched a drop of perspiration run down Henrietta's right temple. "I must confess," she said, "I worry at night, too. So much some nights that I must take a special preparation for my nerves prescribed by my doctor."

"Yes," Aon She Beng said eagerly.

"My husband reassured me that the French would win this war. Our army is small but the generals have set up a strong line of defense. They are determined to beat the Nazis."

"Yes, yes, I know this," Aon She Beng said. "The Japanese? What you know of them?"

Henrietta reached across the table. "Do you mind if I take another cake?" She picked up a pink frosted sweet and brought it to her plate. "You are not to worry about the Japanese," Henrietta said. "My husband has assured me that as soon as France takes care of the Germans, the Japanese will run back to their little island. They are really not to be worried about at all. Jean George has every confidence." Henrietta leaned forward. "I will tell you this," she said. "My husband has met many times with the Japanese and he says they are really quite lovely people. They worry about their family's safety like any man does."

Listening to this silly woman yammering on about what her foolish husband thought about the state of the war was getting on my nerves. Aon She Beng had asked Henrietta to tea for some reason. I didn't have a clue why she'd included me.

Henrietta nibbled on her little pink cake and then put it back onto her plate. A smear of frosting stuck to her thumb. She licked at it with an unselfconscious delight. Putting her hand back on the table she sighed heavily. "There is so much intrigue these days. I am exhausted just thinking about it."

Aon She Beng's ears perked, her backbone straightened. "Yes, exhausting."

"I must rest a great deal during the day."

"You smart woman," Aon She Beng responded and her eyes narrowed with anticipation.

Henrietta sighed again. She looked at me. "Sarah, you must know how difficult it has been for Jean George. First the Governor General's office suspected that he had a spy working in the Archives, and then the Japanese demanded that he hand over confidential information. I don't know how the poor man does it."

Aon She Beng shot me a look. Then her sharp gaze fell on Henrietta. There was no mistaking her interest. "Who is spy?" she snapped.

"Oh, I don't know. Someone was arrested and the French police found information on him that the officials said could have only come from the Archives." Henrietta shifted in her chair. She pushed back at her hair as though strands had fallen loose from her quaff but everything was contained. She cleared her throat. "Oh, I really don't know anything about it. I'm sure I misunderstood what had happened."

"Sarah, you spy?" Aon She Beng asked.

I casually looked back at my landlady and said, with as much of a smooth tongue as I could muster, "There are no spies in the Archives."

"I'm sure there aren't," Henrietta said. "Everyone who works there is lovely. It is such a shame about that poor murdered fellow. How is his fiancé?"

"She like dead woman now," Aon She Beng said. "No one will marry her."

Her harsh words made me cringe. "

So sad," Henrietta said.

"Not sad. It is life." Aon She Beng lifted the plate of cakes and offered Henrietta another tidbit.

"I really shouldn't," said Henrietta, and then she reached out and took another little cake, a chocolate one.

Aon She Beng set the dessert plate back down onto the table. "What information Japanese want?"

"The communists are giving them such trouble in the north. I cannot help but feel sorry for the poor fellows, away from home and defending themselves against such a large and savage country like China." Henrietta sipped her tea. "Jean George said he would have given them what they wanted but the Governor General's office had forbidden him to do so. My poor husband is always in the middle of these kinds of controversies."

"Japanese hungry," Aon She Beng said. "Communists sneaky." She straightened up in her chair slightly. "They both like sleeping wolves. You must walk carefully around them. When they wake up and see you, they eat you." Aon She Beng smacked her hand on the table.

Henrietta jumped and grabbed at her chest as though she'd been shot. After she'd taken a few deep breaths, she said, "Surely, you cannot think they are that dangerous. The communists, yes, but the Japanese, too?"

"They make you fools," Aon She Beng said. "Polite manners only tricks."

"You cannot be serious," Henrietta replied. "They are harmless and quite determined to bring an end to this Asian problem. I don't think they will want to bother with this country. After all, Vietnam belongs to France. I'm sure they will abide by the Colonial rules. In fact, I'm having a small gathering when Jean George returns and he has invited several of the Japanese officers. It would be a wonderful honor if the both of you would attend, as well."

"I come," Aon She Beng said. "I know many important people. These Japanese officers will enjoy meeting me."

This was not something that I wanted any part of. "It would be impossible for me to come. You know how busy the Archives are."

"No," Aon She Beng snapped. "Sarah, you must help me."

"Then it is settled," Henrietta said. Taking the silk gloves from atop her pocketbook she began to very carefully push her fingers, one at a time into the glove. "I really must run. There is another party this evening that I must attend. In this heat I need to rest for an hour or two. Doctor's orders, you know. Jean George will be delighted to hear that you will both come to our party."

Climbing into her waiting car Henrietta waved to Aon She Beng and called out, "I will send you a proper invitation in a day or two."

Aon She Beng nodded politely and said, "That woman has brain of chicken."

"So, why are you going to her party?"

"You not so smart," Aon She Beng said. "Maybe keep your ears open, and you learn more. I tired. Go home."

Thirty-One

THE RAIN CAME DOWN WITH a vengeance several days after Aon She Beng's tea party. The monsoons seemed a terrible punishment to bestow on a country that already suffered such extremes of heat and humidity. During the night the rain beat down so hard on my little house that it sounded as though someone threw metal pellets against my roof.

Traveling through the waterlogged city streets during the monsoon season was treacherous. The wheels of the rickshaw and the puller's feet splashed up huge amounts of water into the carriage as the vehicle slogged through the water-soaked roadways. Most mornings arriving at the Archives, soaking wet and so splattered with muck I looked as though I'd been dragged thought the wet streets.

The documents that had been transported up from Saigon and Hue were now in just as much danger of being ruined as those already stored in the building. The broken windows had been poorly repaired during the dry season, and the roof leaked in several new spots. The heavy winds frequently pushed the rain under a door that opened out into the garden and in some areas of the building, rain seeped through the cracks in the ceiling and trickled down in never ending rivulets.

I'd been hired to preserve and organize documents, yet it seemed that most of my time was spent battling the weather. Insects and rodents had devoured their share of paper before I arrived in this country, but I hadn't realized the toll that weather could take on these ancient communications. I hadn't given up on trying to maintain this crypt of written material though some days it felt like an effort in futility.

Jean George, like a harbinger of ill omens, arrived back to work the same day that the rains hit. He swaggered into the main building of the Archives looking a little more pompous than usual. His pressed shirt had not yet wilted from the humidity and he looked like an administrator who had a motorcar at his disposal. He stepped into the main section of the Archives, something he did not frequently do, and called to us in his booming authoritative voice. "I have important news for you," he said. "Everyone come listen to what I have to say."

Le Sing Dong stood next to me. He had walked to work and his pants legs were soaking. The two porters, quiet, young fellows who always smelled of fish sauce stood on the other side of me. They, too, were drenched from head to toe. They did their job, never complaining. They had single-handedly unloaded the trucks of all the cartons that arrived from the south. We all pitched in to help though these young men really did the lion's share of the work.

Jean George stood in front of us, his arms folded across his chest, his legs spread slightly apart. "The war with Germany is nearly over," he said using his limited Vietnamese language skills, slipping in French words when he was stymied. "France is doing a wonderful job protecting herself."

These were nearly the same words that Henrietta had used when trumpeting her thoughts on the war in Europe. Patriotic rhetoric seemed to be the mode of communication in this country. It was hard to say whether the colonial government intended this to be the case, yet it struck me that if every Frenchman used the same phrasing, it would certainly sound like a united front.

Jean George smiled at the small group that had gathered around him. The two women who sat behind a table all day stood the farthest away, strands of jute in their hands as though they would tolerate only so much interruption from their work.

"Come closer ladies," he ordered.

They took a few steps forward.

"The Governor General's office has personally contacted me and requested that I discuss something with you." He cleared his throat. "Even though the war is going quite nicely, there is an urgent need for more soldiers in France. I've been asked to spread the word to my workers that France would be forever indebted to anyone who joined the volunteer forces to help fight the Germans."

Jean George looked at the two porters and then at Le Sing Dong. No one moved or said a word.

"This would be an opportunity to see Europe," Jean George said. "Hundreds of your fellow countrymen in the south have already enlisted and as you probably know many of them have been awarded medals and have made their parents proud."

One of the porters shifted his weight from one foot to the other. Jean George quickly looked at the young man. The porter remained silent.

The rain beat against the windows with a terrific force. The wind howled. Somewhere near the Archives building, we heard the loud crack of a tree limb crash to the ground.

No one responded to Jean George's call to arms. After what felt like a far too long silence, I said, "We can't stand here all day and listen to the storm."

Jean George looked annoyed that no one had jumped to enlist.

"Sarah, I'll put you in charge of this," Jean George said. "Let me know if anyone changes his mind." He turned to leave, and then hesitating, he said, "I hope everyone understands that if we don't get enough volunteers, the Governor General's office has threatened to order that at least one man in every household will be called up to join the French army."

"They understand," I responded. "They understand very well what's going on."

These words slipped out before realizing what I'd said. Jean George looked at me harshly and then he turned and went into his office.

Le Sing Dong moved closer to me."I cannot leave my mother alone," he whispered. "I am her only provider."

"I know," I said. "Try not to worry about it. You have enough to do in the Archives without concerning yourself with what's happening in Europe."

These words were probably not comforting. He returned to his workstation and began to leaf through one of the cartons that had recently arrived from Saigon. The wind and rain died down slightly. Though no sunlight came through the windows, the day appeared to be a bit brighter.

Thi My's father's health had worsened in the last week and each evening after work, I'd sloshed through the streets in a rickshaw to spend a couple of hours with the poor housebound young woman. She prepared a light dinner for us and we usually spent the remainder of the evening talking softly for fear of being overheard by her father's caretakers. After the women went home, we breathed a sigh of relief. But, on one particularly rainy night, Thi My was more on edge than usual. Every little noise made her jump. Several times during our meal, Thi My quickly looked over her shoulder as though she'd heard someone come into the room.

"What's the matter?" I asked.

"I cannot tell you now." She went back to picking at her food. "
Are you all right?"

"When we are alone I will tell you." She took a swallow of her tea.

Sometime later, the two caretakers came down the stairs, as they often did, without saying a word. They went into the back of the house, gathered their umbrellas and bundles that they carried with them everywhere, and then nodding politely, they left the house by the front door. The wind had picked up again. When the door opened a gust of hot, wet air rushed at us as though an intruder had forced his way into the room. Once the door was closed, the house fell dreadfully quiet, until once again we heard Thi My's father's incessant coughing. His breathing had turned to a high-pitched wheezing, reminding me of the desperate cry of a small animal caught in a trap.

"Thi My, tell me what's bothering you," I said. But before she could respond, Dat Tu appeared in the doorway. The sight of him gave me such a fright it nearly took my breath way.

"Should you be here?" I asked.

"These days I'm everywhere," he said.

"Yes, I suppose you are. How have you been?"

He looked at me with hard eyes. His gaunt figure appeared tired and angry. "I have come to ask for your help."

"You know that the French are suspicious of everyone."

"What I'm asking of you this time is easy, Sarah."

"That's what you always say."

"I promise this is not difficult." He handed me a small bundle of papers wrapped in oiled silk.

I hesitated before taking the package.

"Tonight," he said, "you will stay here. In the morning, when a rickshaw comes to take you to the Archives, leave this on the seat when you get out."

"What is this?"

"Do you want to know more?"

"I might as well hear it all since quite likely some day in the near future the French will shoot me at dawn when they find out what I've been up to."

Thi My sucked in her breathe. We both knew this was a possibility. Though my words sounded harsh and too direct considering all that this family had gone through.

"You're right," Dat Tu replied. "You may be shot. We may all be shot. But the less you know the better off you will be."

The old man shouted out a garbled name from the upstairs bedroom. "He dreams of our mother," Thi My said.

Dat Tu looked angrily at his sister and said, "Let him dream of a dead woman. He will be with her soon."

When Dat Tu appeared in the doorway, I thought that he'd come back to see his dying father. I should have known better. He had severed his ties with his family. Now the only thing he cared about was the revolution.

The old man called out again. The brother and sister stood looking at each other as we listened to their father call out. Then the room fell silent, as though the ragging wind had carried away all sound.

Thi My ran up the stairs.

Dat Tu watched his sister and when the door to the old man's room was closed, he said, "He will die soon. Then there will be one less traitor to contend with."

"But he's your father."

"That old man has turned many good loyal revolutionaries over to the French for favors and profit. I no longer call him my father."

I had hoped that the circumstances would have changed with the father so close to his end. And though my sympathies were with the rebels, it grieved me to see that politics had divided so many families.

"How are you?" I asked.

"We are on the march again. It will only be a short while before we bring the French to their knees. They claw the skin from the backs of the peasants with the high taxes and now they conscript men to fight the fascists in France. The information in that packet has everything to do with what is going to be happening very soon. We will not rest, Sarah. There will be no stopping us now. The French are weakened by the war in Europe. If we don't take advantage of this situation now then we are fools and deserve to be slaves to the French."

When Thi My returned back downstairs, she said, "He was calling out in his sleep. His breathing is weak. I don't know how much longer—"

"Do not expect me to attend his funeral," Dat Tu said.

Thi My sighed. "I will not remain in Hanoi after he is gone," she said. "I have decided to go to the mountains and join the rebels."

Dat Tu did not look surprised. For the first time this evening, I saw a kindness in his eyes. For a moment, he no longer looked like the coarse, underfed rebel who had walked in on us earlier in the evening. There was still a glimmer of the young man that I'd met over five years ago.

Dat Tu put his hand on Thi My's shoulder. "I will meet you at the foot of that mountain and show you the way to the top."

Briefly it felt as though barriers had been broken down and that we could possibly discuss things other than the resistance to the French. In that slight space of time, the only sound now was the house creaking as the storm pushed against the outside walls. As the rain poured down, I stood dumb, unable to verbalize my uneasy feelings about Dat Tu and Thi My's safety once the old man passed away.

"I'll not sleep here tonight," Dat Tu said. "I must keep moving. This is the only way." He shook my hand. "Thank you, Sarah." He opened the door and disappeared into the retched weather.

Thirty-Two

THE FOLLOWING MORNING, I DID as Dat Tu asked.

Though instead of sleeping at Thi My's house for just that one night, I stayed a couple of weeks. Each morning an envelope would be waiting for me when I climbed into a rickshaw.

One morning, a tightly bound scroll sat on the seat next to me. When I arrived at the Archives, a well-dressed man standing at the curb startled me when he extended his hand and said, "How nice to see you again. Let me help you." Unsure of what to do next, I reached for the scroll.

He nodded courteously and said softly, "Leave it on the seat."

I did as he asked and stepped out of the rickshaw. He looked familiar. Thien Nguyen had introduced us last year, though when we met, I'd already been acquainted with his work, having catalogued several of his novels in the Archives.

"I'm Vo Si Tuan," he said.

"Yes, of course. How rude of me. I just didn't expect…"

"No need to explain," he said.

"Are you still writing?" I asked.

"Yes, though I've abandoned the novel. Mostly my writing is smaller pieces now." He glanced at the scroll on the rickshaw's seat.

"I'd like to read some of your recent material," I said. "I don't suppose what you are writing now will find its way into the Archives any time soon."

"It might some day, but for now it's intended for other purposes." He climbed into the rickshaw. "I understand you are temporarily staying with Dat Tu's sister," he said.

"Yes. Their father is very ill." I did not ask how he knew this but now it was clear that the rebels were watching me.

Vo Si Tuan did not seem hurried or in the least bit nervous about our encounter. "Dat Tu has asked me to pay his sister a visit. Please tell her that I'll come by late this evening." He unfastened the buckle of his valise and slipped the manuscript from the seat into it. He snapped it closed and said, "Will I see you this evening, too?"

"Yes, I'll be there."

"Good."

The puller maneuvered the rickshaw out onto the street and the vehicle quickly disappeared around a corner.

In the evening while we ate a light super, I told Thi My about my encounter with Vo Si Tuan.

"It will be a lovely treat to see him again," she said.

The old man's cough had worsened but he was a tough old bird. Who could say, even as ill as he was, how long he could live teetering between life and death. He could not manage business matters and no longer had visitors. Everyone waited for him to die.

Thi My was a quiet, gentle companion. Most nights we played simple board games or would read to each other. After the two women who attended her father left for the evening, we sat quietly in the dim candlelight. It felt as though we were on a deathwatch waiting to hear her father's last cough, his last breath, and quite possibly his last cry for mercy. Thi My and I both welcomed the thought of Vo Si Tuan's visit and we listened intently for his knock.

As the night grew late, we lost hope that he would show up, but then there was a knock at the door.

"I am sorry that I am so late," he said. "The French have set up many checkpoints along the streets and avoiding them takes much patience."

"You are welcome any time," Thi My said.

"That is very kind of you to say."

Thi My hurried into the kitchen and returned with a teapot and three cups. "Have you heard from my brother?" she asked.

"He has set up a newspaper that is being sent throughout the country and even into China with news of the revolution. He works with students from his old school and they are teaching the peasants in the mountains to read and write. The groups are small but he knows that soon more people will want to learn to read. He will need more teachers. He asks that you join him when your father passes."

"Yes, I will join him. It may be soon. Our father has grown very weak. There is not much life left in him."

As though on cue, the wretched hacking of the old man's cough echoed throughout the house. Thi My hurried upstairs. There was urgency in her actions and I knew that she wondered if this would be the night that her father crossed over into the world of his ancestors.

When we heard her footsteps in the old man's room, Vo Si Tuan looked at me and said, "There are large miseries and small miseries, and in the moment they are seldom discernible. Hopefully the revolution will bring an end to needless suffering."

"Are you writing about small or large miseries these days?" I asked.

"Both."

"How many of your stories have been in the rickshaw in the last couple of months?"

"Maybe half, though recently we've had more writers joining the cause." He cocked his head, a slight smile on his face. "You are familiar with my work, then?"

"Yes. Thien Nguyen translated them for me."

"And what do you think of the stories?"

"They are sad stories, but I can tell you are a romantic. You refrain from telling about the brutality of the times but in the end, the cruelty bursts out as though you can no longer hold back the suffering."

"Those were my old writings. I've changed." His face illuminated in the candlelight caught the angry glint in his eyes. His mouth tightened. "Even a romantic bleeds when an arrow pierces his heart. The French, as you know, will not allow the publication of essays. They only want fiction, believing that stories cannot be political. For years, writers like me have been using fiction to get our messages across. There's a certain rhythm and style that comes with telling a straight story. I no longer dance around reality by using the stories of my family and neighbors. I no longer spend time writing fiction. I write about reality."

The old man's coughing did not let up, and I thought, as I had on many other nights, that in his weakened state he would surely die of a heart attack from the sheer exertion of all this coughing. But night after night, he managed to survive these coughing fits. I knew that while Vo Si Tuan and I talked of literature in the living room, Thi My stood at her father's bedside mopping the sweat from his forehead and dabbing the blood that now trickled from the sides of his mouth.

Vo Si Tuan finished his tea. "I cannot stay any longer," he said. "I have enjoyed talking with you. Perhaps we will meet again."

"Yes, I would like that."

After he left, sitting alone, it felt as though a spell had been broken. The nights spent with Thi My were like living in a dream. I'd done this so many times before, cutting myself off from feelings. Then something happened. Feelings stirred again inside me as though I had come to life. The old man's cough sounded more persistent than the night before. I knew that Thi My would not sleep until the two women arrived in the morning.

It would not be easy to leave Thi My. But it was time for me to return back to my place. In the morning while we sat drinking tea, I said, "I can stay no longer."

"This has not been easy for you," she said. "I appreciate your kindness. I've already said goodbye to my father." There was no sadness in her eyes. There were no tears. "The only thing that remains for me now is the ritual to send him into the world of his ancestors."

"When he passes, please send word and I will come right away," I said.

She smiled. "Yes."

I packed up the few clothing items that I'd brought with me and climbed into a rickshaw.

That evening when I got home, everything was as I'd left it. The plants in the garden drooped badly from the beatings they'd endured from the wind and drenching rains. I wandered around in my small garden until the light in the evening sky turned purple, the way it frequently did before a huge storm hit.

I hadn't been home more than an hour when Aon She Beng paid me a visit. There was no mistaking the insistent rapping of her walking stick on my garden gate.

When I opened the gate, and before I uttered a word, she called out, "You spend too long with dying man's family. Not healthy. It make you sick."

I had not told Aon She Beng where I would be staying. It didn't surprise me that this sly old gal had fished around and discovered my whereabouts in the last weeks.

"Nonsense. He's an old man. It's impossible to catch what he has, not until I'm at least another hundred years old."

Aon She Beng snorted her disapproval. "Your tongue smart. Sick bring bad spirit."

"Miss me?" I asked.

"You make me miserable. Henrietta sent invitation. You promised take me. I miss party, I no forgive."

"I'm no mind reader. How should I have known?"

"You have house. You no need stay with dying man's family."

"All right, all right," I said. "When is the tea?"

"Two days."

I knew when I'd agreed to accompany her that I'd regret this promise. It just hadn't occurred to me that it would come so soon. I'd secretly hoped that it would be cancelled. Tea parties in a time of war somehow seemed like another attempt of the colonials to pretend that nothing out of the ordinary might be happening back in France.

"Yes, of course, I'll attend with you."

Aon She Beng looked relieved. "Good." She turned and walked away, stepping carefully along the cobblestones so as not to muddy the bottoms of her silk britches.

I went back into the house, dusted off a few shelves in the front room, and wondered how good the rickshaw drivers were at keeping track of where I might be from one day to the next.

Later that night, the storm that had been threatening all afternoon hit with a frightful noise. The rain poured down, beating fiercely on my roof. I sat near the opened door that faced my garden. The rain splattered into the doorway cooling the air. Watching the storm, I realized how little progress had been made in finding Thien Nguyen's killer. He was in my thoughts every day. He especially had come into my mind while sitting in the evenings with Thi My, though we never again felt his presence in her house. Many mornings while traveling in a rickshaw headed for the Archives, a profound sadness came over me knowing that his smiling face would never again greet me.

The air was unbearably humid. Taking a sip of rice wine, I looked out into the night. Then I thought I saw a shadowy figure standing in a corner of the garden by the potted bamboo. I stepped out into the rain to get a better look. The figure moved closer to me. A quick strong wind drove the rain across the garden at nearly a horizontal angle and the image vanished. I threw back the last of the wine in my glass. I watched a while longer. The figure did not reappear.

The rain subsided some time during the night. In the morning a dreary mist hung in the garden air. A dark sky threatened more rain.

On my second day home, Aon She Beng sent one of her servants to tell me when she expected me to accompany her to Henrietta's tea. Out of respect for Aon She Beng's age, Henrietta arranged to have a motorcar to pick us up.

Aon She Beng wore her finest brocade garment, something I thought was a bit too formal for an afternoon tea. Her hair had been done up in a traditional manner with the massively long tresses twisted and piled high on top of her head. Two carved ivory stickpins held the hair in place. She had to bend quite low to get into the back seat of the car because of the increased height of her hair.

"Don't sit close," Aon She Beng shouted when I climbed in next to her. So, I sat a bit scrunched against the window on the other side of the car.

High winds quickly pushed dark clouds across the horizon. Luckily, there had not been any rain in the last couple hours. A newly fallen tree needed to be removed before we could travel down one road. Aon She Beng clucked and sucked her teeth. "Stupid street cleaners."

I had never seen where Jean George and his wife lived. They thought very highly of themselves, so I knew they would live as posh as they could afford. And it was not a surprise when the driver pulled up to an elaborate wrought iron gate. The house, though stately, had a simple façade.

Henrietta watching from the window at the front entrance, rushed out to greet us and as we drove into the courtyard.

"I'm so glad the storm didn't keep you away. Hasn't the weather been dreadful? Sarah, it is so good that you could make it. I know you've been awfully busy with a sick friend. Is he feeling better? Do you think that my doctor could be of help? He's a wonderful man. Let me know if you need any assistance. I do so like to be useful."

She said this before Aon She Beng and I even got out of the car. It appeared that a lot of people knew what I'd been doing the past month. It made me wonder what else they might know about my business.

"I could not put off this gathering until after the rainy season," Henrietta said while the driver opened the car door. "That would have made it just too much time between my parties. But unfortunately we have had some cancelations and Jean George will not be able to be here either. We'll have a lovely party anyway."

It was difficult to tell if Henrietta expected people to reply to her comments. Actually, I didn't know what the woman expected. Usually her expression was dull and her complexion covered over with a thick powder that caked under her chin and around her eyes exaggerating her crow's feet. Today her eyes were wild looking and her cheeks were flushed.

Aon She Beng got out of the car with quite a bit of difficulty. The ivory pins in her elaborately styled hair pinged against the doorsill as she maneuvered her body out of the backseat. Luckily, her hair stayed in place. I hated to think what would happen if her hair came loose and fell down her back. Aon She Beng stepped onto the sidewalk, her feet so poised and elegant; she could have been mistaken for a princess.

"You look lovely," Henrietta said, though from the expression on her face, I think that Aon She Beng's attire had taken Henrietta by surprise. "Your costume," she continued, "will add so much to the conversation this afternoon."

Aon She Beng looked pleased and cautiously walked to the front door.

Henrietta escorted us into the house where several other women sat on an exquisite velvet settee that looked as though it had recently been the prized possession of French aristocracy. I knew that I'd hate every moment of this gathering. The women on the settee watched

Aon She Beng with nervous smiles. The teacups sitting on the table in front of them were precious-looking things that I would have preferred to dash against the wall rather than to drink from them. But I smiled courteously and behaved myself.

Henrietta introduced everyone and said, "We may have a couple more ladies dropping in later if the weather changes for the better."

The remainder of the afternoon was dreadfully boring; the kind of boring that went on forever and made my bones ache. Drink, opium, or suicide seemed a better alternative to sitting and listening to these women talking, because they only talked about their children and their husbands. They asked Aon She Beng a couple questions about her life style and eating habits and seemed to regard her with a great deal of curiosity, though no one mentioned politics, the war or the rebels.

The promise of rain was fulfilled. This fancy French house seemed sound enough, though when the wind began to blow the windows grew thick with rain that cascaded from the roof. Thunder rumbled so loudly that it rattled a china closet door in the sitting room. One of the guests looked startled as a crack of lightning lit up the darkened sky.

"I must get home," one woman said. "My children are terrified of these storms."

Henrietta did not respond.

"Henrietta, are you all right?" the woman asked, a bit irritated.

"Oh, yes, I'm quite fine," replied Henrietta, and gave her guest an insincere smile. "The tea we are drinking today has come all the way from central China." Henrietta said.

"I really must be leaving," the woman said.

"So soon?" Henrietta replied, as though this was the first time she'd heard the woman's urgent plea that she must depart. "Surely you do not need to be home yet. Aren't your children in school?"

"My youngest is quite upset with these storms and has said that he will not leave the house until the sun is shining. He causes such trouble with the servants that I cannot leave him alone for very long. He simply cannot be consoled."

"How unfortunate," Henrietta said.

"Yes, so you will understand if I leave now."

"I will send along some of the pastries from our party. That would surely make him happy. Your children are so delightful. You must bring them around sometime."

"And we must invite you and Jean George for dinner some night soon. We do so enjoy your company," the woman said and as she stood to leave, her dress clung to her sweaty backside. Pulling the garment free from her legs, she walked to the front door. Henrietta accompanied her. They disappeared through the front entrance leaving Aon She Beng and I to sit alone with the other two guests.

The two women politely smiled. One woman looked at her watch. "Oh, dear look at the time. I still have so much to do this afternoon." She glanced at me. "Where does the time go?"

When Henrietta returned, the two women stood.

"We really have to get home, also," said the shorter of the two women.

"The storm is simply awful," Henrietta said. "Must you go now? Wouldn't it be wiser to wait?"

"No, it's best we leave now." With that said, they proceeded to the front entrance as though they were a single body. Henrietta hurried after them. A servant opened the door. They huddled together nervously talking and when the door was opened a great gust of wind rushed into the house. The heavy brocade curtains in the sitting room rustled and quivered as though someone were hiding behind them. The women hurried out into the stormy afternoon. Henrietta stood for a moment in the doorway looking out into the garden and then closed the door.

When Henrietta returned to the sitting room, she said, "Jean George must have taken our auto someplace on business. I'm afraid you will have to wait until he returns. I am sorry if this will inconvenience you. The storm is terrible."

Aon She Beng had not said much in the past hour. She'd nibbled on the cookies and cakes, drank her tea, and watched the women. There was something other than the storm that had been brewing this afternoon. I felt the tension and I'm sure that Aon She Beng knew something else was going on, too.

"Would you care for a fresh pot of tea?" Henrietta asked. "We may have a while to wait. Or, it is getting late in the afternoon, would you perhaps…" Henrietta looked confused as though she did not how to complete her thought. She sighed heavily and said, "This storm is so upsetting. We might have a small glass of brandy to settle our nerves."

"That would be perfect," I said. My nerves were rankled, too, though it wasn't the result of the storm.

Henrietta smiled ever so slightly. "The afternoons during the monsoons are so dreary." She opened the door to a cabinet and brought out a crystal decanter half full of a honey-colored liquid. "One does need to take a bit of comfort." Henrietta removed three brandy snifters from a shelf and poured a small portion into each glass. "We have a shipment of French brandy sent to us several times a year. It tastes just like home."

Aon She Beng lifted the glass to her lips, smelled the beverage, wrinkled her nose, and put the glass down on the table. I took a hearty swig and felt the warm sensation of the brandy run along the back of my throat.

"This is very good," I said.

"Yes, it is Jean George's favorite. It is from a monastery in the northern part of France."

Henrietta took quick small swallows and finished her brandy before I had even drunk half of mine. She poured another portion into her glass and asked, "Would you care for more?"

"Sure."

Henrietta had been a good host. I could not fault her on that. Yet, much of the afternoon she'd been all over the room straightening first a doily on one table, then rushing out of the room to get a new tray of cookies, returning only to stand near the window fidgeting with the tassels on the curtains. I don't remember if she had sat down during her gathering. Henrietta looked troubled and exhausted.

"Are you alright?" I asked.

"Yes, I'm fine. Why do you ask?"

"No reason, but the weather does put one in an agitated mood. The rain, the dark skies, the constant mess in the doorway dragged in on the feet." I suppose it was the brandy that loosened my lips. Generally

I would not have considered saying such a thing.

"It's not just the weather," Henrietta said. She took a swallow of her drink. "The mail arrived from France this morning. It is hard to be so far from one's home." She sighed. "This country has been quite satisfactory, yet I miss the familiar places of my childhood."

"How is the war going?" I asked.

Henrietta seemed startled by my question. She swallowed a hearty mouthful of the brandy and put the glass down on the table. "I'm afraid things are not going well," she said. "My family has been trying to leave Europe for over a year but have not been able to get their papers in order."

She poured more brandy into her glass and filled mine as well.

"You see, I am a Jew, and I've heard many frightening stories about what has happened to the Jews in Poland and in Germany. My father has relatives scattered in several countries and he has written me that many in his family are missing. Jean George has assured me that the war in Europe will be over very soon and that there is nothing to worry about."

"I didn't know you were Jewish," I said. I thought everyone in the Colony was Catholic. "Is Jean George Jewish, too?"

"No, the poor dear is not. He was orphaned in the first war. His father died in the trenches and his mother died the next year in a tuberculosis sanitarium. He was pretty much on his own from then on. For many years, he worked in the office of my father's export business and then we fell in love."

Henrietta sighed heavily and swirled the brandy around in her glass. "He promised to convert once we were married," she said, not looking up from her drink. "But something always got in the way. And now that we live in the colony, the opportunity to change his religion is impossible."

She took a swallow from her glass. "My father was quite distraught when he learned that Jean George would be taking me to live in French Indochina. He was afraid that Jean George would never convert. I assured my father that it would happen."

Aon She Beng had not said a word, but though I do not think that my landlady understood the subtleties of what Henrietta had said, she knew something juicy was going on and leaned forward to hear more clearly.

"Oh, my story is quite ordinary. Don't listen to me anymore." By now Henrietta had drunk several glasses of brandy. From her slightly slurred speech it was obvious she had had more than enough to drink, though she poured another portion into her glass and swilled it down.

"It must be quite difficult for you here," I said.

"No more than for anyone else. I try to make the best of it. I would love to see my father and mother again. I have four sisters, too. They are all married and have children." Henrietta tipped her nearly empty glass and a small amber droplet slid into her opened mouth.

"We cannot have children you know. Do you think that it's because Jean George is not Jewish? I wonder about this sometimes. We are both healthy, though he does work harder than he should and he is so tired and irritable when he gets home that some nights he has to go out to a men's club to calm his nerves."

The storm raged outside. The windows pinged as the wind blew rain against them. A draft in the room, caused the curtains to move.

Henrietta looked up from her glass and said, "The Nazis are killing the Jews. It's not a rumor. I know it is true. Jean George has told me and he said that he would never convert now."

The front door swung open. Jean George stepped into the entranceway. He closed his umbrella, shook the rain on to the floor, and came into the sitting room. "Has my wife been entertaining again?" he asked. "The car is waiting."

Henrietta stood. She wobbled slightly and grabbed the back of her chair. "You will have to come again," she said. "Maybe when the weather is more civilized."

"Yes," Jean George said. "This weather depresses my poor wife." He paused and added, "Solace in the bottle again, my dear?" He left the room.

Henrietta smiled at me. "You must come to one of my book groups," she said and held so tightly to the back of the chair that her knuckles turned white.

"Let me see you to the door," Henrietta said. "Aon She Beng, I am sorry that you and I did not get a chance to talk more. Did I tell you how lovely you looked today? And your hair, how perfectly spectacular." Henrietta reached out to touch one of the pieces of jewelry poking out of Aon She Beng's hair; she grabbed too hard and nearly pulled it out.

Aon She Beng jerked away, frowned, and then shouted, "You drink too much."

"Yes, I suppose I do," Henrietta said but did not seem insulted by the comment. Henrietta struggled for a few seconds with the doorknob and then when she finally managed to open the door, a heavy gust of wind and rain pelted us. We ran to the waiting car. Aon She Beng hurriedly climbed into the back seat. Bending and slipping she bumped her hair against the car's doorsill causing her great quaff to come tumbling down across her back. Grumbling and hissing she looked as mad as a hornet.

Waving farewell to Henrietta I rushed to get in on the other side of the car.

"Lousy French tea party," Aon She Beng growled. "Drive," she shouted at the driver. She tried several times to adjust her wet hair but each time made it only worse. "French women are stupid," Aon She Beng growled. "They know nothing and they are ugly."

I looked out the window. Visibility was poor and I hoped that the driver would move carefully along the roads. Aon She Beng continued to mumble and wiggle in her seat complaining all the way back home about how uncomfortable it was to sit in wet clothing.

The storm subsided slightly by the time we arrived back home but the rainwater rushed furiously in the gutters. I helped Aon She Beng step over the muddy washouts that now ran between the street and her garden gate. I got her into her yard without too much more damage to her clothing. Her hair had suffered greatly however, and now thin, loose strands clung to her face looking slightly like long, grey worms crawling down from her head.

Once inside Aon She Beng's garden gate, she hobbled away from me and reached for the hand of a servant who had rushed out of the house with an umbrella to greet her. There was no need for me to stick around listening to any more of her complaints. The storm had done me no favors either and it wouldn't have surprised me if we both looked like something that had been dragged up from the river.

I went into my house, peeled off the wet garments and lay down for an afternoon nap. When I finally woke up and stumbled into the front of the house, I found Albee sleeping on my daybed. It didn't surprised to see him. I knew he'd show up again. I went into the kitchen and while I was bent over the stove building a fire to make a pot of coffee, Albee came up from behind me and slid his hands around my waist.

"Miss me?" he asked.

"Always."

"Good, that's why I keep coming back."

"How long this time?"

"A day or two. And then I'm heading south."

"What's going on?"

"Plenty, my dear." He looked weary, though his bloodshot eyes never seemed to lose their spark.

"Been on the road long?" I asked.

"A while."

"So, what's going on?"

"The war in European is not going well. The Nazi's are bombing the hell out the Netherlands and Belgium, and they've skirted the Maginot line. It's only a matter of time now before they reach Paris. France was ill equipped from the start and not much of a match for the German tanks. They expected it would be an old-fashioned trench war. It looks like this colony is in for a bumpy ride, too."

"How do you know all this?"

"Does it matter?"

"Suppose not, but if you listened to the colonials talk, you'd think that nothing could harm them."

"Well, they're wrong and I'm sure in private they're shaking in their boots. They know that once the Germans defeat France, there's no way in hell that things will go on as usual."

"So what brings you here this time?" I didn't expect a straight answer. He usually told me what he thought I should know and then I guess he expected me to pass this information along to his various contacts in the area. Most of the time, I never knew who would carry my words back to the rebels.

He kissed me on the forehead, gave me a hug. His face looked drawn and weary.

"I'm tired," he said. "I could sleep for a year. We can talk more later."

We went to my bedroom and he scarcely had removed his boots before he fell onto the bed and began to snore.

Thirty-Three

AS SUDDENLY AS ALBEE APPEARED, he was gone again. When I arrived home from the Archives the following day, the house was empty and I knew he had moved on to his next destination. The only thing he left behind were a few small chunks of dry mud where his giant boots had been placed just inside the door. There was no lingering manly odor, no shirt needing a button to be sewn on. Nothing remained that would have given a clue that he had once again passed through my doorway.

The rains finally stopped. A cooler breeze blew through Hanoi and life quickly reverted back to a familiar quiet. Thi My informed the rickshaw drivers that arrived at her home to pick me up where I was now living. The manuscripts and letters continued to appear on the rickshaw seats. Several times I watched the rickshaw as it pulled away from me. The runner would quickly pass someone on the street trying to flag it down, then the rickshaw driver would stop on the opposite curb where a man climbed in and they hurried up the street. Once or twice I saw Vo Si Tuan get into the departing rickshaw. Occasionally he waited in front of the Archives building. We exchanged cordial greetings but we never talked for long.

I continued to visit Thi My several times a week. Her life, I believe, had exploded to tragic proportions. The old man, his body refusing to die, had given up eating. One evening between coughing fits, he told his daughter, "I'm tired of my flesh. I only want bones in my coffin. I'll leave nothing for the ghouls to feast on."

"He has begun to talk with his father," she said. "I believe the ancestors are pulling him closer to them. Years ago he joined a funeral club. Every year he puts money aside, handing it over to the club to take care of his burial expenses. Dat Tu was to preside over the ceremonies. My father does not remember what happened between him and my brother. He asks for Dat Tu and tells his father not to worry that the crossing-over money will insure his safe journey into the afterlife."

We sat in our usual chairs, talking quietly. When the rain stopped we once again heard the crickets singing in the night.

"The elder in charge of the funeral club has come to see my father several times this week. He has promised to take over the duties for Dat Tu." Thi My lifted a cup of tea to her mouth, her hand trembled slightly.

"And you? Who is taking care of you?" I asked.

She glanced at me with a slight smile. "I am learning to take care of myself."

I stayed that night and the old man moaned for only a short while after I crawled into bed. I did not hear Thi My go into his room during the night. I believe she might have gotten a bit of rest.

In the morning, an unseasonably hot breeze blew across Hanoi, a peculiar wind for this time of the year and it seemed to make everyone edgy. I didn't bother to eat breakfast and as I climbed into the rickshaw, the dry heat pushed against my face and whipped at my pants legs. I thought the dry wind was a mean trick for the weather to play because everyone knew that the rainy season was not completely over yet. Looking up at the open blue sky, it looked like the prelude to the approaching scorching summer. But June was still only the middle of the monsoon season and there would be more rain.

That night, the rain began again. This year the monsoon season felt as though it had gone on for an eternity. I longed to feel the blistering heat of the sun. The Archives building had sprung a leak in every place imaginable, and I'd grown weary of mopping up and trying to keep all that paper dry. Jean George rarely came to work these days. My secrete wish was that he would soon announce that he had received a promotion. Chances were he had got entangled with one of his women friends and was lying up in her bed.

I missed sitting in my garden. Most evenings, I'd hunker down in the doorway just out of the reach of the rain, drinking a glass of rice wine, looking out into the night. I expected a messenger to arrive at any point with a note from Thi My telling me of her father's passing. So, it didn't surprise me to hear a knock on my garden gate late one night. Sloshing through the muddy path in my garden, I was quite surprised when I opened the gate to see Vo Si Tuan standing in front of me.

It's hard to say how it happened. It might have been the poetry that he brought with him that evening, simple folk tales he had written of love and tradition. Possibly the rain had something to do with it—the incessant beating against my small house—but when he reached out to touch me that night, I did not pull away. We did not know that night if we would become lovers. Neither of us looked into the future. Perhaps we made love to escape from the monsoon. But that night my passion played a trick on me and for the first time in many years, a man moved me in a way that weakened a vulnerable part of my soul and left me asking for more than just comfort for my flesh.

These were complicated times. Only a fool would make plans. Yet, for several weeks, I waited for Vo Si Tuan to return. Though he never did. Then one morning he was standing on the curb when my rickshaw pulled up to the Archives.

"Good morning," I said.

He helped me out of the rickshaw. There was no letter or manuscript to hand over to him though I don't know if he knew this.

"The Germans have marched into Paris," he whispered as I stepped onto the curb.

These words did not fully register in my brain at first.

"We just got the news," he said. "A week ago, a fleet of Japanese ships disembarked from Hainan and had been hovering along the coast near Haiphong Harbor. Everyone had a suspicion that something big was going to happen."

"What now?" I asked though it was obvious to me that the rebels were now going to step up their actions.

"Tell Thi My," he said, "that her brother has traveled to China. I'm headed that way, too. What happens next depends on many things." He climbed into the rickshaw. "Goodbye, Sarah. I wish—" But the runner pulled the rickshaw out onto the street before Vo Si Tuan could finish his sentence. I watched for a short while, but he did not look back.

A sudden gust of rain beat down on me. I hurried into the Archives building. The musty smell had grown stronger as the monsoon season relentlessly stretched on. Every year it was the same. The long wet days and nights made the building smell like a pack of wet dogs lived within the walls. By the end of the rainy season, my clothing would stink of wet rotting paper.

I had no idea whether anyone in the Archives knew what had happened in France, though I'd seen rumors and information fly across this country like a wild fire. Jean George still had his bodyguard, and seeing this nameless oaf sitting in his usual place, I knew we'd probably see plenty of craziness today. I shook the rain from my hair and hurried into the main building.

Le Sing Dong was the first to greet me. From the look on his face it was obvious that he'd heard the news. Quite likely so had everyone else.

"It's true then, France has fallen," he said. This came out as a statement though it could have just as well been a question.

"Yes, this is what I've heard."

"It seems impossible." He shook his head. "How could that be?"

"Anything is possible," I said.

"Now what?"

"Hard to say."

At that moment, Jean George burst through the door. "Sarah, gather up the workers. I have important information. Go on now, hurry." He stood with his arms folded across his chest, one foot tapping the floor demonstrating his authority and his impatience.

I turned to Le Sing Dong, "Get the porters in the back room. I'll tell everyone in here."

The Archives are a quiet, solitary place to work. There are no chattering workers, they tend to their jobs and rarely speak to each other, the paper moves silently from shelf to shelf. Yet, this morning the place was more than quiet. There was an absence of any sound. It reminded me of that empty space between a question and an answer.

When all the workers had been gathered, Jean George said, "I don't have all day. Is this everyone?"

"Yes."

"Well, if you have not heard, the Germans are now occupying Paris. No one knows what that means at this moment, but your work will not change. I want to see you here every day. I want you to follow my orders. When I ask you to do something, I want it done and done quickly. Sarah, is that understood?"

Le Sing Dong gave me a quizzical glance.

I did not respond to Jean George's comment and he repeated, "Sarah, do you understand?"

"Yes, I understand."

"Important administrative information might come through our doors and it is to be treated with the utmost secrecy. My orders will now come directly from the Governor General's office and he will direct our actions. You are to tell no one about the work that you do here. We are now classified a top-secret operation. I cannot tell you any more than this."

I couldn't figure out if what Jean George had said was real or came from his own sense of importance.

"For the time being," Jean George continued, "I want you to carry on as usual." He put his hands on his hips as though he were about to challenge one of the workers and then asked, "Are there any questions?"

No one said a word, and without as much as a grunt Jean George turned and left the building.

In the last couple of months, we'd received more than our share of cartons containing documents and we protected them as best we could against the leaks in the building, the infestation of insects and rodents. There was nowhere else to store more cartons. The Governor General's office had no idea what we were up against in the Archives building. Jean

George certainly wasn't going to convey this information to the Colonial administration. As usual, we were on our own, so rather than complaining about what should have been, I decided to simply go about the day as though nothing out of the ordinary had happened.

No one saw Jean George for the rest of the day. That wasn't unusual. Seeing him lately had been the remarkable event. And at the end of the day when I locked up the building and stepped out into the street, there seemed to be many more automobiles than usual. Every Frenchmen in this country had a lot to figure out. Most of them believed that the war in Europe would never touch them. Now who knew what the future held for them.

I wondered where Albee was at this moment and what he thought about the Nazis in Paris. But wherever he happened to be, he was probably up to his neck in something big.

Thirty-Four

I HADN'T VISITED THI MY in several days. Then one wretched stormy night, after arriving home from the Archive, Aon She Beng banged at my garden gate.

"Thi My's father died." There was a familiar accusatory tone in her voice. "You go help. I sent servant girl. Thi My has no one."

"Yes." It took no time for me to gather a small bundle of clothing before heading back out into the miserable weather.

As we neared Thi My's home, it was clear that the paid mourners had already begun to do their job. A small crowd stood near the doorway, clustered together under umbrellas, their muffled voices only slightly audible above the thrashing of the storm. The flickering candles in the window and the heavy smell of incense marked the beginning of Thi My's ritualistic duties.

The coffin sat in the middle of the living room. The scene reminded me so much of Thien Nguyen's funeral. The darkened room had an eerie look with the thick cloud of smoke from the burning joss sticks, the amber glow of candles casting wild dancing shadows along the walls, and the sweet odor of over-ripe fruit. Thi My sat on her haunches near the far end of the coffin, draped in the traditional gauzy garment, surrounded by a cluster of weeping women.

Thi My slowly raised her head. "He's passing to the other world."

"You look very tired," I said.

"I cannot rest until this is finished. The funeral club will manage all those things that Dat Tu would have taken care of. A messenger has been sent to my father's village." Thi My looked at the coffin. "He has a younger brother. He may pay his respects out of duty. My father did many things to anger his family."

I sat with Thi My most of the night. The rain did not let up. Water ran along the streets in great gushes making it difficult for a funeral procession to take place. But the wise man Thi My consulted about her father's funeral suggested that the burial be held first thing the next day. The mourners gathered at the entrance of the house cried and called out, often sounding like cats begging to come in out of the rain.

Aon She Beng showed up. It was doubtful that my landlady had come to pay her respects to the dead. It was more likely a time for her to collect bits of gossip. She brought a large bowl of fruit and had one of her servant girls scoot all the other fruit and rice cups to one side to place her bowl prominently in the middle of the coffin's lid. Her legs bowed from a childhood bout with rickets, prevented her from squatting, and the old woman stood teetering on her cane in front of Thi My waiting for someone to fetch her a stool to sit on.

"How fortunate that your father still has you to look after his needs," Aon She Beng said and lowered herself onto a stool.

Thi My did not respond.

"You need to be careful." Aon She Beng spoke to Thi My in Vietnamese. It was a hushed tone as though they now both had secrets. "Many thieves come to women who are along. They want your money. They will tell you lies."

The din of the mourners continued to fill the room. Thi My looked up. Her eyes were dull. They were no longer filled with tears. I knew she had turned the world off.

Aon She Beng probably knew this also, though she continued to talk. "These are bad times. The Japanese are everywhere. The Governor General talks like he is an important man. He is weak. He is a useless man. People with property must be careful or they will lose land. We must help each other."

Thi My looked at Aon She Beng with dull confused eyes. "Are you well?" Thi My asked.

Aon She Beng looked at me. "This girl soon find jackals at her door. They take everything. Many greedy people standing in the rain outside her door, waiting. They grab her money."

"She'll be fine," I said.

"No. They steal everything."

Thi My continued to sit, her head bowed, the mourners crying out pitifully.

"I suppose you want to help her," I said.

"Yes," Aon She Beng said and gestured to her servant girl who rushed across the room. Aon She Ben extended her elbow. The servant girl took hold of the old woman and helped her stand. Aon She Beng looked at me. "Thi My has much to learn."

Aon She Beng's rant confused me. After she had left I asked Thi My, "What was that about?"

"Aon She Beng sent a message today that I should combine my father's land in the Mekong Delta with her land. My father did not tell me of this land. I want nothing to do with anything that was my father's."

"What did she say when you told her this?"

"It's against tradition to talk business during these days. I told her we couldn't talk about property before the dead are placed in the ground. Then I said that all my father's property will be given away."

"Maybe you should wait for a while before you decide to do this."

"My mind is made up. After the burial, the papers necessary to remove the property from my hands will be signed."

"And the house?"

"I will sell it."

"Then you must come and live with me," I said.

That seemed to please her and she smiled slightly.

Henrietta arrived later that evening to pay a condolence call. My involvement with Thi My most likely made her feel a social obligation to visit.

"My dear, how terrible about your father passing. If there is anything that I can do, please tell Sarah to contact me." Henrietta gave me an odd grin. "How senseless is death," she said. Then teetering ever so slightly, it was obvious Henrietta was drunk. "These are such uncertain times," she continued. "Terrible times. It seems the end of the world." Tears began to well up in her eyes. Henrietta took out a hanky and dabbed at the droplets. "Thi My, it does break my heart to see you so sad." She blew her nose gently into the hanky. Then, turning to me with a confused and slightly arrogant tone, asked, "Now, what do I do?"

"If you light three joss sticks that would be enough," I said.

"Yes, of course. They have such simple customs," she said. Wobbling to the altar, she managed to light the joss sticks and then returning to where I stood, she said, "I do hope the Germans do not decide to come here. But then, I suppose they'll leave all the dirty work in this country for Japan. Do you think the Japanese will burn books and kick out the Jews, too, like the Nazis? What do you think, Sarah?" She leaned close to me with boozy breath.

"This is not the time or place to talk about such things. You look tired. Go home and rest."

"I cannot rest," she said. "I keep thinking about the burning books." Tears welled up again in her eyes. "I have not heard from my family in such a long time. The news on the shortwave radio is so disturbing. The Jews have now all been taken from their homes. They are forced to work for the Nazis. Jean George told me not to worry that this is probably only temporary. How can I not worry? These are my parents!"

Taking hold of Henrietta's arm I walked her to the door. The mourners standing at the entranceway became quiet except for a small group of women standing on the edge of the crowd. They whispered and pointed. Henrietta looked startled to see everyone watching her. Her arm went tense. Breaking free from my grasp Henrietta rushed out into the rain and scrambled into her waiting car. The driver quickly started the engine and drove his mistress away. Once the car was out of sight, the crying and wailing began again.

The nun did not show up. No one had seen her for many months. The news of Thi My's father's death would eventually reach her no matter where she was. With all that had been going on with the rebels, I just hoped that she was safe.

Early the next day, preparations for the funeral were begun. Thi My asked me to accompany her in the long walk behind the casket. I wanted to believe that somewhere along the route, Dat Tu might be watching, doing his bit to send his father off to be with their ancestors. If he had shown up, I hadn't seen him, and I didn't have the heart to ask Thi My if she had glimpsed her brother.

Thirty-Five

SEVERAL DAYS AFTER THE FUNERAL, Thi My appeared at my door. She brought with her a small satchel of clothing and a bonsai plant.

"It is done," Thi My said. "I want nothing more to do with my father's wealth. The land, the house, everything has been signed away."

"You can stay here as long as you wish," I said.

It was doubtful that such a major business transaction of divesting herself of all the father's holdings could have been concluded in so short a time, though from that point on, we never mentioned the rice paddies that her father owned in the Mekong Delta, the land holdings in the different villages in the north, or the house that Thi My once told me her father secured years ago from a debtor's widow.

Thi My and I lived quietly for a while. If Aon She Beng had not dropped in periodically with the latest news and her worries about the Japanese taking over Indochina, we could have believed that the world had become trouble-free. The streets were unusually empty. Traveling back and forth to the Archives and home again made me think that a large number of people had left the city. I suspected that fear kept the citizens in their homes…fear and the dread of what might happen next.

It didn't take long for Aon She Beng to learn what Thi My had done with her father's wealth.

"You foolish woman," Aon She Beng snarled. "How long farmers keep land? They have too much debt. They have no money to buy seeds, no ox to work farm. They borrow money. Moneylenders will take the land. Your father will never rest now. You make him miserable."

Thi My appeared unfazed by these words. It was difficult to tell if it was her silence or her resolute posture that irritated Aon She Beng more.

"You will become beggar," she raged on. "You are thoughtless and stupid."

"Enough," I said. "Stop it. Thi My did what she wanted to do. It's none of your business."

Aon She Beng glared at me. She opened her mouth to say something else, but her mouth was empty of words. The old woman stood facing Thi My for a short while then went back to her house. Aon She Beng came back several days later, most likely fearful that she'd miss some juicy information. There was never another mention about what Thi My had done.

The following month, quite unexpectedly, Henrietta began to drop by. At first, her visits were only once or twice a week and always in the evenings. I hadn't encouraged her and tolerated the intrusions sometimes with a cup of tea but more frequently, since I had begun to drink again, with a glass of wine. From time to time, she'd bring a bottle of fine French red wine that she snatched from her husband's wine cellar.

"He'll hardly miss them," she said and pulled the cork from the bottle. "I dust them and move them around on the shelves in our basement, something I've done for years. He hasn't a clue what's happening down there. He wants a bottle on the table with his meals and one to keep in his office."

Some evenings, Henrietta showed up drunk and those were the times when she was the most difficult to deal with. Henrietta complained incessantly. She complained about the weather, Jean George working too much, not being able to go shopping in Paris. But her main concerns were for her family and her fear of what was happening to them in France.

With all these visitors, I no longer had the opportunity to sit in my garden, drink alone, and listen to the frog croak in the bamboo thicket on the edge of my koi pond. In the beginning Thi My prepared a simple meal for me in the evenings. Though after a while, returning from the Archive, when I opened the garden gate and did not smell food, I knew Thi My had been out most of the day and might not return that evening. We never talked about where she went.

Aon She Beng no longer acted like a crazy woman yelping and screaming about spirits invading her house. After the rains stopped, Aon She Beng visited me almost nightly in my garden and always with a new bit of information from a neighbor or a servant. "Women alone need be prepared," Aon She Beng said one night. "If Albee here, I not worry."

"But he's not here and I doubt very much if we'll ever see him again," I said.

"You make him go away."

"He's a free man. He can do whatever he wants. He has no strings attached to me."

She sat down in a chair in my garden as though she'd been invited. "You lousy host. Give me tea," she grumbled.

I barely tolerated these visits and didn't think they'd go on forever. The evenings that Henrietta and Aon She Beng both showed up were the most irritating. These two women danced around each other looking for information; Henrietta for her personal safety and her desperate concern for her parents. Aon She Beng worried about how to protect of her property and money.

"My father is a brilliant businessman," Henrietta said. "My mother is an accomplished musician. The Germans will see them as an asset to the government. That they are Jews should not matter. But the news is so terribly confusing. Would the Nazis be so foolish as to disrupt their perfect life of work and art?"

Henrietta drank more heavily with each visit. It didn't take long to deplete my supply of wine. After that she never failed to bring a bottle and we never failed to finish it off. Aon She Beng watched with a critical eye as the glasses were repeatedly filled.

"If France cannot control Germans," Aon She Beng barked, "they no help here with Japanese." She looked directly at Henrietta. "The French too soft, too fat, now you cry, boo-hoo, you scared. Now you understand." There was an angry look in Aon She Beng's eyes that I'd never seen before.

Every night Henrietta said the same thing and each night Aon She Beng became less tolerant.

Too much drinking was going on and I'd begun to feel it. In the mornings, my memory was foggy about what had happened the night before. Sometimes at the crack of dawn, I'd wake up and find myself sprawled atop the covers, my clothes still on with the mosquito net stretched out halfway across the bed. There was no recollection of getting into the bed. Before this, I had a peaceful coexistence with booze, but Henrietta had upped the ante and now I began to pay the price. Many mornings I arrived at the Archives in no shape to handle what was going on.

The Japanese had caused a great deal of trouble for the Governor General's office, and the Japanese Imperial Forces demanded every bit of information we had in the Archives about roads, the rail system, and river routes leading into China. Last year, we'd given them maps. That didn't seem to be a problem. Now the Governor General's office decided to close the Archives rather than to give the Japanese more information. Nothing was to come in, and we were not allowed to let any information out. The Archives building was locked tight and our stacks were declared private. Jean George would not say how long we were expected to stay away from the building. We all stood around watching as the French police slapped a chain and padlock across the door.

Now I had lots of time to kill. Henrietta began to stop by during the day and invite me to her afternoon teas.

"You might consider finding some activities to take up your extra time," Henrietta said. "The Archives may be closed for a long while."

"What makes you think that?"

"It's supposed to be hush-hush but from what Jean George tells me, the Governor General's office and the Japanese are not getting along. The Japanese want total use of all the roads, the waterways, the rail system, and our airports. They even want to establish military bases for their troops. This is going to take some time to work out and my husband has been promised another position if this isn't settled soon. I tell you Sarah, you will have to find something to take up your time or you'll go mad with boredom."

Jean George had not said anything about this when he dismissed us that last day. Though there were no promises about when we'd return, I thought after all these years, the French would not abandon the Archives project now. From my point of view the Governor General's office did the smart thing by securing this information.

"I do wish you'd reconsider and join us today for our book club," Henrietta said.

"No," I replied, and my answer must have been punctuated just right because Henrietta simply shrugged and stepped out on to the street and climbed into her waiting car.

The war in Europe seemed so far away, and though the war between the Japanese and China was only a matter of several hundred miles away, it never seemed that any of this would have a lasting effect on Vietnam. If Albee were here, he could have filled me in on what was happening. But he wasn't here, and though we didn't always agree, it would have been interesting to hear what he thought about the situation. I wondered where he was and hoped that he was safe.

A couple weeks later, we heard that Germany, Italy, and Japan had signed an Axis Pact, and within a day or two a new Governor General of Indochina was appointed, a fellow by the name of Decoux.

Aon She Beng hobbled into my garden that night so agitated she almost tripped over her cane. "What wrong with old Governor General?" she growled. It sounded like a personal offence to have this new appointment.

"He obviously didn't play by the new rules," I responded.

"What Decoux know of this country?"

"Probably nothing."

Thi My sat on her haunches in the doorway. She said nothing.

Henrietta rapped on the garden gate. It was going to be another one of those strange nights. I let her in. She staggered to the middle of the courtyard.

Henrietta was not a sloppy or affectionate drunk. Lately she'd become a bossy, know-it-all drunk. It occurred to me that living with her oppressive husband for so many years was finely getting the best of her and under the influence of alcohol Henrietta simply could no longer hold back her anger.

"They are bombing the hell out of us in the north," she said. Henrietta stood in the middle of the garden. "I mean they have blown up buildings and everything."

"Who has?" Aon She Beng asked.

"The Japanese," she slurred. "We gave them what they wanted, and they just opened fire on two towns in the North. Now what do you think of that?" Henrietta could hardly walk a straight line into the garden. The drunken woman plopped down in a chair and gave me a goofy grin. "Jean George crawled under the bed when he heard this." She laughed like a schoolgirl with a juicy secret. "He's such a baby, that fat husband of mine."

"Did he really crawl under the bed?" I asked.

"No. I was just kidding, but he might as well have, as scared as he was." Henrietta reached into her handbag and pulled out a bottle of red wine. "Here, let's have a drink to lily-livered men and the fine wine they purchase."

"You drink too much," Aon She Beng said.

"No I don't, and neither do you."

Aon She Beng looked angrily at Henrietta. "What you mean Japanese bombed two towns? Where you hear this?"

"Jean George heard it on his shortwave radio. Every night it's the same old crackling sound. I can't hear myself think with that thing blasting. And they said that even though the French have conceded to give Japan everything they wanted, they went ahead and bombed two towns along the border."

"The French will get what they deserve," Thi My said. "But it's the villagers who will pay the price." Thi My looked directly at Henrietta. "Now, maybe the French will understand what it is like to be intimidated."

Henrietta did not seem so drunk now. She sat up in her seat, gave Thi My an angry look and was about to say something.

"I need a drink," I interrupted. "Anyone else want one?"

From night to night, I never knew who would show up at my door or if Thi My would be away for the evening. As the weeks wore on, Thi My began to stay away for increasingly longer periods of time. Some days when she looked so dreadfully tired, she'd come home with her clothing caked with mud. On several occasions while watching her wash her clothing, I ask what she had been doing. My question was ignored and she continued to scrub her dirty britches.

Henrietta and Aon She Beng would comment if they hadn't seen Thi My for a day or two, but they were both so caught up in their own business and worries, that to them it was only a curiosity that they saw her so seldom.

After the Japanese took control of the ports and roadways in Hanoi, my landlady had a constant stream of people coming to her door. I suspected that the hard times had increased her ability to loan money at her exorbitant rate of interest to the desperate. All this activity exhausted her and we saw her less frequently. Henrietta, though, still came several times a week. Actually, I think she just liked the idea of having a drinking buddy even though I'd begun to cut way back on my consumption of booze.

I got used to her special knock on my garden gate, like a secret code: two loud knocks and three short snappy raps. There was always something for her to complain about.

"No one wants to come to my tea parties. Most of the ladies hardly come out of their houses any more. The poor dears are frightened of the Japanese soldiers that march up and down the streets."

"Yes, it must be a disappointment to you," I said, watching her skillfully remove the cork from a fresh bottle of red wine.

She poured us each a glass, and in the garden, with only the glow of a single candle near my chair, the wine looked awfully dark, almost black. I lifted my glass. "To better times."

"Yes, to better times." Henrietta took a swallow of her wine and held the glass up seeming to examine its quality.

"Aon She Beng must be very busy," Henrietta said. "She even had visitors this evening. I saw them when I drove up. In fact, you know one of them…Loc Dang Hung, the murdered translator's older brother. Remember him? That family must still be suffering if he's coming to her for a loan. You know that's why everyone is at her door."

"It's hard for everyone."

"I thought that things would get better for that poor family. Jean George tried to help him get a job after the murder of his brother. The fellow came by our house often enough, and my husband tried very hard to get him something. But, in the end there was nothing that Jean George could do. I don't know what happened. They had a falling out one night. It was terrible, with hollering. I couldn't hear everything they said. But they were both very angry." Henrietta lifted the glass to her lips. She sniffed the wine. "Do you think this is a bit sour? Some of our wine is so old that it's turned to vinegar and we've had to throw it out. Such a waste."

Something Henrietta said made me uneasy. It wasn't about the wine; I couldn't tell a bad one from a good one unless it had already turned nasty. But what she said about Loc Dang Hung clanked around in my head.

"When did he come to your house?" I asked.

"I don't remember…maybe before his brother had been killed. But then, you know I remember him coming even after I'd been to the funeral. Oh, that was such a scene. Do you remember? All that crying and carrying on. So terribly sad to see the young die."

Henrietta sat quietly for a while. She sipped the wine. "Jean George told me that he felt sorry for the brother," she said. "He told me he even wondered if he had a responsibility for the family's welfare. I think that's why he was so determined to try to help Loc Dang Hung find a position." Henrietta took a couple hearty swallows of her wine. "But his hands were tied. There was simply nothing he could do. The poor fellow did not like to hear that. He came by several times in the evening when Jean George was out on business. He frightened me and would not believe me when I said my husband was not at home." Henrietta furrowed her brows and poured herself another glass of wine. She seemed so intent with the story she did not offer to refill my glass.

"I told Jean George about how Loc Dang Hung's late night visits bothered me. He said he'd put a stop them. And that was the last I saw of him until tonight. My heart nearly stopped when I bumped into him coming out of Aon She Beng's garden. The poor man's lost an unnatural amount of weight. It looks as though his brother's death has turned him nearly mad. His eyes are so sunken in now, he looks like a lunatic." Henrietta sipped the wine. "No, I think this bottle is fine. Don't you?"

Thirty-Six

LIVING WITH THI MY HAD begun to feel similar to what it was like when Albee stayed with me. He came and went and I never knew when to expect him back. Now my new houseguest disappeared for days, only expecting a roof over her head and nothing else when she returned. When I offered her food, she took frightfully small portions or refused to eat at all. And then she retreated to the back room where she fell onto the bed and I wouldn't see her again for hours.

In the dry season it doesn't take the land to dry out and for the rickshaws to kick up large plumes of dust as they traveled the dirt roads. The rhododendron bush bloom profusely and I found myself most days sitting in the bright sun wondering when the Archives would open again. Henrietta might have been right about the possibility of me going mad with nothing constructive to take up my time. But, I refused to get involved with her afternoon gatherings. Quite likely, from what she said, it might have been only the two of us. There were a few more shoppers on the streets now that everyone seemed to have gotten accustomed to seeing so many Japanese soldiers strutting about, though there were not as many shoppers and pedestrians as there used to be.

I had no way knowing what was going on with the rebels. Thi My told me nothing. Though I was sure she knew plenty. I felt left out. I missed Albee and Dat Tu. Even as peripherally as I had been involved with what they did, they made me feel that I had a purpose. I was miserable sitting around like an old woman waiting for someone to throw me a crumb. That was when I decided to have a chat with Aon She Beng about Loc Dang Hung. Henrietta's comment the other week left me with many unanswered questions. I'd have to approach my landlady cautiously about her business. But it was worth a try.

Aon She Beng rarely opened her gate these days, complaining that too many people bothered her, and that she had to take on a couple new house servants. So, when I knocked on her gate, I knew that there would be an unfamiliar face. However, I did not expect such a young girl to open the gate. Barely tall enough to reach the latch, a child stood in front of me, a frail little thing, dressed in clean but somewhat shabby traditional ao dai pants and shirt with a mandarin collar. Her face was freshly washed but her hands were dirty. The little girl looked at me, but said nothing.

"Well, who is it?" Aon She Beng called out from inside the house.

The child remained mute and then quickly turned and ran back into the house leaving me alone at the entrance. "You stupid child," Aon She Beng barked. "Go stand next to your mother, you worthless thing."

"She did a lovely job," I said. "I think that little girl has great potential."

"Oh, it's you," Aon She Beng grumbled.

"Disappointed?"

"I tired. I have no time for visits."

"I thought you would like some company."

"You lie. No one visits me unless they want something. What you want?"

"Don't you think that's a bit rude to talk to your company like that?"

She gave me one of her familiar frowns. "I always rude. Takes too long to be polite."

"Yes, you're right. It does take too much of your time to be polite."

I sat in a chair across from Aon She Beng. My landlady grumbled again, then looked at me suspiciously.

I smiled and said, "The other night, Loc Dang Hung was outside on the street. He looked very tired."

"He unlucky man. All fools are unlucky."

"Is he ill?"

"He will live very long time." Aon She Beng leaned forward, looking me straight in the eyes. "Why you want talk about him?"

"When I saw him, I thought about Thien Nguyen and wondered

how the family was doing."

"They worse," she said. "The mother cry all day. His sisters give husbands dead babies. Loc Dang Hung try cheat me and tell me his brother refuse to stay in the grave."

Aon She Beng could not resist passing along a good bit of gossip, and once this old gal got started, she could go on for quite some time. All I had to do was feed her the right questions, to shine a light on her as the aggrieved moneylender, and she'd tell it all.

"He lie and say when his brother died his family would come into a fortunate situation. The father made much debt. Loc Dang Hung say he pay soon. He tell me not worry. He only needed money to bury brother."

"Did he say what kind of good fortune? Was it money or property?"

"He say position of importance would change family's fortune."

"What did he mean by that?"

Aon She Beng ignored my question and continued with her story. "I believe him. I loan him money. After funeral, he come back. He say he need more money. He only give promises. Next month I pay you, he say. I poor old woman. I need my money, I told him."

"And he came back last week for more?"

"He cannot pay. His family suffers. He owes money to many lenders. Not only me."

I knew that Aon She Beng stood by her word. I shuddered to think about all the times this old money lender had removed people from their homes and taken over their land, making entire families share-croppers on their own property. I didn't want to think about this. Instead I asked, "What did Loc Dang Hung mean when he said that his brother would not stay in his grave?"

"You know nothing about my country."

I waited for her to say more but she looked at me with an expression that had become all too familiar, a look that dismissed me and made me feel the fool.

"Maybe you find answer in drink," she said. "Now, go. I tired. Many visitors come to ask for money." Aon She Beng stood up and hobbled to the back of the house.

I hadn't left Aon She Beng's place more than a few seconds when I saw a smart young Vietnamese couple dressed in business attire knocking on her gate. The man looked nervously over his shoulder and when the gate opened, they hurried into the courtyard.

Upon returning home, Thi My was waiting for me in the garden. She'd been gone for three days this time and looked a mess. Her hair, tied back with a strip of rag, was littered with leaves and twigs. Her pants and shirt were wrinkled and filled with dirty scuffmarks and there was a nasty cut below one eye.

"Where on earth have you been?" I asked.

She looked at me. There was a contented expression on her face. "I've come to say good-bye."

"I wish—" Words failed me. I'd grown so fond of her, though I knew in these troubled times that she'd eventually join the rebels the way that her brother had done.

"There's going to be an uprising," she said.

"I'll come with you."

"That would be impossible." she said, and rubbed the back of her neck. "I am so terribly tired. I have to lay down for a while and then I must go."

"Something has come up. I want to ask you a question," I said. We had not talked about Thien Nguyen in quite a while. To do so felt like it would be opening a wound but it was quite likely that I might not get another chance to talk with her again. "The document that Thien Nguyen gave you…did he say if he'd shown it to someone else?" I might have asked her this before, but I couldn't remember.

Her expression did not change. She looked at me with tired, dark eyes. The fresh deep cut on her cheekbone made her look like a stranger, someone that I might not recognize in a year or two. "He said he told his brother about something that would prove the French were deliberately withholding food from the people. Loc Dang Hung could never see the French as harmful to this country."

"Did he say anything else?"

She shook her head. "Please, I am so tired. I need to lie down."

"Of course. Do you want me to wake you?"

"No," she said and went into the back bedroom.

Thi My did not come out for the evening meal. In the morning she was gone. I worried about her safety. There would eventually be an insurgency but I wondered what kind of role a delicate young girl like Thi My could play in such a situation. I wondered when we'd see each other again.

For the next couple days, I listened for news about the rebels. The French tried to keep information about rebellions hushed, though eventually the news got out. Now that the Japanese were in the picture, it was difficult to know how the French would handle any insurrection by the rebels.

Henrietta hadn't been by for over a week. Aon She Beng had her hands full with her business. One day when returning from food shopping, I saw two Japanese officers step into Aon She Beng's garden. The little girl who had opened the gate for me stood in the entranceway. Our eyes met briefly before she closed the gate.

I rambled around in my house for several days, doing nothing, missing Thi My, when I got the courage to visit Loc Dang Hung. A bevy of questions were rattling around in my head. It was time to dig deeper and try to find out what he knew about the murder of his brother.

The rickshaw wheels wobbled slightly as the puller dodged the trolley car that ran down the middle of Hang Dao Street. The shoppers were an excited lot this afternoon carrying home a few more food items in the baskets that dangled from the shoulder poles. I suspected that an Asian country making demands on the French had begun to excite the locals into feeling hopeful about what might happen next.

Arriving in front of Loc Dang Hung's home, it surprised me at how desolate the area surrounding the residence now appeared. No one walked the street. Several giant Gingko trees that lined the walkway had been blown over during the monsoon and were in various stages of being cut up and hauled away. I stepped out of the rickshaw and knocked on the door. A wizened old woman opened it slightly, allowing me to see only a slice of her face. The ghostly grey of her skin, the starkness of her thin pointed nose, and her hollowed cheekbones made me wonder if she were indeed real.

"Loc Dang Hung," I said, and the door slowly opened.

A great musty stink billowed out from the house making me wonder when the door had last been opened. Candles flickered in one corner and undulating wisps of incense smoke slowly danced across the room. Loc Dang Hung sat on his haunches in a far corner of the room smoking a cigarette. He lifted his head and looked in my direction.

Henrietta had seen Lock Dang Hung several times and her description of him was quite accurate. His eyes, sunken so deeply into his skull, looked as though he might have gone blind. I could not judge the pallor of his complexion from where I stood, nor could I see how diminished his body had become, but from the expression on his face, he looked like a man on the verge of insanity.

"Why are you here?" he asked. His voice rattled with congestion.

"I worked with your brother," I said.

"I know who you are. Why are you here?" This time his voice sounded threatening.

"I have some questions about your brother's murder."

"You can ask him yourself."

"What do you mean?"

"He comes every night to our house and makes the fruit rot on the tree in the garden. I would offer you a cup of tea but he's made the water in our well smell foul and no one can drink it. Thien Nguyen has decided not to stay with the ancestors but instead he's chosen to haunt his family and make our lives miserable." Loc Dang Hung took a puff of his cigarette, the smoke swirled above his head in a long ghostly stream.

"I don't understand," I said.

"Nor do I. The elders that I've consulted have said that I'm mad to believe such a thing. But they do not see him. I do. Our mother is nothing but bones and refuses to get out of her bed. She says he stands in the doorway of her room at night. Since his death, each of my sisters has lost a baby in childbirth. They say that something touched their bellies making them shudder and their blood run cold on the night before the babies were born. Our family is cursed. Stay the night and you will see for yourself."

I did not question that the water, the fruit, the dead babies had taken place, though I doubted that Thien Nguyen had been the cause. But I played along with Loc Dang Hung and asked, "Why do you think he has chosen to do this?"

As he looked at me, the madness in his eyes grew stronger. "My brother's angry because he did not listen to me. I told him the rebels would cause nothing but trouble and he continued to ignore my warnings."

"Why? What happened?"

"The rebels are greedy and treacherous."

The madness in his eyes flared with anger. The old woman who had let me into the house began to busy herself with lighting an incense stick at the altar.

"Get out, you old witch," Loc Dang Hung shouted in Vietnamese. The woman rushed to the back of the house. "My mother's sister," he said, "a worrisome woman who believes she can appease the spirits." He turned and faced me. "Why did you come here? Do you want to steal my house? Pick my bones before I'm dead?"

"Your brother found something in the Archives," I said.

His mad eyes darted away from me.

"Did he tell you about it?" I asked.

"About what?"

"You tell me."

"Whatever he found, the rebels killed him for it. Now he is angry at me because I did not take better care of him and insist he follow my warnings." Loc Dang Hung glanced down at the cigarette between his fingers.

"I saw it," I said.

"You saw what?"

"The document."

Loc Dang Hung sat as still as a statue. "Where is it now?"

A long stream of gray smoke floated up from the cigarette and curled into many ringlets before it disappeared.

Then taking another chance with my hunch that Loc Dan Hung knew more than he was telling, I said, "Did you tell anyone else what your brother told you?"

Loc Dang Hung's head turned slowly in my direction. His eyes met mine. He then stood and without saying another word walked out of the room.

The old woman rushed past me and opened the front door for me to leave.

Thirty-Seven

THE DAY I RECEIVED THE message that the Archives would be reopened; there was also news about a major rebel uprising in the south. The French had gathered up all their extra police and army recruits from Hanoi and sent them to Saigon. Thi My had put herself in terrible danger. It was such a helpless feeling waiting to hear from her. I wanted to jump on a train, head south, thrash through the jungle to bring her back to Hanoi.

The news of the skirmishes also had a strange effect on the people in Hanoi. Everyone walked more quickly as they did their daily shopping. The French looked ill at ease, frequently glancing over their shoulders, worried that at any moment the rebels might start something.

But nothing happened in Hanoi. The city continued to go on pretty much as it always had. My rides to the Archives in a rickshaw were uneventful and there were no longer bundles of documents or envelopes waiting for me on the seat.

Everything looked normal that first morning in the Archives. The two women who repaired the manuscripts were already busy at their workstation. From the piles of debris gathered on the floor, it was clear that someone had been hard at work scooting around the dust and fallen plaster that accumulated during our absence.

There was a God-awful musty smell in the building. The Archives had never been closed for so long, any way on my watch, and it was quite likely another level of mold was growing atop the old stuff.

My work had gone from being a professional librarian-archivist to that of a charwoman. Working alongside the staff clearing clutter, we picked through the ruined manuscripts and documents, and every night I arrived home smelling musty. Even my cigarettes had a foul flavor. Rice wine seemed to be the only thing that covered over the musty smell of the Archives. After a couple swallows, the smell dissipated.

The news from the south was confusing. No one knew for sure how far this insurrection would spread. My nerves were on edge waiting to hear something from Thi My.

Henrietta's visits were still down to once a week, or less. When she arrived there were no longer bottles of Jean George's wine tucked away in her handbag. I got the distinct feeling that she preferred to keep her husband's stash to herself and most evenings she'd arrived with a strong smell of booze on her breath..

Aon She Beng rarely came by any more, though I heard her quite often, her voice carrying over our common wall, cursing at a client who had asked for more money when nothing had been paid on a past-due loan. I'd seen Loc Dang Hung enter her courtyard a couple of times. Once he brought a small sack of rice and on another occasion he had an armful of fresh produce. He looked more emaciated than ever. On our last chance meeting he looked to have lost so much weight that the clothing hung from his body. I tried to talk to him one evening as he left Aon She Beng's place. He looked at me with nervous eyes and ran down the street disappearing into an alley.

After a while living alone again seemed natural. The nights ran together and except for a slight shift in the direction of the hot breeze in my garden, not much changed. The rebels continued to wage war against the colonials but I never learned the full story. It was impossible to find out where Thi My ended up or whether the brother and sister ever made contact.

Late one night a stranger came to my door. The insistent knock on the garden gate roused me from a sleepy state. When I opened the garden gate, I thought it was Thi My. The slight figure of a woman stood in front of me, her black clothing blending in with the night. Yet, it was not Thi My.

"I have a message," she said.

"Come in," I offered and braced myself, fearing the worst.

Stepping into the flickering light of the lone candle in the garden, her clothing, ragged and over-sized for her stature, was caked with mud. The tops of her shoes were worn through and held onto her foot with jute twine.

"Thi My has been captured," she said. "We promised to inform each other's families if anything happened. The French overran our stronghold in Vu Lang where we had been helping with the wounded. She's been taken to the Con Doa prison colony."

My heart stopped when I heard this news. Yet, there was hope. At least Thi My was still alive.

"If you see her brother, tell him what has happened. Though I'm sure he knows by now. A full battalion of soldiers attacked us. Hundreds were arrested and those who got away fled into the hills."

I could not speak. Then looking at the young woman, who appeared not to have eaten in days, I found my voice. "Would you care for a bit of food?"

"No, there are other families to notify. Please, do what you can to help Thi My." The young woman opened the gate and rushed into the night without glancing back.

My hands trembled so badly that I could not pour myself another drink nor light a cigarette. My only thought was of Thi My sitting in prison. Such terrible stories circulated about places like these, penal colonies set up by the French years ago when they'd first settled in the area. Now the rebels were taken there like so much cattle and stuck in cages. I could not believe what had happened, though something like this was inevitable. Thi My also knew what to expect when she joined the rebels.

It was impossible for me to sleep. In the morning I made plans to travel south by train to intervene on Thi My's behalf. The Archives could rot now. Nothing else mattered. The only thing that concerned me was Thi My's release from prison. The rest of the world could go to hell. I sent a note to Jean George by way of a messenger telling him that I'd be away for an undetermined amount of time. Working for the French had its privileges and I easily got past the checkpoint and purchased a train ticket.

I paid no attention to anyone sitting in the compartment with me. The trip seemed endless and the farther south we went, the more fearful I became for Thi My's safety.

Soldiers were everywhere along the route. When we stopped at a small outpost, a contingency of French Foreign Legionnaires climbed aboard the passenger cars. They clambered for seats in the compartments and an overflow of bodies crowded into the walkways, leaning against the open windows puffing on Gaulloise.

Arriving in Saigon in the morning several days later, I was reeling from fatigue and my clothing stank from the strong French cigarettes the soldiers had smoked. As soon as I got off the train, I headed for the ticket booth inside the train station.

"When does the next train leave for Con Dao," I asked the sleepy clerk behind the counter.

"There are no trains to Con Dao. It's an island." The clerk looked at me as though I was crazy.

"How about the closest station."

"This is it."

"Well, how could I get there?"

"I do not know," the clerk said indifferently.

Climbing into a taxi I asked the driver to take me to a hotel. And though all I wanted to do was find Thi My, I was exhausted. Securing a room, sleep overcame me as soon as my head hit the pillow. When I awoke, sunlight blasted through my hotel window as though a spotlight had been turned on me. The room was beastly hot. My pillow was soaked with sweat. Splashing my face with water from a pitcher on the dresser, I then slipped into fresh clothing, and went downstairs.

"How can I make arrangements to get to Con Dao?" I asked a very old Chinese man standing behind the reception desk. He looked at me with dead eyes and said nothing. Repeating my question still did not get a response.

"That would be very dangerous," someone standing behind me said. "And an especially difficult trip for an English woman."

I turned and saw a delicately built man with a pencil-thin mustache.

"American," I corrected him.

"Ah, yes, and why would you want to go to Con Dao? Most people want to get out of that place."

"Exactly."

"Maybe I can be of service. My name is Peter Montague."

He glanced in the direction of the clerk and said to me, "There is only military transport to that place."

"Surely there are other ways of getting there."

"I'm afraid not."

"This is ridiculous."

"There is perhaps something," he said. "There are no guarantees, but if you would like, I could inquire on your behalf. There are special concessions for the English, Americans, and, of course, the Japanese and the Germans, too. We have many people of interest in our country now and our new officials are very willing to cooperate if it is within their interest."

There were no other alternatives left to me. I knew no one in Saigon.

"Give me until tomorrow," he said. "I'm sure something can be arranged."

"I suppose there is no other choice," I said.

Peter Montague smiled. His wisp of a mustache looked so thin, as it stretched out across his face, that it appeared to be the outline of his upper lip. "I am very discrete," he said and lit a cigarette. "Would you care to tell me why you want to travel to Con Dao?"

"No, I would not."

He smiled. "I understand. Let me see what I can do."

"Thank you."

"Then, until tomorrow," he said and crushed his cigarette into the ashtray. "In the meantime, let me make a suggestion for your dinner tonight. Two blocks north and across the street you will find the food is excellent and if you tell them that Peter Montague sent you, they will treat you with special care." He nodded politely and left the hotel lobby.

By dinnertime the brilliant late afternoon sun had turned everything orange. The heat, always more miserable in the south than up north, made me nauseous. I had no appetite and picked at the food in the plate. The place had a decent bar and I ordered several shots of whatever it was that the bartender suggested. There were a few other diners in the place, but no one made eye contact. After returning back to the hotel room, it was impossible for me to keep my eyes open.

In the morning several businessmen stood at the reception desk when I arrived downstairs. I quickly walked past them and sat in the seat next to Peter.

"I have good news for you," he said. "I have booked a berth for you on a military train that is used only by the French officers and their families. It leaves this evening and will arrive in the afternoon at the port used to disembark for Con Dao. I can give you the name of the general in charge of that section but I cannot give you any guarantees that you will be allowed on the island."

"Thank you."

"I hope your purpose in going to that place is important enough for you to be taking this trip."

"Why are you doing all this?" I asked.

"Let's just say sympathies in this country are complicated and I like to help ladies in need."

"This is very kind of you."

Peter stood up. "The clerk will make arrangements for you to be picked up this evening and taken to the station. Perhaps we will meet again on your return trip."

I expected him to tell me at that point that I owed him money for making these arrangements, but he simply walked out the door.

Waiting became a painful endeavor. Napping was impossible. I had no patience to read. As the sun slipped low in the sky, someone came to get my luggage and brought it downstairs. A younger man stood behind the reception desk. He escorted me to a waiting taxi.

Arriving a short time later at the station, the driver carried my valise onto the train and handed it to the conductor who escorted me into a small compartment. A bed had already been made and a crystal class and a decanter of brandy waited for me on the bedside table. The conductor put the valise on the shelf above the bed and left.

After several glasses of the brandy, I crawled into bed. The clacking of the wheels against the metal tracks and the sweet taste of the brandy in my mouth lulled me to sleep. The night passed fitfully. I woke-up several times with a heavy feeling in my chest and sense a miserable feeling of panic and dread that it was impossible to sleep. I lay in the bed most of the night, my eyes wide open, crawling out from under the covers when the morning light radiated around the heavy blinds that covered the windows.

Then the train stopped in the middle of nowhere. Small poorly constructed buildings lined one side of the tracks. Army trucks soon rolled into view, kicking up huge clouds of dust. Soldiers clambered out of the train and gathered in long lines across the dusty soil. There was a faint odor of salt in the air. I knew we must be near lands' end. A porter came into my room, took up my bag, and escorted me out of the train and into a small shed. A young soldier sat behind a lone desk. He seemed surprised to see me.

"You were on that train?" he asked.

"Yes, I want to see someone on Con Dao."

"That is quite impossible."

"I want to see the officer in charge."

"He sees no one without an appointment."

"Young man, he will see me. I will not leave here until he and I talk."

This boy-soldier had quite likely gotten through his military life so far without having made too many difficult decisions on his own, and he wasn't sure how to handle this one. The porter put my valise on the floor, gave me a quizzical look, and left the building. The young soldier stood and seeing that I was not going to leave, said, "I will get someone." He left me standing in the middle of the room.

Soon several officers entered the shed. "A problem?" the largest of the three men said.

"I want to see someone who has been taken to Con Dao, a very dear friend of mine who has been wrongly arrested."

"Everyone is guilty who is in that prison," he said.

"We'll see about that," I spat. "I am to arrange for her defense."

"Impossible," he barked.

"I work for the Colonial government and I know people who are very powerful," I snapped back at him. The longer I stood in that shack, the stronger and the more resolute I felt. At the beginning of this journey, it was not clear to me what to do or say. The only thing I knew for sure was that I would exhaust my resources, no matter how meager. And I would not back down from anyone. "If I do not get in to see my client, the authorities in Saigon and Hanoi will certainly hear from me."

I don't know if he believed me or if he just decided not to take any chances, but after conferring with his companions, he said, "I'll let you see your friend. You can take the next boat with the new prison guards. Maybe you will want to become friendly with some of them, they could be quite helpful." He laughed hard at his comment and elbowed one of his companions in the ribs.

"Very helpful," one of the other men said and let out a horselaugh.

"You'll get in this time, but do not expect to get in again," the big man said. He looked harshly at the boy-soldier clerk and barked, "Take her to the ship and see that she goes nowhere else. You will follow her everywhere and if she must attend to herself in the lady's room, boy, you attend with her."

One of the officers gave out a great laugh. He seemed to be having a lot of fun with my situation.

The young soldier took up my valise and quickly left the shack. I followed.

"Idiot," I heard the officer mumble as he stepped out the door.

The ship was a rusted troop transporter. The soldiers were crowded so close together that no one could sit. Confused to see a woman on board, the men attempted to give me as much space as they could, but we were still almost nose-to-nose. The young man assigned to accompany me tried to stand close to me but as the boat shifted in the water everyone moved from one side to the other. And there were a few who were not seaworthy and the air soon stank of vomit.

Finally, we landed on the island and my escort half-trotted me up to the main gate. After a short conversation with a guard, the gate opened and we stepped inside the prison. Another guard led us to an administrative office where the young soldier explained that his commanding officer had given me permission to see a prisoner. There were no questions other than to ask for the prisoner's name. When I gave it to them, someone picked up the telephone and mumbled into the receiver.

"This will take a bit of time," the clerk said. "Have a seat."

It was almost an hour later when someone said, "She's ready. We'll escort you to the visitors' room."

I stood up, my heart raced. My only desire was to hold Thi My and to assure her that she would get home.

We entered the visitors' room. That was my first disappointment. I thought she'd be waiting for me, that gentle smile greeting me. Instead, it was a miserably stark room and we had to stand waiting this time for at least another half hour. Eventually a door clicked open. I braced myself.

At first I thought they had brought the wrong woman to see me. An emaciated, limp figure was dragged into the room. Surely the soldiers had brought the wrong person. This was not Thi My. The woman's hair had been shorn, her arms were tied behind her back, and her legs dragged along the floor apparently too weak to support her feeble body.

"Thi My?" I asked.

Her head slowly rose in recognition of a name, of a voice. Her face was badly bruised. A long gash ran down one side of her face.

It was difficult to imagine that she could see, for her eyes were nearly swollen shut.

Then our eyes met. "Thi My!" I gasped.

My breath caught in my chest. I attempted to rush to her side. A soldier grabbed my arm. He would not let me near her. Blood was caked everywhere on her clothing, and I knew that this could not have all been her blood. A strong odor of urine permeated the room.

"I'm going to get you out of here. I promise. I will do everything to get you back home safely."

Her eyes rolled back in her head. She swooned, making it awkward for the soldiers to hold her upright. "She needs medical attention," I shouted.

"We have doctors here," the soldier said. "She has refused to eat. This is her choice."

"Enough," the clerk said, "The visit is over."

"No," I shouted and watched horrified as the soldiers dragged Thi My out of the room.

"You've seen your friend," the clerk said. "Now be on the next boat returning to the mainland. It is best that you not return. These are dangerous prisoners and it is disruptive to have people coming onto the island."

I'd never felt so helpless. The only thing in my mind was to get Thi My out of this wretched place.

The boat returned me to the mainland quickly but it took several hours to catch the train back to Saigon. It was an agonizingly long wait. When I finally got to the hotel, the old Chinese man was standing behind the reception desk. He asked no questions and handed me a room key.

The hallway outside my room smelled of stale cigar smoke and whisky. I lay on the bed. My head ached. With my eyes closed the vision of Thi My being held by those brutish soldiers broke my heart. At some point I mercifully fell asleep. In the morning, I had no clear plan of action, but if Thi My was not removed from that place, she would die. Peter was nowhere to be found the next day and when I asked after him, the clerk said, "I know no Peter Montague."

"Surely you must know him. He was here almost every day."

"I am sorry, Madame, but I know of no such man."

Though I waited several days, he never showed up again. I decided to venture out on my own and made several attempts to arrange appointments with various Colonial administrators. When they learned that I'd come on behalf of a prisoner in Con Dao they refused to see me. Several lawyers listened to my story but said they would not get involved.

"I suggest you go back to Hanoi," one lawyer said. "These are not the times to attempt the release of a friend from a prison colony. The rebels are holding steady and the French are determined to break their backs. Stay out of this or you will find yourself carried away to one of these places."

One door after another closed on me, though I continued to stay on in Saigon for another couple of weeks looking for someone to help me with Thi My's case. When my money ran out, there was no choice but to return to Hanoi.

On the trip back, my compartment was filled with a rowdy bunch of French businessmen. They never stopped drinking, and though they offered their booze to me, I lost my taste for it. At night, after they'd drunk several bottles between them and had fallen into a sloppy stupor, I went out into the hall, stood by an open breezeway and let the wind dry my tears.

Thirty-Eight

RETURNING TO HANOI, I HEADED straight for the Governor General's Office hoping that someone could help get Thi My off that horrid island. There were several senior clerks who frequently come to the Archives asking for assistance in finding specific information. It was now time to call in favors.

But everyone gave me the same reply: Thi My had confessed to being a member of the Viet Minh. Thi My would have to stand trial.

"She was tortured," I said repeatedly.

No one would intervene.

Weeks went by. I exhausted every French government office. I even went to the newly established Japanese military offices. They were the worst. By now I'd thought we might see some dislodging of French power and that the Japanese would have some say in these issues. They found my story comical. One officer told me in good English that the petty problems of the Vietnamese were of no concern to them.

On my second round of visits to the French government offices, the clerks were ready for me. Not one door would open. I'd more than hit a brick wall; I'd fallen into a hole.

Going back to work at the Archives, my heart wasn't in it. It sounded like Jean George missed me because now he had his hands full with the demands of a Japanese soldier who had been assigned to the Archives. This fellow didn't work, not like everyone else in the place. He was there to gather information requested of him by his superiors. Maps were his main concern, followed by anything related to sections of the country where the Japanese might set up outposts. Anything that he deemed important took precedence over what we were working on. Now everyone had an opportunity to jerk us around.

During the day, there was too much going on to think about what might be happening to Thi My. The nights though were difficult. The horror of seeing Thi My bloodied and bruised would come back to me with such force it would take my breath away. A bottle of rice wine remained untouched in my cabinet; getting drunk only exaggerated the devastating image. I sat in the dark most evenings, always with the image of Thi My's face keeping me company.

Aon She Beng sent a servant to my door shortly after I returned from Saigon asking me to join her for tea. I knew she most likely had heard what I'd been up to and wanted to get more information. In the back of my mind, I hoped she would have an idea about how we might get Thi My out of prison. I arrived next door with renewed expectations.

"You bring bad spirits from that lousy place," were her first words to me as I passed through her garden gate.

"What are you talking about?"

"Thi My make misery for everyone. She bad daughter."

"The misery is the world we live in."

"You know nothing." Aon She Beng snapped those words at me as though she'd cracked a whip. "Her father never rest in grave. He unlucky man with foolish son and daughter. No respect for ancestors."

"I guess it would be useless to ask you to help get Thi My out of prison."

"She made bad choice. No one help her. She cursed. Only bad will come now."

"I want Thi My to be safe," I said.

"The French never release her. Dat Tu make this trouble. He lives in disgrace."

"I don't think he sees it that way."

"He foolish man. The communists brainwashed him. When he grows old and sees what shame he brought his ancestors, he will go mad."

"Did you invite me here to lecture me?"

"I brought you here to tell you the French will not release Thi My because Dat Tu abandon his family. The spirits make him pay."

"Ridiculous."

"You will see," she said. "The spirit world is restless. Soon they come to your house. You will understand then what I say."

I didn't see much of Aon She Beng after that. She didn't send a servant requesting my presence again either. From time to time there was still loud conversations coming from the other side of our common wall. It was probably her money lending business that kept her busy.

Loc Dang Hung came to mind once in a while. He looked miserable the last time I'd seen him. I couldn't help but wonder how he and his family were doing now and if they knew about what had happened to Thi My.

The work at the Archives was about as bad as it could get. Then one of the porters, a young man who always smelled of fish sauce, came to work wearing a Japanese military jacket. Jean George made a stink about a civilian wearing a uniform, but the more he pressured the young man to remove the jacket, the more resistance he got. Finally Jean George gave up and let him wear whatever he wanted.

It had been weeks since I'd been to that horrid prison. Realizing that no one in Hanoi would help me get Thi My released, I began to inquire about Thi My's trial date. No one gave me a straight answer about that either. First one clerk said in a month. Another clerk said no one knew when the trials would begin. One clerk refused to say anything.

"Can I go see her?" I asked.

"Visitors are not allowed," was the only answer they would give.

I hated every minute I spent in the Archives. Nothing pleased me. All I wanted was to see Thi My safe and living in Hanoi. I had thought about looking for the nun to see if she knew how we could get Thi My out of jail. Who knew where she was these days.

Then one evening arriving home from the Archives, I found the nun sitting in my garden.

"Oh, my God, I'm so glad to see you," I said.

She smiled. "I'm happy to see you, too."

She was dressed in a nun's robe; her feet were bare, though her hair had grown back.

"Have you heard about Thi My?" I asked.

"Yes, many have been captured."

I did not know how to respond. The bloodied image of Thi My rushed across my vision. "Let me make you a cup of tea."

"There is no time for tea. We need your assistance."

I could see in her eyes that circumstances had changed her a great deal since we'd last met. Her face was drawn; her checks sunken and her eyes had gone cold.

"What? What do you want me to do?"

"Julia is very ill. We've brought her to one of our camps in the hills, but we cannot stay with her much longer. You will have to come and attend to her."

"What's wrong?"

"Malaria."

"You couldn't bring her here?"

"No, it would look too suspicious."

"How bad is it?"

"She's quite ill. I have secured some medication to bring with us. We must move quickly. Take nothing with you but money. It might be needed for bribes along the way. A truck is waiting. Please, hurry."

I briefly thought about getting a message to Jean George to let him know that I'd be away for a while. Though at this point, I didn't care if there would be a position waiting for me when I got back. Other than rescuing Thi My, the only thing that mattered now was getting Julia safely back to Hanoi.

When the nun told me we'd ride in a truck, I thought we'd share the front seat with the driver. Much to my disappointment, the front seat had already been filled with three slight men and the driver. We were directed to the back where the nun and I sat on the bare wooden surface under a heavy canvas tarp. The air was stifling. Dust billowed up through the floorboards. To make things worse, the driver stopped numerous times along the way to pick up bags of rice that were piled around us. On the last leg of the trip, we had to contend with caged chickens that squawked and fluttered frantically, filling the air with feathers every time the truck hit a bump in the road.

We traveled through the evening. I tried several times to converse with the nun but we were either jostled from side to side and banging into the walls or we were choking on the thick dust, gas fumes and feathers that filled the back of the truck.

When we'd reach a checkpoint, the nun and I ducked behind the bags of rice and fluttering chickens, while the police pulled back the canvas to check for contraband and rebels. The police flicked torches across the inside of the truck. The light sliced through the darkness. The chickens, crammed tightly in their bamboo cages, squawked and fluttered. Luckily, the authorities were satisfied with what they saw, or didn't see, and the driver started up the truck and we drove off again.

At one point, the driver shifted into a low gear and the truck began to climb a steep hill. The bags of rice and chicken cages shifted slightly. We traveled for several hours, climbing, climbing, and then we stopped.

The driver threw open the canvas flap. We'd traveled through the night. A dull grey morning light filled the sky.

"We're here," the nun said. "We go the rest of the way on foot."

Scrambling out from the back of the truck was a bit of a feat considering we'd been sitting on the wooden floor for so many hours. My poor joints ached, but grabbing a good mouthful of fresh air was delicious.

The nun handed the driver a few coins and taking up the ends of her robe, she headed into the jungle that flanked both sides of the road. I hurried after her. We only went a short distance when sweat poured down my back. The nun raced through the dense underbrush, carefully pushing the vines and branches aside, hardly leaving a path to follow.

We had traveled for nearly two hours when we stopped. The nun reached into a pouch hanging from her waist and handed me a small packet of rice enclosed in a banana leaf.

"Eat," she said. "We still have a long way to go."

I hadn't eaten in many hours and devoured the meager offering.

Monkeys chattered overhead. Birds flew from tree to tree calling out with unusual shrill cries. I heard footsteps near where we sat, but there was nothing to see and the footsteps faded.

The nun took the empty banana leaf from me, folded it neatly and tucked it back into her pouch. "We leave nothing behind," she said.

"Are you rested?"

"Yes."

We walked for several more hours. The daylight shifted in the jungle like colors in a kaleidoscope. A deafening chorus of birds screamed as we passed under a canopy of trees. At one point, a wild boar dove into a thicket in front of us, its fat tail snapping angrily several times before the beastly thing disappeared.

It was impossible to know how far we'd walked when I heard the faint sound of a woman crying. Soft and low at first, the words were unintelligible. The nun quickened her pace. Soon we came to a clearing where we were greeted by a small group of men and women.

Several makeshift shelters had been erected along one edge of the jungle. Hammocks hung from the trunks of the stronger trees. From inside one of the shelters a woman called out again. It was Julia. Her voice sounded like that of a small child whimpering.

"Mommy," she called out miserably and began to cry.

It sounded as if she were in a great deal of pain. I hurried into the shelter.

"Oh, Julia." I touched her forehead. She was burning up with fever. Her eyes were wild with delirium. "We'll fix you up. We brought you medicine."

"Mommy," she called out again.

"It's alright, shh. It's all right."

Julia grabbed my hand, clenching my fingers so tightly that the knucklebones crunched together.

"We have to give her those pills now," the nun said. "She's going out of her head."

Julia fought us all the way. So fearful of something in her delirium, it took five people to administer the medication. One of the women brought a pan of water and a rag and we swabbed her down. Julia continued to whimper and call out, her cries blending in with those of the wild animals. It seemed that some birds in a nearby tree responded to her with distress cries of their own.

Someone hung a hammock for me near Julia. I lay there all afternoon watching my friend squirm and gyrate in her fitful state. Sweat poured from her forehead. When it was time to give her another dose of medication, she did not fight so strongly, though she looked at us with utter terror. One of the women brought a tin cup of liquid for Julia to drink. She swallowed some, though much of the beverage ran out of the sides of her mouth. Julia appeared to be locked into a horrible dream and flailed as if trying to keep something from coming near her.

Night comes quickly in the jungle, there is no warning. One minute there was light and the next minute darkness engulfs the world.

A camp fire glowed from under one of the lean-tos. The smell of food roused me from the hammock. The nun had taken off her robe and now wore the traditional peasants garb. With her back to me, squatting on the ground near the flame, it was impossible to distinguish her from her companions.

"Join us," she said and handed me a smoldering tuber impaled on the end of a stick.

I took it and sat down on the ground. "What next?" I asked.

"Tomorrow we leave. Two men will remain behind to help bring Julia back out to the road where a truck will be waiting to take you into Hanoi. Hopefully, she'll be well enough to be moved within several days."

"Where are you going?"

"Deeper into the mountains. Many of our leaders were arrested in this last uprising. We have no choice but to draw back and regroup."

"How far into China did Julia get?"

"Quite far. She decided to return to Hanoi. She wanted to go back to America. Our paths crossed as she and her companions were making their way back to the coast. I joined up with them. While we were camped in one of the valleys, Julia became ill. At first, she could travel on foot. Soon we had to carry her on a stretcher. That's when I decided to ask for your help. Caring for her was too risky."

The tuber cooled enough for me to eat and though it tasted bland, the roasting added some flavor. I knew that there would not be much else to eat for days so I chomped away at the pasty flesh.

"I went to see Thi My in the prison," I said.

"There are many in the prisons. Thi My knew the danger." The nun continued to eat. She did not look up at me. A crazy chatter of monkeys in the trees overhead broke the dark silence that had fallen on us. Julia cried out. One of the women dipped a cup into a pot of brew sitting on the edge of the fire and took it to Julia.

"What is she giving her?" I asked.

"It's a local remedy, termite larvae steeped like a tea. It's probably what has saved her life so far. When you get her back to Hanoi, she will continue to recover with the Western medicine."

The nun and I stood watching the fire. Pale trails of smoke rose into the air. A burning bundle of wood snapped. The night went silent, and then Julia grunted loudly and shouted, "No, go away."

Startled by the pitiful plea, I hurried to her side. She was not as feverish as she had been earlier in the afternoon. Her clothing was sweat soaked. The rest of the night she slept fitfully, grinding her teeth and breathing heavily.

The jungle noises grew louder. Bats flitted about in the trees. One fat flying creature swooped down into the shelter, the glow from the fire reflected off its wings. I went back to where the nun stood poking a stick in the embers of the fire pit.

She did not look up as I approached. "Vo Si Tuan has been arrested," she said. "It happened about the same time that Thi My was captured."

It had been such a brief affair. It surprised me that anyone knew about it. But perhaps Thi My mentioned my involvement with Vo Si Tuan or maybe the novelist had renounced me as an offering of his commitment to the movement.

"Where is he being held?" I asked.

"No one knows."

A trio of bats swooped close to the fire. An animal near the camp cackled oddly and something else whooped. The unfamiliar noises of the night echoed again and again.

"I must sleep now," the nun said. "I have a long journey ahead of me. You need your rest, too. Here is Julia's camera. It was the only thing on her when we met up. I carried it for her when she became so ill." The nun reached into a canvas bag hanging on a tree limb, removing the camera and a few rolls of film. It felt like the nun had just handed me a piece of Julia.

The fire had nearly burned out. "I wish you luck," the nun said and passed through my shadow on her way to the edge of the clearing.

"And you be safe," I responded.

"Thank you."

Julia woke me several times during the night with her moaning and talking. In my sleepy state her word sounded coherent. Though it was only the fever talking.

In the morning, a heavy mist hung in the air, dew coated everything, and only Julia's shelter remained standing. Everything else had been removed. The lean-tos, the hammocks, everything had been taken down. Julia and I were now alone except for two young boys sitting on the edge of the small clearing.

Though Julia's fever lessened, she was still quite ill. Her eyes fluttered open from time to time. One of the young boys brought a cup of the liquid from the pot that had been left by the fire pit. We managed to get Julia to take the pill and to drink some of the potion. We lay her back in the hammock and she slept for the rest of the day hardly moving at all.

We spent two more days watching after Julia. On the third morning, the young men chopped down a small tree and quickly cut off the limbs. They tied Julia's hammock to either end of the pole. Without disturbing her, they hoisted the pole onto their shoulders and began to carry her through the jungle. I quickly followed.

It was a miserable trek. The young men slowed the pace a couple times waiting for me to catch my breath. Thick clouds of insects frequently swarmed around my head. I had to put a hand over my mouth and nose to keep them from flying up into my nostrils. Animals of all kinds scurried away from us. We startled a small deer that jumped and ran through the tangled jungle vines disappearing like a spotted ghost. A family of large rodents squealed and scurried across our path.

Then something strange happened. The young men stopped. They looked at each and motioned for me to be quiet. I heard movement. Footsteps. The young men cautiously placed the pole between the cruxes of two trees. Julia's hammock rocked softly as though she were caught in a gentle breeze. They looked into the jungle, watching for something in the tangle of green.

We didn't have a weapon. I feared that a tiger might be crouching behind a tree. We waited. I moved close to Julia totally unprepared to protect either her or myself from anything wild. Then through the thick green of the jungle three Japanese soldiers appeared. They did not have their guns drawn and there were no bayonets on the ends of the rifles. They looked at Julia in the hammock and then turned their eyes on me. We stood perfectly still. Everyone appraised the situation, cautiously, wordlessly. It was difficult to know whether these soldiers were scouts. They could have even been lost, or perhaps they were deserters.

One of them took hold of the bag that the nun had left behind for me. The only thing it contained was a couple of chloroquine pills, enough to hold Julia until we returned to Hanoi and several roasted manioc tuber. The soldier grabbed the food from the bag. It was obvious they were starving. Saliva dripped from the corner of one soldier's mouth. He wiped at the drool with the sleeve of his shirt and grabbed one of the tubers.

The soldiers hungrily ate the roasted vegetable as they ran deeper into the jungle. My two companions hurriedly took up the pole once again and trotted at a faster pace through the tangle of vines. It wasn't easy to keep up with them and though I'd lost sight of them several times, we finally reached the road. Thankfully the truck was waiting for us just as the nun had said it would be.

The driver quickly opened his door and helped Julia out of the sling and to a standing position. We managed to get her into the front seat. Julia had no idea where she was. The driver said nothing but glanced at us curiously from time to time. He appeared worried when we hit a couple of nasty ruts and Julia's head lurched forward.

It was odd, but for some reason, we did not encounter one roadblock on our way back into Hanoi. And if we had been stopped, Julia and I hopefully would have been no more than a curiosity. Once we reached the outskirts of the city, the driver assisted me in getting Julia into a rickshaw. She had begun to speak more coherently between her sleeping bouts, but complained of a headache and groaned periodically. I had never been so happy to see anything in my life, as when we reached the gritty street outside my house.

Several neighbors stopped to watch when the rickshaw pulled up in front of my gate. Aon She Beng, coming back from shopping, quickened her pace as she watched me assist Julia out of the rickshaw. Julia stumbled, nearly falling to the ground. Someone gasped. Julia placed a hand on the wall to steady herself while I opened the gate.

"I feel sick," she said.

"You'll be fine now," I replied. With one of Julia's arms slung over my shoulder, we managed to get into the house without too much difficulty. Julia flopped down on the day bed, groaning several times before falling asleep.

Aon She Beng wasted no time knocking on my gate.

"Where you find her?" she asked.

"Non of your business."

"She look dead."

"She's very ill."

"I have good medicine. I will send servant to help make her well."

"That's very kind of you but I can manage."

"I hope she no die. She never make my picture."

"Well, that is important, now isn't it?"

Aon She Beng furrowed her brow, her lips pinched tightly together. "You look sick. Sleep. We talk tomorrow." She turned and slowly walked back to her house.

I closed the garden gate. My body went limp with fatigue. My feet felt nailed to the ground. My arms were heavy. With great effort, I stepped over the threshold of my doorway and stumbled into a chair. Julia was breathing heavily. I closed my eyes and saw nothing but darkness.

Thirty-Nine

I DIDN'T KNOW HOW LONG I'd slept. When I next opened my eyes, the first thing I saw was Julia propped against the wall looking at me.

"Thought you'd fall out of that chair at one point," she said. Her voice sounded raspy, as though she'd been doing a lot of shouting.

The back of my neck ached. "How long have you been awake?"

"Who knows, and I have no idea how I got here. You'll have to fill me in."

"How do you feel?"

"Woozy."

"Want a cup of tea?"

"Would love one."

For the next couple days, I took care of Julia. It made me nervous to think about leaving her alone though she slept most of the time. We had no visitors except one afternoon when Aon She Beng's servant brought us a special sauce, a thick, dark concoction that made the house reek of rotten fish.

"Don't even think about feeding me that," Julia said.

"I guess it's her way of making sure you don't die on her. She still wants that photo session you promised her."

"Some things don't change, do they?"

Eventually I'd have to get back to the Archives. Jean George had gotten used to my coming and going without any notice. So I knew he wasn't going to give me any grief about my absence. Besides, he had enough to do at the Archives without concerning himself about my business. The political jostling back and forth between the needs of the new Governor General's office and the Japanese making demands for information kept him hopping.

As I traveled to the Archives, there appeared to be many more Japanese soldiers on the streets than I remembered. There were fewer French women walking with parasols accompanied by servants carrying their packages. In the early morning hours there would usually be a rush of colonial women shopping to avoid the afternoon heat.

The runner parked the rickshaw at the same curb where Vo Si Tuan would frequently be waiting. I wondered if things would have worked out for us if the times were different. We had not fallen in love. Though it might have happened. I sat in the rickshaw cab remembering our only night together and realized that the rickshaw puller stood on the street waiting patiently for his money. I paid him and went into the Archives.

Just as I opened the door, I heard shouting.

"Don't come here again," Jean George bellowed.

The scene was confusing. I saw Jean George, his bodyguard, and a quite thin man standing with his back to me. The bodyguard clinched his fists. He moved towards the other man. The man with his back to me turned. It was Loc Dang Hung. His eyes were wild with anger. He glanced at me. For an instant it looked as though he was about to say something but he left the building without another word.

"I don't want him anywhere near me," Jean George shouted at the bodyguard. The angry look on Jean George's face frightened me. I had never seen him so angry.

This incident disturbed me while at the same time it piqued my curiosity. It was time to pay Loc Dang Hung another visit. I wanted to know what was going on. Jean George would never tell me. And I had a strong feeling that it had everything to do with Thien Nguyen's death.

But first I had to get through my first day back at the Archives. The place didn't look to be in that bad of shape. The floors were passable now, swept clean of all the plaster and debris. Windows that had been stuck closed were opened. Fresh air filled the Archives. Sunlight glowed in the room. Everyone was busy doing what they were hired to do.

"Good morning," Le Sing Dong said as he came from behind one of the shelves. "We missed you. Is everything all right?"

"Yes, things are fine," I said.

"The place looks good, don't you think?"

"It's remarkable. You're to be congratulated."

"Is Jean George going to replace the broken windows?" Le Sing Dong pointed to the wall where most of the wind damage had occurred during one of the more devastating storms.

"I don't know. He looked like he had his hands full this morning. Did you see Loc Dang Hung?"

"Yes, there was quite a fight. Loc Dang Hung tried to get to something in here. He started to pull manuscripts off the shelves shouting that we had information that killed his brother."

"I only caught the last of it," I said. "Did he hurt anyone?"

"No. He didn't get very far because Jean George's bodyguard pulled him back out into the administrative area. He didn't try to hurt anyone. He just insisted on looking for something."

"Did he give you an idea what it was?"

"No. He just started to run through the place grabbing documents and shouting that Jean George lied to him."

I looked around the room. The young Japanese soldier that had been assigned to the Archive, stood, arms folded across his chest, watching me. "How's he doing?" I asked.

"A couple of times he ordered us around like he was the boss. Now that you're here, I think he'll behave himself."

"You've had your hands full," I said.

Le Sing Dong smiled. "I like my work."

"That's good."

Luckily, fewer documents arrived in my absence. There were quite a few manuscripts that still needed repairing and I concentrated on that aspect of the job. Le Sing Dong would have plenty to do, translating at least three boxes of Vietnamese literature into French; the boxes had arrived some months earlier, during the worst part of the rainy season. The poor guy hadn't had a chance to do his job properly, but with avchange in the season, he could begin to decipher what had arrived and we could organize it accordingly.

This first day back at the Archives did not pass quickly nor did it drag, it just thankfully ended. I knew that there would come a time—

and it wouldn't be long now—that I would simply quit the Archives. I had no idea what I'd do after that, but it was time for me to move on.

When I arrived home, Julia was sitting in the garden near the fish-pond, a cup of tea in her hand.

"I forgot how lovely this courtyard is in the evening," she said.

"You look much better."

"I'm getting there."

"Want something to eat?" I asked.

"Maybe a bit of broth."

I went into the house. Julia slowly got up from her seat and followed me.

"How was it going back to the Archives?"

"Strange, very strange." Before I could say any more there was a knock at the garden gate. "The last thing I need tonight is company," I said and went to see who had come to visit.

Henrietta stood in the evening light, a small bundle in her hands and a rather stupid look on her face. "Jean George said that you had returned to work," she said and craned her neck to look inside the courtyard. I knew she'd come calling to get a look at Julia. By now probably half of Hanoi knew that my friend had returned from some long journey and that she'd come back deathly ill.

"I brought you some fresh bread from our kitchen. Mind if I come in?" Henrietta said and handed me the bundle. "I won't stay long."

"I suppose," I said as she stepped into the courtyard.

"Where is your friend?" Looking into the doorway of the house, Henrietta smiled. "There she is." With a conspiratorial whisper, she asked, "How is she? I do hope there are no long-term effects. I have heard stories where people never recover fully from malaria and they suffer for years."

"She's recovering quite nicely," I said. "Would you care for a cup of tea?"

"I'd prefer something a little more lively."

"Sorry, all out of the lively stuff."

Henrietta looked disappointed and I could smell on her breath that she'd already been drinking. "I don't like hot beverages in the evening," she said. "They make me sweat all night. I can hardly sleep."

"Yes, yes," I said, wishing that I had pretended that no one was at home.

"Yoo-hoo," Henrietta called to Julia. "I brought you some fresh bread. My cook is amazingly talented. She's learned to bake as good as any chef in Paris."

I went into the house and Henrietta followed close behind.

"Oh, you do look so well. I thought from what everyone was saying, that you'd look a lot worse. But you look quite normal."

Julia cleared her throat. "I am normal."

"I do hope you don't mind that I've barged in on you like this. But Jean George is at his short wave radio again tonight. I cannot bear to listen to what's going on in Europe. Such awful stuff is happening. It makes me cry every night. And I still have not heard from my parents or my sisters."

"What is happening?" Julia asked seriously.

"It's dreadful. The Germans are firebombing London and the Jews were forced to leave Warsaw. I suppose Indochina might be the safest place in the world right now. Jean George has assured me that things will get better very soon now because Chiang Kai-Shek has banned the communist party in China. All the trouble makers will be rounded up and hopefully it won't be long before we're back to normal."

"Jean George says all of this?" Julia asked.

"Yes, he knows quite a bit about world politics because he listens to the radio every night."

I heated some fish broth for Julia. "Henrietta, would you care to join us for a light supper?"

"I've already eaten, but I do wish you had a bit of wine."

"Sorry," I replied.

Julia gave me a quizzical look. "No wine?"

"That's right. All out."

"What a shame. Tonight I would have liked a bit of a drink myself," Julia said.

Shrugging my shoulders, I turned my attention to Henrietta. As long as she had come all this way to see Julia, it wouldn't hurt to tap her for information. "Did Jean George say anything about Loc Dang Hung visiting the Archives today?"

"No, my poor husband said he had a terrible day. He rarely tells me about his work, but a couple days ago Loc Dang Hung came to our house. He caused such an uproar with the servant girl. She had strict orders not to let him in. He knocked her to the ground and pushed his way into the house. There is certainly something very wrong with that man. If he is not careful Jean George will have him arrested."

"Sounds serious," Julia said.

"Oh, it is very serious. We cannot have these people barging into our home and making demands. I don't even know what it is that he wants. My husband is at his wits' end and is quite tired of this ridiculous situation."

Henrietta didn't stay too much longer after she'd related all of her daily woes to us. Quite likely it was her thirst that got the best of her and she went home.

"So, what is this, no booze in your house?" Julia asked when I returned from securing the gate.

"A lot has changed since you've been gone," I replied. "Drinking used to make me forget. Now it makes everything worse."

I hadn't thought to tell Julia about Thi My's arrest until now. It was most likely my way of avoiding the sadness. It broke my heart each time I retold the story. And rage burned inside me every time I thought about my failed attempt to getting her out of prison.

"Thi My's been arrested," I said. "I tried to get her out but it doesn't look good."

"I heard that the French had captured a great many rebels," Julia said. "I ran into one group after another that had had been lucky enough to escape. Most of them were scrambling to get either deeper into the mountains or out of the country altogether and into China. One night we camped with a small band of rebels who were deciding what direction to go in next. It seems most of the leaders had been caught in the net when the French swooped down on the rebel camps."

"Thi My wasn't a leader and she wasn't lucky enough to get away."

Julia's eyes glazed over. Suddenly she looked quite pale. "I am so tired," she said, "My head is throbbing. I have to lay down." Julia got up from her chair and slowly walked to the back bedroom.

Sitting alone now in the quiet house the incident this morning with Jean George and Loc Dang Hun came to mind. It had me puzzled. It was still early. The sun had just set. So I decided to pay Loc Dang Hung another visit. Something serious had gone on between them and I was convinced that it had everything to do with Thien Nguyen's murder.

The evening air was deathly still. The humidity was stifling. It was a long ride across the city. It wasn't the possibility of bandits that bothered me, but the large number of Japanese soldiers marching up and down the street that made me uneasy. I did not share the same confidence that Henrietta had in the future of this country.

When the rickshaw stopped outside of Loc Dang Hung's home, I told the puller that I'd give him extra money if he waited for me. He agreed. A dim light glowed inside the main room. I knocked. The door opened slightly. Loc Dang Hung stood in the doorway. Even in the dim light it was easy to see the anger in his eyes. "Why are you here?" he asked.

"I want to talk to you."

"I have nothing to say. Go away."

"You must talk with me. Your brother was very dear to me. Tell me what made you so angry with Jean George. I know it has something to do with your brother."

"This is none of your affair. There is enough suffering in our house without you making us more miserable."

"Have you heard about Thi My?" I asked.

He looked at me with such an angry expression that I worried he might strike me. "She made this decision of her own free will. If my brother were alive, he would have gone to prison with her. We no longer have sympathy for her."

"Where are your sympathies?" I asked. "Are they with the Colonial government?"

Loc Dang Hung's expression went from angry to hopeless in an instant. His body language changed from the stiffness of contempt to that of limp resolution. My words had hit a sensitive nerve.

"What did Jean George promise you?"

"There have been too many promises," he said.

A mournful cry came from an upstairs room. Loc Dang Hung quickly looked behind him. Something shifted in a darkened doorway. We heard the scream again. Footsteps quickly scurried across the floor in the room above our heads.

Loc Dang Hung looked back at me. Fear flashed in his eyes. "Leave us alone," he said and slammed the door shut.

Forty

JULIA SLEPT MOST MORNINGS WHILE I headed off to the Archives. Her health improved though fatigue continued to plague her. Our evenings were usually quiet. Henrietta visited infrequently. Aon She Beng never came by for a chat. Instead, some evenings she sent a servant with a message that Aon She Beng wanted us to visit her. Sometimes my landlady sent a bundle of fresh herbs and vegetables.

The Archives had become a low priority for me. My main concern now was to seek legal assistance for Thi My from the Governor General's offices. Yet, no one would budge. After all this time I was still no closer to getting her out of prison.

When Julia felt strong enough to travel, we attempted to get train tickets for Saigon. But all rail travel had been stopped except for those passengers with special business outside of Hanoi. Visiting prisoners did not fall into that category.

Once Aon She Beng saw Julia getting around during the day, it didn't take her long to send word that Julia should prepare her camera to make the photograph that was promised.

"Looks like she wants that birthday present," Julia said. "Why don't you come along with me?"

"You need the help?" I asked.

"No, just thought it might go quicker if the two of us were dealing with her."

"Nothing makes dealing with my landlady quick or easy, but I'll tag along."

Julia slept late as usual. When finally emerging from her bedroom, Julia complained that the daylight hurt her eyes. She sat in a dark corner sipping a cup of tea waiting while her system adjusted to the brightness of the noonday sun.

Then Julia went to her bedroom returning dressed in fresh clothing, her camera hanging from her neck. With a sigh and a bit of a smile, she said, "Well, let's go immortalize your landlady."

Julia's camera had been the only possession that came back with her from the trek to China. The Remington typewriter and her clothing had most likely been left in the jungle or in a village somewhere along the way.

Aon She Beng served us a small lunch and many cups of tea while her servants helped her dress for the photograph. It seemed to be taking forever when one of the servants rushed out from the back room. Grabbing my hand, the servant insisted that I follow her. At the end of a short corridor Aon She Beng stood in the doorway of her dressing room.

"I look important?" she asked.

"Yes, very important."

She turned around to display her long brocade garment, the same garment that she'd worn to her longevity celebration. The intricate gold-embroidered flowers on the fabric glistened even in the dim light of this windowless back room. Her gray hair had been twisted and mounded on top of her head. The tresses, piled high and fastened in place with long, thin ivory sticks, slightly resembled a crown .

"You look like a queen," I said.

"I know," she replied.

Aon She Beng walked past me and into the room where Julia sat waiting. "You take picture now," she commanded.

"Indeed," Julia replied and lifted her camera to take a candid shot.

"NO!" Aon She Beng shouted. "I must sit."

"Very well," Julia said, but the camera clicked again and again. I hoped Julia had gotten the shot that she wanted.

Aon She Beng sat in the chair that a local carpenter had made for her longevity celebration last year. It was a hefty chair that took up nearly a quarter of the living room. Aon She Beng shouted to her servants that a golden footstool should be brought for her swollen feet. With all this regalia, she certainly did look regal.

"Is there enough light?" I asked. "Looks kind of dark in here."

"I like the shadow across her face," Julia said. "It makes her look mysterious."

Aon She Beng shifted in her chair. "I want best picture," she demanded. "Not mysterious."

"You'll love my photograph," Julia said. "I'll make you look very beautiful."

"Good," she said and lifted her chin arrogantly.

Julia took a half-dozen shots and then said, "You are now immortal."

Aon She Beng smiled and motioned to one of her servants to bring her a cup of tea. "You think I am beautiful?" she asked Julia.

"Yes, very beautiful," Julia replied.

More tea with little sweet cakes was set on the table in front of us. I didn't know how much more liquid my poor bladder could hold though the sweets made my mouth water just to look at them.

"I saw a woman in China who reminded me of you," Julia said.

"Was she important?" Aon She Beng asked. "Quite important, though not in the same way that you are important. She had grey hair like you and had seen many years. A very tough woman and she was given the power to be a general over many of the guerrilla fighters."

"You see this woman?" Aon She Beng asked.

"Yes, and she let me take her picture, too."

"She not dressed good as me."

"No, she dressed very simply but that did not matter to her. Once she had been a prosperous farmer's wife but she'd seen too much trouble and decided to do something about it."

Aon She Beng took a small bite from one of the little cakes.

"The Japanese took her husband's land," Julia said. "Several of her sons were killed. She was left with no choice but to defend her country. They call her the 'mother of China's guerrillas'. She can shoot a gun as well as any soldier. I saw it for myself." Julia looked pale. I recognized the familiar glassiness that came over her eyes when she became overly tired.

Aon She Beng smiled. "I would make good general."

"Yes, you would," I agreed. "But I think your photographer is getting tired and it's time we leave."

"You made this important day," Aon She Beng said as we stepped though the doorway.

Once inside my house, Julia collapsed onto the daybed. "It's taking me forever to get back to normal. I don't like being so dammed weak all the time."

"Be patient," I said.

"Easy for you to say," she snapped.

We had this discussion many times. In the end Julia only got more frustrated and weaker.

"Was that a real story about the woman in China or did you make it up?"

"It's true. But then, I haven't told you much about what I saw." Julia lay on her back and even with her eyes closed, it was easy to tell that she was still in her sour frame of mind. "Maybe seeing all that stuff made me sick. War is so ugly. I don't care if I ever see another gun, a soldier, or army truck again as long as I live. I've had enough." She rolled over.

I'd had enough of this country, the heartache, the disappointments and I'd had enough of the Archives. So, just like that, I resigned. I told Jean George that Le Sing Dong could handle anything that came up and that I'd not be coming back. He didn't argue with me. He was quite likely on his way to another administrative position.

There wasn't a lot to do after that. I napped most afternoons. Julia and I didn't talk much but when we did, she told me bits and pieces of what she'd seen while traveling in China.

"What happened between you and Tex?" I asked her one night.

"He went on his merry way with a section of the British Army that was constructing a road into China from Burma. And you'd never guess what Sherman was really up to. That mousey little guy with his baby face was in some kind of Special Forces. It seems he had some real important deciphering skills that would help the U.S. government keep track of the Japanese. He was working under cover and to keep up the ruse he had to get to China on his own. Truthfully, I thought he might have been some kind of pervert on the lam from the authorities. You just never know."

"You run into Albee while you were up there?"

"I heard about a few Americans, and Russians, too, who were moving about in China. It's a big place and I never met up with any of them. There were a few women I wanted to get in touch with, but they were usually in an inaccessible Godforsaken village or miles away from Shanghai on the Mongolian border. But no, sorry, Sarah, Albee and I never crossed paths."

I kind of liked having nothing to do. I'd saved a great deal of money over the years. Finally there was time to read the books that I'd brought with me when I first came to this country. They weren't in very good shape, but I read them and when a page fell out of the book, I carefully replaced it.

Julia developed her photos. Aon She Beng was thrilled with the results and said, "I make best subject for photographer."

Julia had not shown Aon She Beng the candid shots that she took before the formal photo session. Julia called those unbiased photographs. I didn't think that Aon She Beng would have agreed. They depicted my landlady as comical, confused, and really more like a madwoman ranting at the camera.

Julia joined me in haranguing the colonial government for information about Thi My's trial. We always got the same empty replies. Occasionally, we took a chance and stopped by the Japanese official headquarters and tried again to get them to help us. Everyone gave the same answers. There was no information. "Come back another time," they said repeatedly. As the weeks went on, another response had been added to the pat replies: "A report is being drawn up and will be available soon."

And then in August, on a miserably hot and muggy evening, Henrietta brought us the news. She arrived pale and nervously pulling at her fingers as though they pained her.

"Have you heard?" she asked as she stepped into the courtyard.

"Heard what?" I asked.

"They've all been shot."

"Who?"

"The whole lot of them that had been arrested in the insurgence."

It took only a split second to realize what Henrietta had just said.

My mind went white. I could not catch my breath. My heart raced frantically.

"Julia!" I screamed.

Julia hurried outside. "What? What happened?"

"They've killed Thi My," I managed to say. "They've murdered her."

Henrietta stood motionless in the opened doorway of the courtyard. I looked at her. "You're wrong," I said. "How could they do that?"

"I just heard about it from Jean George. He said all the Colonial administrators were told about it. I knew you would want to know as soon as possible."

I could have scratched Henrietta's eyes out for telling me this terrible news. I could have killed her with my bare hands.

"You," I screamed, as though she had done the deed herself. "Oh, Julia, how could they?" I said.

Tears would not come, sand scraped across my eyes instead of water. A knife had been plunged into my heart.

Forty-One

IT TOOK ONLY SEVERAL MINUTES before one of Aon She Beng's servants came running to see what had happened. Standing next to Henrietta, the servant waited to hear what the fuss was about.

I couldn't talk. Words stuck in my throat like brads from a thistle.

"What?" Julia demanded.

Henrietta stood in the opened garden gate looking dumbfounded. After a short pause, she said, "They executed Thi My."

Julia glared at Henrietta.

The servant quickly left the garden. Though before returning to Aon She Beng, the woman whispered something to a small crowd gathered around the silk merchants stall across the street. A woman screamed—a mother, a sister or a wife; someone else who felt a knife stabbed into her heart. There was a great clamor of shouts and cries. They knew that the execution of one meant the execution of all the prisoners.

Ignoring the anguished crowd, Henrietta said, "I'll make you a cup of tea."

"Don't!" I shouted.

"Isn't there something I can do for you?" Henrietta said.

"You've done enough."

I could not bear to look into Julia's eyes fearful that my own pain would reflect back at me. A throbbing pulsated in my ears. I was nauseous. I retched. Nothing came up.

"You look like you're going to pass out," Julia said and closed the garden gate.

I took a deep breath.

Then above all the noise we heard Aon She Beng's banging against my garden gate with her walking stick. Henrietta looked at me, startled.

"Let her in. It's Aon She Beng," I said.

Henrietta lifted the latch and the gate swung open. Aon She Beng stood in the doorway leaning heavily on her cane while a servant girl held onto her other arm. "Who caused all this trouble?" Aon She Beng demanded.

"Thi My has been executed," I said, though I was sure that her servant had already told her the news.

Aon She Beng stumbled slightly. "Many mothers cry tonight."

I glanced at Henrietta. She looked bewildered. I don't believe Henrietta understood the impact that this news would have on us. Gossiping and being the first to tell the big news of the day seemed to be her main line of interest. Now as the reality of the information settled in, she went pale.

The next days and weeks melted into a blur. Julia and I hardly ate. Any rapping on the gate went ignored. I would not talk to anyone, not even Aon She Beng.

"I'm going back home," I told Julia one evening after we sat through an afternoon watching shadows slowly move across the garden floor. I had neglected the pond for weeks. The fish had long since died. The water sat stagnant and deeply green with great gobs of algae, and the frog hadn't made any noise in weeks.

"Kansas City?" Julia asked.

"Maybe, eventually," I said. "This country asks too much of a soul."

"When do you think you'll pull up stakes?"

"Before Christmas. I haven't seen a pine tree in years. It would be awfully nice to have a piece of sweet potato pie."

"Henrietta's going to miss you and you'll break old Aon She Beng's heart."

"They'll get over it. But…" A huge wave of sadness washed over me. I could not finish my sentence. We sat in silence for quite a while longer before I could speak again. "I have some regrets. Maybe if they'd found Thien Nguyen's murderer I might not feel so defeated. That one really sticks in my craw."

"How long has it been?" Julia asked, though if she thought about it for even a second, she would remember that the murder took place several days before her arrival in this country.

"Too long," I said.

"There's still time," Julia said. "You don't have to be out of here by any particular date. We could still do some digging around."

"You serious?"

"Yeah, why not."

The thought of finding Thien Nguyen's killer struck me as a real possibility. "I always believed that Loc Dang Hung knew more than he was telling us."

"We could try again. Visit the family. Maybe time has changed their attitude." Julia looked quite sincere and enthusiastic.

"Might be a bit intimidating with both of us."

"We're not going to threaten the guy, just ask questions," Julia said.

The next morning started out slow as usual. My spirit felt renewed and energized thinking that we might get more information from Loc Dang Hung. He gave me the willies the last time I spoke to him about his brother's murder. It certainly felt like he was holding back information.

The French police had made the sketchiest of inquiries into the murder. They seemed to have lost interest only a week or two after their superficial investigation. In the meantime, so much had happened that the murder was now old business to them. But I hadn't forgotten. I still cared and wondered how Thien Nguyen's family felt now that Thi My had been executed.

As we approached Loc Dang Hung's house, it struck me how quiet, almost eerie this area had become since the murder. There were no passersby and no rickshaw traffic. It was difficult to explain. The area just didn't feel right.

We got out of the rickshaw. Loud angry voices came from inside the house as we approached. I knocked on the door. The place went silent. We waited. I knocked again.

"We're not leaving," Julia shouted.

I knocked several more times before an ancient, bent-over woman unlatched the door and opened it wide for us to enter. The front room was as dark as it had been during the funeral; a few candles flickered on the floor near a small shrine.

Loc Dang Hung stepped out of a darkened doorway. He didn't look as crazed as he had when we'd last met, though his eyes appeared tired and he was still so terribly thin. "Again?" he asked. "Why don't you leave us alone? Haven't we suffered enough without having to deal with your questions?"

"I haven't gotten any answers that make sense," I said. "I'll ask my questions until I'm satisfied."

"What would satisfy you?" he said.

"If we knew who murdered your brother," I replied. "All we have now are questions and they keep me awake at night."

"In my world, sleep is no comfort," Loc Dang Hung said.

"Maybe it's your conscience," Julia said.

Loc Dang Hung glared at her. He looked nearly inhuman with eyes sunk so deep into his face, his stick-thin neck poking out of his garment. "What do you mean?" he asked.

"You pretend to know nothing, but you know a great deal," Julia said.

"The rebels killed my brother."

"You know that for a fact?" I asked.

"Who else?" Loc Dang Hung said, not taking his gaze from Julia.

"Why would the rebels want to kill him?" I asked.

"There are many petty political groups struggling for power and they would do anything to get the information that my brother found."

Loc Dang Hung did not know what he'd just inadvertently admitted.

"Thien Nguyen showed you what he found, didn't he?" I asked.

"No," he snapped. But it was too late and he realized what he had just admitted.

"But you said that Thien Nguyen found something," Julia said.

The room went so silent, so undisturbed by sound that the breath moving in and out of my nostrils became a roar in my ears. Loc Dang Hung's eyes frantically darted about the room realizing now that he could not take back his words.

"I know what he found," I persisted. "It was a document, wasn't it?"

Loc Dang Hung stood perfectly still.

"I saw the document," I said. "He gave it to Thi My before he was murdered."

"Where is it now?" he asked cautiously.

"Does it matter?"

"No," he said.

"Did you tell anyone else about this document?"

He glanced slyly at me. "I thought you were a smart woman. Haven't you figured that out?"

I was caught off-guard. Julia looked at me. And then the answer hit me like a blow to my chest…Jean George. It could have been no one else.

"When Thien Nguyen showed me what he had found," Loc Dang Hung said, "I told Jean George, but said nothing to anyone else. Not even to our mother. Thien Nguyen wanted to convince me that the French were starving our people by turning the rice harvests into fuel."

"What did Jean George say?" Julia asked.

"He called it a communist lie and said that Thien Nguyen had fallen in with the rebels."

A thin trace of the noonday sun slowly crawled over the threshold of the open doorway like a snake of light slithering into the house.

"What did you say to that?" I asked.

"Jean George promised to find me a position if I kept him informed of suspicious activity."

"And you did as he asked?"

"Thien Nguyen had become foolish. He stopped listening to me, his older brother. I could not stop his arranged marriage into a family where the only son was an active revolutionary. Someone had to be concerned about his political involvement. He would have brought shame to our family if he continued to be involved with the rebels."

"Sounds like you did it more for personal gain," Julia said.

Loc Dang Hung looked at Julia with such viciousness I thought that he might strike her face. "I went to Jean George to get help for my brother," he said. "It was my duty to take care of him."

"Did Jean George help you as he promised?"

"No," he said. "Now my family is ruined. Our mother must move to the country and live with her brother. I'm ordered to report to the mines on the northern coast to work off our debt. We've lost our house. We have nothing."

We stood silently while the sunlight continued to creep across the floor.

"Are you satisfied now?" Loc Dang Hung finally asked.

I didn't know how to respond. I felt sheepish about what I said next, though I realized there was no other choice. I wanted to shake up Loc Dang Hung to try to get more information. I took a deep breath and said, "Have you heard about Thi My?"

Loc Dang Hung did not move a muscle. There was a blank expression on his face. He turned and left the room.

"Any doubt now that Jean George had something to do with Thien Nguyen's murder?" I asked Julia as we left the house.

"No, none at all. But why?"

We were in a country that protected colonial administrators. No one would have listened to our suspicions. Any official, even if we could get someone to listen, would ask for proof. We had none.

It was on the ride back from seeing Lok Dang Hung that my mind was made up to leave French Indochina. Before, perhaps moving back to the States had only been fantasy, wishful thinking. It was clear that we would never learn the full story about Thien Nguyen's murder. There was no longer any reason for me to stick around. When I told this to Julia, she said it was time for her to leave this part of the world, as well.

Aon She Beng had become ill. The doctors called it weak blood. Herbalists, both local practitioners and some from nearby villages, brought her one concoction after another trying to fortify her system. Nothing seemed to work. Most of her days were spent in bed.

"I hear my ancestors calling me," she said on one of my visits with her. "You'll drink some of that nasty tea the herbalists bring and you'll be up and giving us all a hard time the way you always do."

"No," she said.

My landlady did not look well. She was pale; her hands trembled as she took a sip of the herbal tea. Her skin looked transparent, showing black veins laying flat against her bones.

I'd planned on stopping by the Archives to confront Jean George one last time about Thien Nguyen's murder. There were still so many unanswered questions. I think Julia and I both realized that we'd never get a straight answer from him.

In the meantime, Julia booked us passage on a small freighter. The captain told her that there were a few problems with the departure time. Though he assured us his vessel would get underway within the month.

"I'm heartsick," said Henrietta when we told her of our plans to leave Vietnam. "Why? Why would you go back to America? It's perfectly lovely here, and really quite safe. I will miss you terribly." She went on a crying-jag every time we saw her. As a result, we got more than the average number of invitations to her gatherings. Thankfully we were always too busy to attend.

I decided to travel light and began to give away all my possessions. Aon She Beng's servants had first choice of everything in my house, the dishes, the furniture, and clothing. Henrietta took a few pieces of jewelry as mementos of our friendship. The more that I got rid of, the better it felt.

Julia and I never did stop by to see Jean George. I couldn't stand to look at his face one more time, or even breathe the same air as him. The unanswered questions would have to remain unanswered.

The captain of our ship repeatedly changed the departure date. "It's not me," he told us. "The Japanese have closed the harbor. No one can leave. We'll get underway in a day or two, or perhaps next week."

"It's a good thing you didn't get rid of the beds," Julia said. "Or we'd be sleeping on the floor."

My little house was so empty that any movement caused an echo. Life was simpler with almost everything that I owned either given away or sold. After so many delays, Julia and I were more than ready to get underway. I fretted in my sleep, frequently waking up in the middle of the night thinking that someone had come into my room. There never was anyone there but it took me forever to fall back to sleep.

The day after the sea captain told us that our departure had once again been postponed for another week, a distraught female messenger banged on my garden gate early one morning. "Please, open. You must come. Please!"

I opened the gate. Henrietta's servant stood in the entrance. The woman was terribly insistent. I spotted Jean George's bodyguard standing near a car parked across the street.

"What on earth is wrong?" I asked.

"Something terrible has happened," the woman said, her breath heavy, her face pale, and her eyes red from crying. "Please! Henrietta needs you. The car is waiting."

"Just a moment," I said and rushed into the house to get Julia.

"Something's happened and I don't want to go by myself."

"This better not be her way of getting us to one of those tea parties," Julia grumbled.

We climbed into the back seat of the car.

"What's going on?" I asked the bodyguard and realized that he had never spoken a word in my presence.

"There's been a murder."

The servant sitting in the front seat wept uncontrollably. "Jean George," she sobbed.

"I don't believe this," I said.

"It is true," the bodyguard said.

"Who did it?" Julia asked.

The driver, as cool and detached as ever, explained, "A witness said that a mad man rushed out from an alley and stabbed him in the heart. His wife is hysterical and insisted that I come to get you."

"Where were you?" I asked.

"He wanted to drive himself last night."

Many vehicles and rickshaws filled the driveway in front of Henrietta's house. A police guard stood on either side of the front door. When we got out of the car, a crowd standing on the curb rushed to see who else had come to the big French estate.

The guards gave Julia and me the once over. The servant who opened the door said we were friends of the family. We were let into the house and taken up stairs to Henrietta's bedroom. I knocked softly on the door.

"Come in," Henrietta responded.

We opened the door. Henrietta lay prostrate atop a huge feather-stuffed mattress. Her hair was a mess and she was still dressed in her nightclothes. As we stepped into the room Henrietta whimpered, "Oh, Sarah, they have murdered my husband!" She sobbed with such violence that the bedposts rattled.

"What happened?" I asked.

"The communists killed him!" she screamed.

"Why would they want to do that?" Julia asked.

Henrietta continued to weep.

I sat on the bed and put my arm around Henrietta's shoulder. I'd never really touched her before. It surprised me how tight her back muscles felt even with all the extra flesh that she carried. Henrietta placed her head against my temple and whispered, "What am I going to do?" Her breathing came in clutching gasps. "I will so need my friends now."

"How did this happen?" I asked.

"He went out to a late-night meeting," Henrietta said, pausing briefly to wipe her nose with a hanky. "He decided to drive himself and gave the bodyguard the night off. The terrible thing must have happened after he left the meeting on his way home. Luckily, it occurred close to Blossom's dress shop. She's the one who rushed here last night to tell me what had happened."

"Were there witnesses?" Julia asked.

Henrietta bristled in response to Julia's question. "Blossom said she saw a thin shadow of a man running away." The tears stopped flowing. Henrietta took a deep soulful breath and said, "I'd like to get dressed now. I've cried so hard my chest hurts."

Julia and I went downstairs. Even at this early morning hour, it appeared that the news of Jean George's murder had quickly spread through the city because when we went into the parlor, four women from Henrietta's social circle sat huddled together talking softly to each other. They looked up when Julia and I entered the room.

"It is terrible," one of the women said. "Have you seen the poor dear?"

"How frightening to have this happen, and with the Japanese behaving so unpredictably."

"One just doesn't know what to think these days."

The woman on the far end of the room, the youngest of the group said nothing and seemed dazed by the situation. I hadn't seen her before and wondered if she might have been the latest of Henrietta's recruits of fresh blood to help civilize this country.

A maid came into the room with a tray of tea and small cakes.

"How very thoughtful of Henrietta," one of the women said and poured a cup of tea. The other three women seemed more interested in the cakes and they each took one.

Julia and I sat opposite the women waiting for Henrietta to come down from her room. It felt like a very long and tedious wait with no one knowing what to say in the midst of all this chaos. Finally, Henrietta arrived. She looked composed. Her hair had been combed, her summer dress was perfectly pressed, and her face freshly powdered with a touch of color on her lips.

Julia and I watched the women as they took turns hugging the new widow. Julia leaned in close to me and whispered, "Which ones do you think Jean George slept with?"

"You're about as irreverent as they come," I chided.

Julia shielded her mouth with her hand so that the other ladies could not hear what she had just said. When she gave me one of her goofy grins, it was clear to me that Julia had returned back to her old self.

"How did you find out?" one of the women asked Henrietta.

Henrietta repeated the same story she'd told Julia and me upstairs.

"Did Blossom see who did it?"

"Only a shadow. By the time she got there, the murderer had vanished in the dark."

"Like a rat into a hole," one of the women said.

"Yes, quite," another woman chimed in.

"Do they suspect it was the communists?"

"I'm sure it had to be one of them. They are causing so much trouble."

The young woman, the new member of the group, asked, "How is Blossom?" Her words were simple and punctuated with what sounded like a thoughtful mention of a troublesome discovery by one of them. But after Julia's off-the-cuff comment, I wondered just how innocent her words were.

Henrietta said nothing and sat down in one of the winged back chairs. The four women scurried around getting her tea, placing a piece of cake on a dish, and fluffing a pillow for her back. "You poor dear," one of them said.

"Let's get out of here," Julia whispered to me.

I nodded and stood.

"Henrietta," I said, "Julia and I are leaving."

"No," she shrieked and looked startled as though something had suddenly frightened her and she began to sob.

"We'll come another time."

"Please don't go."

"These fine women will take good care of you. I'll stop by later."

The other women closed in around Henrietta, gently stroking her as though she were a lost child.

"There is nothing to worry about," one of them said. "We will not leave your side and the police have guards outside your door. There is nothing for you to be frightened of."

When we stepped out of the house, Julia said, "Can't say I'd like all that smothering. Though it looks like Henrietta could get used to that kind of treatment."

The small crowd of curious onlookers outside the house had grown larger. Some sat on their haunches looking as though they might spend the day. Several women heading to market with huge baskets of produce dangling from shoulder poles paused to take in the scene. A small contingency of Japanese soldiers marched down the middle of the street forcing everyone to move up onto the curb.

Julia and I stood out of the way until the last soldiers passed and then we walked up the street and found a rickshaw. When I first decided to leave Vietnam, it seemed like there was little time to prepare, but with all the delays I'd begun to wonder if we'd ever get underway. So far, I had to unpack twice as our departure dates were repeatedly changed.

"I'm not going to miss this place," I said.

"Don't kid yourself. As soon as we're headed out of the harbor you'll start to pine for these good old days."

The Japanese forces had more than doubled in size during the past week and the roadways were now clogged with troops and long convoys. Our rickshaw was forced off the road several times by long contingents of marching soldiers before we finally reached my street.

"What do you think's going on?" Julia asked.

"You could fill an ocean with what I don't know," I said. "But it does seem to be getting awfully crowded with the Japanese army."

"Kind of takes your mind off the murder, doesn't it?" Julia asked.

"Takes my mind off a lot of things."

After we got home, Julia suggested that we try to fly out of Vietnam. The next day we went to the airport to see about booking a flight. That proved to be futile. Nothing was going in or out of the country, the ticket agent told us. And when we inquired why, the man could not give us a straight answer and said he was just following orders.

Aon She Beng, even in her unwell state, visited us periodically hounding me about the rent money she'd be losing when I left. She wanted to know why I was doing this to her.

Once I'd decided to leave Hanoi, each delay annoyed me. I'd lost interest in finding Thien Nguyen's murderer and I wasn't going to stick around to find out if the police would do a better job at finding Jean George's murderer.

Julia and I were now consumed by our travel problems. We knew that something was going on and figured Japan tied up the harbor and air travel for military reasons.

One day, the Japanese troops disappeared from Hanoi—no ships in the harbor, no troops marching in the streets, and the skies were empty of airplanes. Unable to leave the country, we visited Henrietta from time to time, though with each trip to her house, I hoped that it would be my last.

"What is going on?" I asked Henrietta as we sat in her parlor drinking tea and eating her prized cakes. "Have you heard anything from all the socializing that you do?"

"If Jean George were here..." she said. Her eyes became silky with tears. She took a deep breath. Dabbing at the tears with a handkerchief, she said, "Oh, I do feel so vulnerable without him around."

"Yes," I said. "It must be quite an adjustment."

"How do you and Julia do it? Living alone for all these years, don't you feel frightened without a man around?"

"I just don't think about it," I replied.

"It's on my mind all the time," Henrietta said.

"You'll be fine."

Henrietta put her teacup onto the table. "I've decided to bury Jean George in Hanoi. He loved this place so much. This is what he would have wanted."

"When?"

"This Sunday. A priest is making the arrangements for me. And the women from the Social Club will prepare the food for afterward. It's too late for a proper wake. The investigators insisted on keeping his body for such a long time." Henrietta clutched at her chest and breathed in short puffs. "The knife was left in his chest," she said. Catching her bearing, Henrietta continued. "They are trying to trace its origin. But I don't know why they wanted to keep my husband for so long." Henrietta took a sip of tea. "I wish you were not leaving."

"It's time," I said. "The world is in such bad shape, if we don't do it now, who knows when we'll get another chance. It might already be too late. But we're going to try to get back to the States before Christmas. There have been so many delays, we might not get there until well after the New Year."

"Jean George said that something big was about to happen and that all the shortwave radio operators were talking about it. No one knew what it was. He said that everyone suspected that the Japanese were going to make a big move against the US or the British territories."

"Do you know how to operate the shortwave radio?" Julia asked.

"I used to sit and listen and watch when Jean George first got the thing, but it's been a while since I've worked with it."

"Would you mind turning it on?"

"Why?"

"Maybe we'll hear something," Julia said.

"Most of what we heard was in Japanese."

"Let's try. We know that something is going on and it's certainly worth an effort."

"I suppose," Henrietta said. She got up from her chair and opened the door to a closet revealing a professional radio system with a microphone and many dials. Flipping a switch, loud squeaks blurted out of the speakers. She twisted one of the large dials. The high-pitched noise became lower in tone. We heard very distant voices. Henrietta flipped a couple more switches and worked the dial.e The voice came in more clearly. She turned up the volume. Though the voice was faint, we could only make out two words.

"Disaster…Burning…"

"What are they talking about? Where? Can you get this in any better?"

"I'll try. It sounds so far away. Jean George must have set this up for long distance. I'm not sure how to get it in any better." Henrietta turned a few more dials. The background static became a loud high-pitched squeal. When she turned the dial the other way the background noise subsided slightly allowing us to hear more clearly.

And then through the fog of garbled noises we heard an American voice, "Japanese…" The voice faded to static.

Julia looked up at me and said, "Could it be possible?" She looked at Henrietta, "Try again," she demanded.

Henrietta twisted the dials. Great screeching and gurgling noise roared out at us. She turned the volume down and soft undulating hisses emanated from the speakers.

We heard voices, words that faded in and out of the static.

"What are they saying?" Julia asked.

I leaned in close to the speaker. A lone voice, sounding so terribly far away, repeated the same message. The words were swallowed in the static. We did not hear words, only the frantic tone in the speech.

Henrietta continued to manipulate the switches and dials. "This is so frustrating," she said and turned one of the larger dials ever so slowly. The voice sounded less distorted. Henrietta leaned back in her chair and looked up at me. "I heard…" she said. The color drained from her face. "This is awful," she whispered. "Did you hear?"

Julia and I leaned in closer to the radio. "Disaster…Mayday…Japanese attacked Pearl Harbor." The voice garbled, fading in and out, repeated this message over and over.

Julia whimpered, "No. Oh, my God, no. We are at war now?"

The afternoon light faded. A servant woman came into the room with another tray of tea and small cakes. No matter how much more Henrietta fiddled with the dials and switches, the signal faded into garbled and crackling noise. The radio continued to squeak but nothing substantial came across the airways. We sat close to the radio for hours, waiting to hear more information. My ears throbbed from the tension, from not knowing, from the fear of another world war.

Afternoon turned to evening and then the night came. We spoke hardly a word to each other after that. Henrietta manipulated the dials trying to get a better signal. The cakes on the tray remained uneaten; the tea turned cold. The signal grew stronger in the evening, but it was the same message.

"I'm very tired," Julia said.

"Why don't you stay the night," Henrietta suggested.

"Nice offer," Julia responded, "But I need my own bed tonight. We are at war."

I feared what Julia said was true. There could be no other conclusion.

Henrietta insisted that her bodyguard drive us home.

We stepped out into the night. A dense canopy of stars hung above us. I wondered how many other shortwave radios had picked up these distress calls. Had the Jews in Europe hopeful of defeating the fascists heard this message? Were families listening to their radios back in Kansas City wondering what it would all mean in the morning? Who had told President Roosevelt that this horrible thing had happened? And who would tell the mothers and wives, the fathers and husbands, the daughters and sons, about the many dead.

The bodyguard, a man who still had no name, quickly drove us back to my house. The night was absolutely silent. When I closed the car door, it sounded like the crack of a whip and the shadow of a small creature scurried along the wall before we opened the garden gate.

Julia and I said nothing to each other. She went directly to her room. I could not bear to go into that back bedroom where the air would surely be miserably hot and I sat in the garden a few minutes to soak up the silence.

When I went into Julia's room, she sat on the bed, a dozen or more undeveloped rolls of film scattered across the covers.

I sat next to her.

She took my hand.

"I can't do this again," she whispered.

We sat for a little while sharing my last cigarette, and then I went to my room. I did not bother to light the lamp but fell onto the bed. I thought about the document that had been stuck into the quilt in my closet. It didn't matter now who I'd given it to. In the dark, my mind raced frantically remembering Thien Nguyen, Thi My and Dat Tu's lovely wife. Their deaths could not have been prevented, no matter what I'd done with that document. Thien Nguyen's murder would never be solved; war and politics had put a stop to that. I'd come to this distant land trying to rid myself of personal pain and found only deeper hurt and misery. Loc Dang Hung and I both knew Jean George had everything to do with Thien Nguyen's murder and though morally I could not condone what I feared Loc Dan Hung had done, in these ragged days of disquiet and uncertainty, I believe he took revenge for his brother's death in the only way that was left to him.

The air, thick with humidity, pushed against my chest. I laid in the dark and eventually sank into a drugged-like slumber.

"Sarah," someone softly called my name. "Sarah, darkness is leaching across the world."

Opening my eyes, Thien Nguyen stood at the foot of my bed. He extended his hand to me. I could not move, not even a finger. Dreams are like shadows. They bend and twist, and there is no reasoning why something happens. He hovered above my bed. I wondered if he had come to me as a harbinger. Had he brought me a warning? Then I felt myself lift off the bed. My neck strained to hold my head up; my limbs were weightless. We rose high into the night sky, floating through the stars that stung my skin like bites of angry insects. Still we went deeper into the night.

I thought we would go on for an eternity but then a dense cluster of stars blocked our passage. I looked back from where we had come. The war flared up from the earth as though petrol had been poured over burning coals. Like beasts given a taste of their first kill, warriors lunged at the earth with sharpened teeth. Rivers of blood overflowed their banks.

Drifting so high above the planet, I could not hear the screams, though I knew there must have been horrible sounds coming from the maimed and dying. I decided to stay in the stars until this terrible time had passed. Losing sight of Thien Nguyen, I'd begun to fall back down through the stars. Searing pain from the burning stars ripped at my elbow, my belly, my thighs, every part of me now felt the wrath of the heavens as I descended to earth. The screams of children, the most haunting of all sounds, pierced my ears first. The world trembled and roared with explosions.

I awoke with a horrible fear that if I opened my eyes, everything that I had seen would be true. The room, still in darkness, like a tomb, my body heavy with the burden of my dream, I struggled to get up to go into Julia's room.

Her breath was soft in the dark. The smell of cigarette smoke lingered in the air. I lay next to her, a comfort I'd never allowed myself until now.

"I'm frightened," I whispered.

"I am, too."

We lay braced against the dark waiting for the morning light. There were no more dreams. There were no more ghosts. There was only the humid air and the memory of weightlessness before the war.

About the Author

MARGARET MENDEL LIVES IN NEW York City. She has an MFA in Creative Writing from Sarah Lawrence. Many of her short stories have appeared in literary journals and anthologies. Her debut novel, *FISH KICKER* was published in 2014. She has worked in the mental health field for more than twenty years, but now devotes her time to writing. She is an avid blogger and photographer. Not only does she drag a laptop wherever she goes, but she also takes a Nikon camera with her as well. Many of her photographs have appeared in websites, in online literary journals, e-magazines, and some have become book covers. Read more about Margaret on her website at http://www.pushingtime.com/

Did you enjoy *Pushing Water?*

If so, please help us spread the word about Margaret Mendel.
It's as easy as:
• Recommend the book to your family and friends
• Post a review
• Tweet and Facebook about it